ELEVEN

'A great read, showing not only Mark's sense of humour but his brilliantly acute observation of human nature . . . Sad as well as funny with a fascinating set of characters. It really is difficult to put down. If you like Nick Hornby or David Nicholls this is a must-have for the summer' *North West Evening Mail*

'By turns moving, hilarious and always heartfelt – the kind of book Nick Hornby fans will adore' *Daily Telegraph, Australia*

'Hugely recommended. Gentle, compassionate, unusual and thought-provoking' Chris Cleave

BULLET POINTS

'Brilliantly hilarious and hilariously brilliant . . . William Boyd and Woody Allen have a bastard lovechild and his name is Mark Watson' *Stephen Fry*

'It is unnervingly accomplished' *Observer*

'A fledgling Nabokov for the Big Brother generation' *Independent*

A LIGHT-HEARTED LOOK AT MURDER

'An intelligent, humane and desperately funny tale' *Independent*

'Packed with brilliant observation' *The Times*

'Will Self with humility' *The List*

the KnOT

MARK WATSON

SIMON &
SCHUSTER

London · New York · Sydney · Toronto · New Delhi

A CBS COMPANY

First published in Great Britain by Simon & Schuster UK Ltd, 2012
A CBS COMPANY
Copyright © Mark Watson Productions Limited 2012

1 3 5 7 9 10 8 6 4 2

Simon & Schuster UK Ltd
1st Floor
222 Gray's Inn Road
London WC1X 8HB

www.simonandschuster.co.uk

Simon & Schuster Australia, Sydney
Simon & Schuster India, New Delhi

A CIP catalogue record for this book is available from the British Library

HB ISBN: 978-1-47111-343-7
TPB ISBN: 978-0-85720-032-7
EBOOK ISBN: 978-0-85720-033-4

Typeset by Hewer Text UK Ltd, Edinburgh
Printed and bound by CPI Group (UK) Ltd, Croydon CR0 4YY

To Paul

PROLOGUE

You are at a wedding at a country church one Saturday. The bride and groom are friends of yours from university, the latest in a long line to tie the knot over the past couple of years. The women's high heels sink slightly into the soft ground of the churchyard, where gravestones bear faded names. The crowd trickles through the enormous bell-shaped door to be met by those unmistakable church smells: old wood, stale flowers, dusty books.

You watch the players preparing for action. The vicar in his stifling robes has another wedding to do after this one; the photographer sprinkles fag-ash onto the sacred grass. The organist tootles away in welcome, sending surreptitious texts in between tunes to arrange the delivery of his new fridge. You're aware that almost identical scenes are being played out simultaneously around Britain. You've been to five weddings this year, and came close to getting married yourself once: you're at the sort of age where these events seem to litter the calendar, especially in the summer months.

The service rattles by. The vicar pauses mock-theatrically for a second after inviting the congregation to declare if they know any reason why the couple may not be joined in matrimony. There is silence and everyone laughs. When he pronounces the lovers married, applause and gentle whooping ring around the old beamed roof. The photographer, forbidden to use his flash during the service, fiddles with a long lens. The mother of the groom bats away a tear as the organist bashes out the recessional and the married pair walk triumphantly through the beaming ranks of their friends.

At the reception in a nearby hotel you sit next to a man you vaguely knew at university who is now an anaesthetist. There is soup, chicken, booze. The best man's speech includes a handful of jokes he plundered from a website the night before last. The photographer, still on duty, prowls the function room for informal shots of relatives. He dampens his hunger with a spare bowl of soup, meant for someone who cancelled at the last minute. Eventually the dining gives way to dancing, tentative at first, then energetic. Some of the older people are now sitting with cups of tea at the fringes of the room discussing recent family developments, nibbling doubtfully at slices of the freshly cut cake. You kiss the groom on the cheek. You dance with the anaesthetist until he slopes off to the Gents and you don't see him again.

By now you have had four glasses of wine and consider the day a big success. In a heady mood you join in the dancing. The longer the dancing goes on, the more completely you forget about the organist, the vicar, the waiters, the photographer: all the people for whom the wedding, the biggest day of the participants' lives, was simply a stint at work.

The photographer has been on his feet – or occasionally his haunches – for seven or eight hours by the time he finally packs the various lenses into their cases and stashes them in his bag. On the memory card of his camera are more than five hundred pictures of people he doesn't know. Unnoticed by anyone, bag slung over his shoulder, he leaves the celebrations. He loads the bag carefully into the boot of his Escort. He sits at the wheel for a few moments, poring over an aged book of roadmaps: he's never quite got used to these new navigation gadgets. When he snaps the light off again, he realizes how long a day it has been.

He smokes a last cigarette, stubs it out in a plastic ashtray and starts up the engine. It will be late when he gets home.

This has been my Saturday-afternoon routine for more than thirty-five years. I've heard Mendelssohn's march more than a thousand times. I have seen marriage vows broken on the same day they were made, witnessed a jilting at the altar, slept with a bridesmaid when I should have been taking her picture, watched a man die of a stroke as his newly wedded daughter was leaving the church. I don't think there is anything that can happen at a wedding which I haven't seen.

And yet of the tens of thousands of people I have photo-graphed, very few would recognize me if they saw me today; in fact few would remember that I was ever there. That may sound a pessimistic thing to say, but being invisible has had its advantages.

Part One

I

I was born in 1950 and given the inauspicious name of Dominic Kitchen. I am seven years younger than my brother Max and nine years younger than my sister Victoria. Being the youngest member of the family by such a margin gave me a lingering feeling of being permanently behind everyone else, especially my brother. If I found something out, Max would already know it; whatever I achieved, he would either have done it already, or looked into it and deemed it unworthy of his attention. In short, I'd turned up too late. Max himself did everything possible to encourage me in this belief.

On one of London's many Park Streets, where we lived at number 40, a lot of houses had been bombed a few years earlier, and many of the others – as Victoria once cheerfully remarked – were so ugly that they ought to have been. Between the uneven semis, London's austere post-war sky hung like a bowl of dirty water. There was a corner shop where Victoria worked at weekends; a bit further along, a pub called the Shipmate fuelled up the Irish labourers who were plastering the area back together. Finsbury Park itself was half a mile down the road, and it was here I went with my mother on Saturday afternoons, to bob to and fro on the wet swings, while everyone else was at the football. My father was a sports journalist, covering Arsenal for the local paper, though his writing style suggested a much grander audience. When I think of being very young, I remember lying in bed in the corner of Max's room he had reluctantly surrendered to me, listening to Dad downstairs wiring his reports to the office. 'Arsenal Defeated by Virtuoso Goal.' A patient chuckle, as his words were misheard at the other end. 'No, no: "virtuoso". V, i, r . . .'

My earliest memory is being lifted up by Dad to throw a scrap of bread at the one duck hardy enough to brave a foul February afternoon.

The duck watched me throw the bread for some minutes before sidling over, as if humouring us. 'Here he comes!' said Dad, holding me out over the water like a trophy. 'What lovely luck, to see a duck!' This was easily the funniest sentence I had heard in my four years, and I squealed with laughter. A few minutes later he repeated his success – 'what a great hoot, to see a coot!' – as a snow-white forehead emerged from rushes. And then on the way out of the park, 'I never heard of so many birds!' as a well-aimed throw of more bread brought a bickering pack of pigeons to our feet. Every boy looks for proof of his father's greatness: mine was Dad's ability to make up rhymes.

He had a fine head of black hair which never went grey, and glasses which gave him the appearance of intellectualism. 'These,' he used to say, tapping them, 'saved me from the Army.' On winter afternoons his glasses misted up and he wore a red-and-white football scarf, knitted by Mum years before. Mum had no interest in football; her only opinion on the game was that a man ought to wear a nice scarf when watching it.

It wasn't until I was six or so that I was allowed to make my first visit to the Arsenal ground with Max and Dad. I was given an old scarf of Max's and tottered along apprehensively behind him, amid a gang of shouting, smoking, laughing men in cream coats and hats. I had no real enthusiasm for the game; just a strong sense that, if I managed to enjoy it, I would raise myself in their estimation. The stew of the crowd thickened through the narrow streets leading up to the football ground, and strange ingredients were thrown in: hollering programme-sellers, policemen on enormous horses. It felt as if everyone were converging on the stadium not for entertainment, but for some serious and frightening purpose. Max talked showily about different players, ignoring me as best he could, and sighed each time Dad took my arm to guide me around a new obstacle.

'That,' said Max, pointing at a sign for Victoria Street, 'was named after our sister.'

'Really?'

He snorted. 'Of course not. My God, you're thick.'

'No need for that, Max,' said Dad, too mildly to make any impression on my brother. Neither of our parents raised their voices as a rule, and certainly not to reprimand Max, who was top of his class, talented at cricket, and would end up at Oxford.

He was a streaky, wily kid, with greasy curls and an expression of cunning which scarcely ever relaxed. They say if you see the boy of seven, you see the man, or something like that: I'm getting fuzzier on these things as I get older. Anyway, it was certainly true of Max. In the faded leather album of my baby photos, Max's face appears creased in calculations of what I will cost him in attention. It's a fox-like face, unboyishly nuanced and knowing, and it seems already to know the high-flying life in store: the pin-striped shirts and monogrammed pens, the financial operations, the easy, cynical banter with blonde divorcées in West End nightspots.

When we got inside the stadium, the mass of bigger humans was even more daunting: thousands of white faces packed together, so tightly it was impossible to look at one and say which body it belonged to. Dad went off to join his colleagues in the press box, and though I heard him say 'Look after him', I knew Max had no such intention. The terrace was jammed with limbs and bodies; behind me a boy of about sixteen was using my shoulder as a shelf to get a better view. There was a vast roar as the teams took to the field, and it swelled as the game progressed. Each surge of noise had a threatening quality; I felt as if the shouting were out of control, might sweep me physically off my feet. Max joined in hoarsely, his just-broken voice rising in confident yells. I wanted desperately to pee, but could not ask my scornful brother where to go, and would never be able to make my way back.

Eventually there was a goal, and the men all around us yelled louder than ever, rocking with delight. The crowd staggered this way and that across the terraces, like a pantomime horse whose actors are going in different directions; I lost my footing and cracked my knee on the concrete. Tears sprang into my eyes as a stranger yanked me to my feet. Max glanced across in distaste and, with a demonstrative sigh, beckoned me to follow him. Without taking his eyes off the game he led me up the long slope of steps and delivered me to the press box. Dad was hunched over his notebook scrawling the strange hieroglyphics used by journalists before computers arrived.

'What's up, Dominic? Not enjoying the game?'

I shook my head wretchedly.

'Come and help me with the report, then.'

The atmosphere of studiousness in the press box was comforting. The journalists sipped mugs of grey tea and conferred with each other. 'Who took that shot?' 'Danns, I think.' 'Oh well,' said Dad, 'they'll never know, anyway, they weren't here.' A laugh from everyone. The journalists were all bespectacled and kindly-faced, like him: for some while afterwards I thought all reporters had the same pair of glasses, the way firemen had helmets. In between his note-taking, Dad amused me by pretending to speak to various imaginary characters under the desk. 'It's a goal, Mr Mole!' A couple of the other reporters tried to join in: 'Close game, Mr Mole!'

'That doesn't rhyme,' I objected.

'He's right, Clive,' said Dad, and everyone laughed again. I was delighted to find that, here in his workplace, Dad was the person everyone listened to.

'Perhaps you oughtn't to come until you're a bit bigger,' he suggested as he left the box, shaking hands with each of his colleagues, and I nodded gratefully. What I really wanted, though, was not a reprieve from football, but the secret of enjoying it, as everyone else seemed to.

The next time Arsenal played, I stayed at home, watching Victoria prepare for a party by trying on hat after hat from her formidable collection. My mother bustled about in the kitchen, baking a cake and singing in her absent-minded way, *'The way your smile just beams . . . the way you* something-something.'

Dad and Max came home at half past five, Max full of shrill bluster about the referee – 'Bloody idiot should have brought his guide dog!' With them came Mr Linus, our next-door neighbour. Mr Linus was athletic-looking, nimble, as thin as the washing line that hung in his garden. He was an antiques dealer, with a moustache like the ones sported by pilots in war films. His wife was the physical opposite: pink and flabby as a blancmange, slow-moving, always propping herself heavily against the fence to gossip loudly with my mother. Although he sometimes went to the football with Max and Dad, Mr Linus supported the rival team, Tottenham.

'So, has Dominic been down the Arsenal yet, or is he doing the decent thing and holding out for a proper team?'

'No, Dominic doesn't like football,' Max called from the hall.

'Doesn't like it? Blimey O'Reilly,' said Mr Linus, sipping his tea.

This was the first time it was spoken as a fact, and almost from that moment sport and I became official enemies. But it was still the key to Max's acceptance, so from time to time I tried to join in his noisy skirmishes with other teenagers on our street. One Sunday afternoon they were kicking a tennis ball around; some lump of a youth hoofed it into the garden of an unfriendly old couple who were renowned confiscators. There were general groans. Max summoned me from my vantage point in our patch of front garden.

'Reckon you can get over that wall?'

My heart sagged. 'I'll try.'

'If you can get the ball back,' said Max, 'you can play.'

I scrambled over the wall, skinning my knee, and scampered onto the forbidden lawn expecting to be shouted at. I fetched the ball and got back over the wall and the game went on just as before. Not sure which team I was meant to be on, I ran around after the rush of shrieking boys, always a few steps behind, never getting to kick the ball.

'I thought you said I could play,' I said to Max, next time there was a pause in the game.

'You *are* playing. You just aren't any good.'

There was a worse snub early in my first year at secondary school. Max was a prefect by now and about to apply to Oxford; at night, he studied soundlessly under the

Anglepoise lamp, whose white glare nudged at the edges of my eyelids as I tried to sleep. If I shuffled around, or fell asleep and started to snore, he would sigh peevishly. 'Can you not be quieter? I'm trying to work.'

Towards the end of the Christmas term we were playing rugby, as on every Wednesday afternoon, on a pitch which successive weeks of matches had raked up into a broth of mud. It was horribly cold and my hands were pink and stiff and caked in dirt. At one point I had shoved them down my jumper, only to be passed the ball; I fumbled it and was knocked down enthusiastically by a twelve-stone boy who already had a moustache. When at last it was time to go I ran to the pavilion where we were meant to change before being ferried back to school in ancient creaking buses. The changing rooms smelled sourly of sweat and of liniments used by older players, the stench of sport: it hung so densely in the air that I doubt they have got rid of it even now, more than forty years on. The floor was strewn with clumps of muck shaken from boots, and little puddles of water left by those brave enough to stand in the icy showers. Sometimes the class troublemakers would sweep your clothes off the changing bench into the puddles: this was called 'puddling', and everyone went out of their way to be friends with the boys who were best at it.

That afternoon my fingers were so leaden with cold that I struggled to do up the buttons on my shirt, and saw with alarm the other boys getting ahead of me in the race to be dressed. My right boot was tied with a double bow, and I'd

run the laces along the underside to make sure they stayed
fastened: one of the pieces of advice Dad had given me on
my first day. Now, mud was packed down so thickly along
the bottom of the boot that I couldn't get at the laces, and
my freezing fingers picked in vain at the knot. I tugged at
the boot, more and more furiously, but it was so filthy that
it was impossible to grip. I sat in my shirt, tie, shorts and
boots, comically half-dressed, mud on my hands, feeling
the cold grip of panic.

The engines of the buses were growling outside and
the quickest boys were already on their way. One or two
glanced pityingly at me. The changing room emptied, the
boot was stuck, and I wanted to weep. In desperation I
tottered outside, my boots as useless as ice-skates on the
hard ground. I had no plan, just a vague hope of finding
a teacher who might help me discreetly, but then I caught
sight of Max.

He was walking with a mate, a rogue called Rowlands
who was sometimes to be found lurking around our
kitchen, accepting handouts of cake from Mum. Now he
cupped an illicit cigarette in his hand. 'Max!' I called.

'Hey,' said Rowlands with a mocking grin, 'is that
Kitchen Minor?'

Max shrugged and walked on as if I were not there.

'Yes!' I called after them. 'I am! Max!'

'I believe it *is* your brother, Kitchen,' said Rowlands,
clawing his hair out of his eyes.

'Good detective work,' said Max, still not looking
round.

'Max, help!' I shouted, but the two of them went on their way.

My cheeks burned; the wind whistled through the pavilion and lashed at my exposed legs. The bus driver honked at me to hurry up. I went back into the changing room, gathered up my jumble of muddy sportswear, and hobbled miserably across the car park. The sight of me half-dressed brought a throaty chorus of mirth from the thirty or so boys on the bus; even the teacher broke into a grin. 'An interesting interpretation of the school uniform, Kitchen,' he said. 'Might you have taken off your boots and put your trousers on?'

'I couldn't get them off,' I muttered. This was received with even more laughter. I sat in the one remaining seat next to an unpopular, odd-smelling boy called Stephens, looked out of the window and pretended not to cry.

When we got back to school things were even worse; I had to trail across the playground in my disarray, avoiding everyone's eye. I'd begun to feel as if I would be dressed like this well into my adult life. By the school's imposing black gates I looked for Mum, whose fingers could have unpicked a knot tied by the devil himself. Although the school was close enough to us to walk home, she liked to come and collect me, the youngest of her children. But today something had detained her, and here instead was my sister Victoria.

She was wearing a hat, as usual: a red beret, beneath which her hair flicked at the tips of her ears. She had a Louise Brooks haircut, very short and even; it was too short for Mum's liking, one of several traits our mother found unbecomingly boy-like. Victoria wore a green double-breasted coat with large black buttons, which I'd heard our mother describe as 'an extravagance'. The colour alone was a shock to the eye. In the middle of the dowdy grey-and-brown crowd she stood out like a living person in a waxwork museum. Her large lips curled into a quizzical grin as I neared.

'Dommo! What the hell happened?'

'Stuck,' I muttered.

'Was Max not around?'

'He ignored me.'

'I'll kill him when we get home,' she said, shaking her head. 'Right, hang on for dear life.'

She gestured to the school gates. I gripped the ironwork and Victoria clamped her hands around the gooey edges of the left boot, prising it from my foot quite easily. Behind me, what had begun as further jeering was beginning to die away. Victoria was twenty, and there was an ease about her which none of the boys – and in fact few of the parents or teachers – could match. She turned her attention to my other foot.

'Christ,' she said, wiping mud from her hands onto her own boots, 'this is a stubborn little fucker.'

A wolf-whistle came from one of the watching crowd behind me. Victoria's head swivelled, reminding me of one of the birds in Finsbury Park, and her glinting eyes sought out the whistler, a rat-faced youth called Sanderson. She shot him a look of such disdain that his face went bright red in half a second. The other boys' braying now fell on him, and I felt my back straighten. Then I lurched sideways, almost thrown off my feet, as Victoria gave a mighty tug on the boot.

'I told you to hang on!' We both laughed; she wiped her hands again and renewed her grip. I looked at her fingernails, painted red, now smeared with dirt. She gave a little shout and tore the heavy boot away from my foot.

'Victory is ours!'

There was good-sported clapping from a couple of the watching parents, and she wiped her brow with the back of her hand in an exaggerated gesture, like a mountaineer at the summit. Then from somewhere among the spectators came the voice of Rowlands, my brother's friend. 'Heard you were good with your hands!'

Neither I nor my classmates could have said exactly what this meant, but Rowlands' gang began to laugh. It was now Victoria's turn to colour. Then she drew back her left arm and let the boot fly. In front of the startled spectators it skimmed through the air and struck Rowlands clean on the ear. He yelped and staggered backwards, his hand pressed to the side of his head. There was an uproar of laughs, shouts and cheers. Victoria scooped up my school bag and grabbed my arm.

'Shoes on! Let's run!'

Like an outlaw's sidekick I charged down the road with her, heart pounding in my ears as I ran to keep up, exhilarated. We ran until we reached the Shipmate on the corner of our road, panting and laughing wildly.

'Well, Dom,' she said as her breath came back, 'don't tell Mum, but we may have to go shopping for a single boot.'

After this celebrated episode Victoria became a regular talking point among my peers, and sure enough my own status in the class rose accordingly.

'Kitchen, why is your sister's hair so short?'

'Does she have boyfriends? Who does she go out with?'

'Kitchen, do you sleep in the same bedroom as your sister?'

I tended to evade these questions as well as I could. Partly this was because of some desire to protect Victoria's privacy, as if she were a film star and they were news-hounds, rather than eleven-year-old boys she would never meet. But in truth Victoria was almost as mysterious to me as she was to my classmates. This was not, as in Max's case, due to aloofness, but simply because as a twenty-year-old woman she might as well have been a member of an entirely different species.

I always had the impression she could appear or disap-pear at any time. Although she lived with us I sometimes barely saw her for days at a stretch. She smoked cigarettes at breakfast and cooked her own meals at what seemed impossible times in our generally orderly household; I would marvel at the smell of toasted cheese wafting up from downstairs at midnight. In the bedroom next to mine, on Saturday nights, I heard her and her friends holding noisy post-pub chatter I couldn't follow.

'Mark my words, in a few years, *all* models will be like that. They'll all look like ghosts and be as skinny as fucking rakes.'

'You'll be all right, Vic. You've got hair like a boy.'

'I haven't got a bum like a boy. Look at it.'

'You've got a lovely arse. I wish I had those curves.'

'Well, none of us is going to be a model, anyhow. So let's finish this cheese off, it's not going to eat itself.'

Where Max was at pains to shut his world away from me, Victoria allowed me unexpected glimpses of hers. One Saturday afternoon she called me from upstairs. 'Domino!'

I was sitting on my parents' longest-serving piece of furniture, a pea-green Chesterfield, running my fingers up and down the pattern of holes in its body and half watching some war film or other. Arsenal were playing at home, so I was on my own. Mum was preparing a casserole for evening guests; the smell of cooking meat poured from the kitchen, and her singing lilted over the puff and hiss of the heavy old kettle. 'Something-something-something, the something *vie en rose*.' At the sound of Victoria's voice, I rose straight away and scampered up the stairs.

'Dom!' the voice called again, muffled and distant: I realized it was coming from the bathroom. 'Be the best brother ever and get me my book, will you? It's just on the bed, there.'

I pushed open the door of her bedroom. Inside it was, as always, like a lost-property box. Dresses and hats and shoes lay haphazardly around; plates bore the remnants of barely remembered snacks. On the bed was a little green packet of tablets, and as she had said, the book: *Lolita*. It was a heavy hardback with a cover in primary colours. I picked it up and knocked tentatively on the bathroom door.

'Come in!'

I nudged the door open. Victoria was lying in the bath, cocooned in soupy, foamy water. Baths were another thing she seemed to indulge in at entirely unpredictable times of the day. Her head rested against the wall with its grid of brown tiles, installed in the fifties and already dated. The tips of her shoulders, reddened by the hot water, were just visible above the water-line. At the other end of the bath her shins rose out of the water, and her feet rested next to the taps. Although nothing else of her could be seen over the high sides of the tub, I averted my eyes with what I imagined was gentlemanly discretion. Victoria laughed at my coyness.

'You can look at me! I saw you naked the day you were born!'

Her eyes, deep brown – almost as dark as her hair – shone with amusement. She had a roundish nose, soft at the tip, and today she had bright red lipstick on. It was an attractive face because of its overall effect rather than any specific feature, which I suppose was true of Victoria in general. Her attraction for most people seemed to lie in some quality impossible to miss, but equally impossible to describe.

I let my eyes rise from the messy heap of her discarded clothes and come to rest upon Victoria herself.

'What am I missing downstairs?' she asked. 'Any excitement?'

'Mum's making a casserole.'

She laughed softly. 'Yes, I smelled that. I should think they can smell it in France.'

Water gurgled in the pipes behind the wall.

'Want to see something secret?' she asked.

Her left leg rose slowly out of the bath, a pink foot brushing against the porcelain tap with its swirling 'H'. Just above the rim of the water, a little way up from her knee, I could see a small green and brown mark. I had forgotten my embarrassment now. I leaned closer and the mark, at first hard to make out, revealed its shape.

'A tortoise!'

'It's a tattoo.' Victoria patted the tiny head proudly with a forefinger. 'What do you make of that?'

She had always been fond of tortoises, and sometimes during the holidays she looked after one belonging to her friend Maudie. She would take me outside to watch it shuffling indifferently around our little strip of garden, poking its head into clumps of grass and bush. I stared at the image inked on her thigh.

'It's excellent,' I said after some consideration.

She laughed. 'Thanks, Dom.'

'Where did you . . . get it?'

'A bloke in Willesden.'

'Did it hurt?'

'It did, rather.'

My mind struggled to paint the scene from the limited palette of my imagination: a big, bald man sticking a needle into my sister's flesh, in a dingy room in a part of

London I had never been to, while the radio played pop music and people stood around smoking and discussing sex or parties.

'Penny for your thoughts.'

'Really?'

'Well, it's just a phrase, but if you insist on being paid to talk to me, I'll see what I can do.'

'I was just wondering if Mum and Dad know.'

Victoria let a soft whistle of amusement through her teeth. 'Of course not! Can you imagine? Not that it's any of their business. But imagine the fuss. *You don't know him from Adam!*' She retracted her leg slowly and the tortoise vanished from sight. 'If word got round at church, poor old Mum would hardly dare go up for the communion.' Her eyebrows lifted with an affectionate scorn, and the dark eyes shone at me again. 'So, Dom, you must take this secret to the grave.'

Our mother was still singing her 'something-some-things' downstairs. We listened for a moment.

'It's not their fault,' Victoria said, nodding vaguely in the direction of the singing. 'They grew up thinking you weren't allowed to do anything, you mustn't spend any money. They find it hard to understand that we . . .'

In the middle of this sentence, the front door swung open downstairs; there was a pair of thuds as Max kicked off his shoes, and a few low words exchanged. Mr Linus made some quip and gave a barking laugh to support it, and Dad responded with a rueful chortle. I sensed that Arsenal had lost. Victoria picked up the novel and, as I slipped out of the bathroom, tapped her nose to remind me of our pact.

What made me begin to idolize Victoria was her rebellion not so much against authority – all that was on a pretty minor scale – but against the polite routines of our household and of everyday life in general. She was the one who animated our family. She insisted on observing Midsummer's Day with a picnic and finding a sledge-worthy hill as soon as it began to snow. Every year she took me to Bonfire Night at Alexandra Palace, which our mother had always avoided because the noise of fireworks reminded her of bombs dropping.

'You only live once, Dom,' she used to tell me, 'and some people don't even do *that*.'

On the way to Southwold for our annual holiday, she started endless games and kept running jokes alive from year to year. She painted her room black, organized strawberry-picking, took herself off to open-air concerts or underground art exhibitions. Lying sleepless in my bed as Max worked at the desk in the corner, I would hear her heading out for the night and wish, wherever she was going, that I could go too.

Not so long ago – in 2003, or one of these increasingly odd-sounding years – I was taking photographs at a marketing awards ceremony. It's the kind of job I never have much appetite for: pointing the camera at leering middle-managers as they pose, stinking of aftershave, with their

worthless trophies. The event was over and I was packing my camera into its case when somebody tapped me
on the shoulder and said my name, tentatively: 'Kitchen?'
I turned around and after a short effort recognized the
speaker. It was Rowlands, the boy hit by the boot.

To see a man at the wrong end of his life, having previ-
ously encountered him long ago when it was all still to
come, is a disquieting experience. The decades had claimed
most of Rowlands' long hair; he had shaved the grey fuzz
into a skinhead style ill-suited to a man of his age. For a
moment I felt glad of my own unkempt mop. My brother's
old classmate was paunchy these days, and wore a dinner
jacket that was slightly too small.

'Dominic Kitchen! Little Dominic Kitchen! I thought it
was you. Never forget a face. Ha, ha.' He was drunk, and
leaned unpleasantly close to my face as he spoke.

'Rowlands?' I had never known his first name, I realized.

'Pete Rowlands.' He extended his hand; for a nasty
moment I thought he might give me a business card. 'So,
you're in this game these days? Taking the pictures?'

'I'm a freelance photographer,' I said. 'Mostly weddings
and so on, but I also . . .'

But he hadn't really been interested, and moved the
conversation in its inevitable next direction.

'What became of Max in the end? We stayed in touch for
a while. Haven't seen him now for, what, forty years!' He
grinned as if the relentless passing of time were a pretty
funny thing.

'He manages sportspeople. Part owns the business.'

'Sportspeople! Any I'd have heard of?'

'Cricketers, mostly. And he runs corporate events. Very rich, anyway.'

Rowlands chuckled. 'Bet he is! Clever bastard, Max! Give him my regards.' This platitude becomes more and more hollow as you get older. Then his eyes flickered craftily.

'And of course,' he said, 'there was that beautiful sister of yours . . .'

I felt my voice get stuck in my throat and swallowed several times to loosen it. A piece of good fortune released me from the conversation, however: one of the evening's prize-winners was trying to attract my attention. He wanted to be snapped once more, holding his ugly engraved vase. I seized the chance. 'I'm sorry, I'm still on duty . . .'

Rowlands pressed his sweaty hand against mine again. 'Of course. Duty calls. Ha, ha. Well, as I say. Regards to Max.'

He waddled back into the throng of drunken executives and disappeared from view. I stood there for a short while, unable to believe that it was indeed more than forty years since I had last seen him. For a few moments, I almost convinced myself it simply couldn't be true; that it was still some much earlier year, and all I needed to do was knock on a bedroom door to see Victoria again. Then the prize-winner struck a pose, and with unsteady hands I slung the camera strap around my neck.

II

When you're young, the family routine has the air of absolute permanence and rightness. Certain components of the weekend slotted so reliably into place that it never struck me they might not be the same in everyone's house. Victoria worked at the corner shop, came home drunk from the Shipmate and crashed her way up the stairs. Max read maths books at the dinner table. Dad dictated his football reports patiently down the phone line, still finding time to play chess with me. He would end the game with a cheerful quip. 'Good and bad news, Dominic. Bad news is, it's checkmate.'

'So what's the good news?'

'The good news is the same. But it's only good news for me.'

Mum observed all this activity from a certain distance. She cooked a roast on Sundays, knitted, and made a hobby out of domestic economies: keeping bars of soap until they were as thin as fingers, walking four miles to the shops and back to save the bus fare.

But when I was twelve Max went to Oxford, and things began to change.

On a very warm afternoon late in September, we all went together to deliver Max to his new home. The three children sat uncomfortably in the back, thigh to thigh against the hot leather like potatoes baking in an oven, surrounded by Max's belongings in cardboard boxes. Victoria had woken late and missed breakfast; she munched on a sweaty-smelling cheese sandwich. Dad was in even chirpier spirits than usual and kept singing snatches of a song, something about the banks of the Cherwell.

Max gritted his teeth each time it started up.

'Where did you get that bloody song from?'

'This is a momentous day!' Dad said. 'First Kitchen to attend Oxford in more than seven hundred years!'

'Oh, stop singing it, Harry, if it's annoying him.'

'He might as well get into the spirit,' Victoria chimed in, muffled by the sandwich. 'He'll soon have a gown on and be singing and buggering merrily away.'

'Victoria, that's enough, thank you.'

'I think it's pretty much enough from everyone,' growled Max.

Given that Max had been anticipating Oxford for years, tunnelling relentlessly towards it by the light of the Anglepoise, I was surprised at what a bad mood he seemed to be in. His face looked sore from over-shaving. He was noticeably distracted when Victoria began our customary travel game, reading the letters off the number plate of a Fiat as it passed.

'Ladies and gentlemen, your letters are G-H-O.'

Once the number plate had been called out, the players had twenty seconds to make the longest possible word containing its letters in the right order.

Max tugged irritably at a lock of his over-treated hair. 'Do we have to?'

Victoria glanced at him in amusement. 'Not got a good one?'

'All right, *ghostly*.'

'Seven letters! Is that the best you can do?' Victoria nudged me, bringing me into the joke.

Max shifted irritably in his warm patch of seat. 'What's your word, then, genius?'

'*Ghettoization*.'

'What on earth does that mean?' Mum swivelled round, baffled.

'It means putting people in a ghetto,' said Max sullenly, looking out at the motorway.

'Putting them in what?'

'Separating them, in other words. Isolating them,' Victoria elaborated, 'like, for example, women in certain establishments, or . . .'

'Shut up.'

'. . . in certain universities.'

'Shut up, Victoria. I'm not in the mood.'

'Never mind,' said Mum. 'I shouldn't have asked, anyway.'

Max, still smoothing his hair with restless sweeps of one hand, glared at us and resumed his looking out of the window. Victoria and I exchanged a grin. Max wrinkled his nose as, with antagonistic gusto, she finished off the cheese sandwich.

The centre of Oxford was clogged with little cars dropping off serious young men and their belongings. We were directed to a pale stone building. Above the entrance to the stairwell, names had been written in a fussy hand which made them look as if they had been there a hundred years already.

1. *KITCHEN, M.*
2. *SHILLINGWORTH, T.*
3. *RODWELL, J.*

I still think of the few moments I spent looking up at my brother's name next to 'Shillingworth, T.'. To think that at the time this name meant nothing to me gives the memory a peculiar quality, almost makes me doubt that it comes from my own life.

We spent an hour or so carrying belongings from the car into the bare room. I stayed close to Victoria, who hefted boxes out of the boot two at a time under Mum's wary glance. 'Careful. Get Max to help with that one.'

'I'm fine,' Victoria muttered.

'She's like a boy, she really is,' lamented Mum, watching Victoria stride across the quad.

No sooner had Max got settled in his new digs than he became noticeably impatient for us to leave, but Dad had made tea and continued to savour the occasion. Pausing to look out of the window onto the deserted lawn, he said, 'I bet there have been some famous figures in this room, over the years.'

Max grunted non-committally.

'Wordsworth was at this college, I believe, wasn't he?'

'Cambridge,' muttered Max.

'Perhaps he was looking out of this very window,' Dad went on, ignoring him, 'as he wrote – what was it – *Earth has not anything to show more fair . . .*'

'It was London,' said Max, 'and he was actually at Cambridge.'

'My point exactly,' Dad nodded. 'What a marvellous history.'

'Still, Oxford and Cambridge are the same sort of thing, aren't they,' said Mum, earning a rancid look from Max.

When at last he could decently be rid of us Max saw us out into the yard, and there we encountered 'Rodwell, J.'. He was short, had hair that was already receding, and spoke in a brash, clipped voice which reminded me of people on the radio.

'I've just met the other chap,' said Rodwell. 'Tom Shillingworth. Very nice fellow. Do you know, he already plays cricket for Surrey.' Rodwell's little eyes gleamed excitably behind the spectacles. 'Think we've struck lucky, landing next to him!' This, again, was a moment I would look back on many times.

'It's all been a bit much, today,' Mum said quietly on the way home. This was a phrase she often used at the end of a day of even moderate activity. Sometimes she gave the impression life itself was a bit much.

I glanced at Victoria, who had closed her eyes and was leaning against the window. Outside, the sun was beginning to set a pretty pink over the tarmac flatlands of the motorway. For the first time I could remember, there were only four of us: it was as if a hand had reached into the car and plucked Max away.

The next evening was another warm one. Victoria came home at about teatime and went straight out to the garden to check on Hercules, her friend's tortoise. She was wearing a straw summer hat, sandals and a red gingham dress which inched up as she crouched on the ground and shook out the contents of a bag salvaged from the corner shop. The tortoise immediately began to chew at a lettuce leaf, and she ran her hand approvingly over its shell.

'Not the same without Max, is it!'

'No,' I said, 'it's better.'

She cackled at this. It was always a good, adult feeling, making her laugh.

Our next-door neighbour Mrs Linus appeared at the fence, a washing basket in her chubby arms. Her face was wide and pink; she breathed distractingly loudly even when at rest. Although she was probably the same age as our parents, I imagined her twenty years older.

'Max gone to Oxford, then, 'as 'e?'

She was one of those people whose main conversational pleasure lies in the reiteration of known facts.

'Yes. Went yesterday.'

'Brainy one, i'n' 'e!'

'He certainly is.' Victoria smiled politely and turned back towards me as if to continue our conversation, but Mrs Linus's attention had been caught by Hercules the tortoise. 'Been lumped with 'im again, 'ave you!' She watched in amusement as the tortoise started to sniff around the empty bag. 'Funny little thing, i'n' 'e! What's 'e eat?'

Victoria smiled with obvious effort. 'Oh, lettuce and so on.'

Hercules had now wandered halfway into the bag, and was jerking his head around, trying to shake it off. Mrs Linus cackled. 'Stupid little bugger, i'n' 'e!'

'That tortoise may be stupid,' said Victoria, 'but he is likely to live to at least a hundred. He'll be here when you and I are long gone.'

That brought the conversation to a halt, but it was reanimated by the dashing figure of Mr Linus, who appeared on the lawn wearing a white cap and a pair of sunglasses. 'Blimey O'Reilly, Pat. Gonna be out here all bloody night?'

'I was just saying about Max, gone up to Oxford.'

'Yes, yes. Anyone'd think he'd been knighted.' Mr Linus gave us a wry twitch of his eyebrows. 'Bet you're getting sick of the subject, eh!'

'Oh, we've been sick of it for quite a while,' Victoria replied breezily.

Mr Linus laughed and turned his attention to me. 'Now, Dom, I know you're not a football fan, but ask your dad if he happened to see the Spurs score yesterday!'

I said I would. Mr Linus nodded approvingly, raised his cap to Victoria and put his hand on Mrs Linus's arm. 'We've got to be going, love.'

We watched them go back across the lawn, at Mrs Linus's waddling speed. Mr Linus waited patiently as she bent over to put her washing basket down by the line and straightened up again as slowly as a cruise liner. He took her arm again and guided her inside.

That was the last time we ever saw Mr Linus. Three days later he left for ever. It was weeks before Victoria and I found out, though, and even then only through corner-shop gossip. One day she came bounding up the stairs with even more vigour than usual and hammered on my door. 'Dom! Sensational news!'

She waited until dinner before confronting our parents. 'Is it true that Mr Linus has gone?'

There was a pause. They looked at each other and set down their cutlery, as if by prior arrangement.

'I believe it is,' said Dad in the end, frowning at the boiled potatoes on his plate.

'Why?'

Dad shook his head. 'We've no idea.'

'Are they getting *divorced*? You must have talked about it.'

'There's talking about it, and there's sticking your nose in,' said Mum. 'We've been round to make sure Mrs Linus is all right. We haven't been prying.'

'Cracking bit of beef,' said Dad, not bothering to disguise his intention to close the conversation down.

'Goodness.' Victoria's dark eyes were dancing. 'Drama on Park Street! I wonder what it was? Has he run off with a Czechoslovakian dowager? Or perhaps he's in trouble with the law and has done a bunk? Or perhaps . . .'

'Perhaps it's none of our business,' said Dad.

Victoria's cheeks smarted at this uncharacteristically tart put-down. She took a large chunk of meat and chewed it resentfully. There was a long lull punctuated only by cutlery clatter and averted eyes.

'I can't see how it can *not be your business* to ask after people who are pretty much your closest friends,' Victoria muttered at last.

'No, well,' said Mum, 'there we are.'

'Lovely bit of beef,' Dad confirmed, and that was that for the biggest conversation topic of recent times.

After dinner, Victoria and I adjourned to her room, where I perched on the edge of the bed while she shoved open the window and blew cigarette clouds into the night. We received dispatches from Dad's football report as he dictated it downstairs. 'Arsenal were saved by the capricious mistress of the penalty kick. C-a-p . . .'

'Do you think they actually know what happened and just won't tell us?' I asked.

'It's funny. I mean, the Linuses have lived next door since before I was born, I think. Dad and Mr Linus go back for ever. But in all that time I'm not sure they've ever discussed anything but football. I've never known them actually have a conversation.'

'*Capricious*,' Dad was saying again downstairs. 'It means

full of caprice, unpredictable.' Perhaps I was imagining it because of our discussion, but there seemed to be a certain flatness about his voice. I wondered suddenly whether he missed having Max to take to the football, whether it had been disappointing to him the way I'd turned out.

'On the other hand,' Victoria speculated, 'it could be that they just don't like discussing scandal at the dinner table.'

'Why is it a scandal?'

'A divorce is still a big hoo-hah in these parts. You're meant to tie the knot and then stay together till death, if not longer. That's what Mum and Dad are doing, all right.'

Our parents had met just before the outbreak of war at a dance in Holloway. On the morning of the dance a local prankster, with some grievance against the organizers, put notes through the letterboxes of every house in the area saying that it had been cancelled. He missed out Dad's house because it was partly hidden from the main road, and Mum's because her parents had a ferocious dog, so they were the only two people who turned up. Finding themselves standing on the deserted parquet floor, with music echoing dolefully around the room, they eyed each other for a few moments before Dad uttered what was to become a celebrated line in our family history: 'Well, I think it would make sense for us to go for a drink.'

The anecdote was dusted down so often by relatives that I felt as if I'd known it all my life. They were married a year later, on a Saturday afternoon in front of a few dozen people invited by my grandmother, who drew up a non-negotiable guest list as well as picking the date and the dress. Mum told me once that, as she walked down the aisle, she recognized so few of the people lining the pews that she briefly feared she had been taken to the wrong church. In their wedding photo, which I passed every night on the way up to bed, Mum's smile was wary, attention-shy, with a trace of relief at the approaching end of the formalities. She and the bridesmaid held bouquets stiffly away from their bodies as if they were pokers. When I was young, I found it hard to believe that the real scene had taken place in colour, that the flowers had been lilac and lavender and the grass green, instead of the roughly graded greys of the photo. Dad, wearing very round glasses with lenses so thick they resembled a pilot's goggles, beamed boyishly next to a strapping best man, a friend who would be killed in Belgium a couple of years later. Both sets of parents, standing arms folded and straight-backed like a clump of oak trees, eyed the photographer as if he had broken in uninvited.

'Mum was barely eighteen,' said Victoria. 'You can see why she's worried about me getting left on the shelf.'

'You won't be.'

'Thank you, Dom. And what makes you so sure?'

'Well, you're . . .' I searched my brain for something I was sure would go down well.

'You're larger than life.'

She squawked at this. 'Larger than life! Well, that's exactly what every man is looking for.'

I sensed my compliment had misfired. 'Sorry.'

'No, I'm charmed.' Victoria grinned and ruffled my hair. 'Right, I'm supposed to be getting ready for the pub. If I can find anything to wear.' The two of us looked at the huge heap of her assorted garments on the floor. 'My *hips* are certainly larger than life at the moment.'

I lay awake that night listening to the low voices of my parents downstairs, wondering whether they were talking about the Linuses. I was awake when they came up to bed; Victoria was still out somewhere.

Sometimes when I was younger, I had half opened my eyes after Mum pulled the blankets up over me at night, and caught her looking at me with a strange, fierce expression of love. Later on in life I would occasionally glimpse the same tender look on her face, and in those moments I realized how pretty she was, how Victoria had inherited her full lips and brown eyes. But she maintained an almost identical pose and expression in every photo taken of her: that small, conditional smile from the wedding snap, and – in later years – an arm laid rigidly on the shoulder of one of her children.

There are no pictures of that other face of hers, and as hard as I try, I can't picture it any more when I close my eyes at night.

Mr Linus's disappearance seemed to herald a time of change.

As long as I could remember, the family had gone to Southwold every summer for a holiday. But at the end of his first year at Oxford Max announced that he was going off with some friends, including the cricketer Shillingworth, whose family owned a farmhouse in

Provence. The news caused Victoria to stare darkly into her bowl of porridge.

'He's fallen in with the Little Lord Fauntleroys.'

On the drive up to Suffolk Max's absence seemed to weigh heavily, as it had that first time we dropped him at Oxford. In his place Victoria had brought her friend Maudie: the owner of Hercules, but an un-Herculean figure herself. She was very thin and mumbled so quietly you weren't always sure she had spoken at all. It soon became clear that she was not a natural at the number-plate game.

'For example that one, its letters are C-T-L. So, you see, it could be *cathedral*.'

'Or *control*,' I put in helpfully, 'but *cathedral* is obviously better.'

'Oh dear,' said Maudie, crossing and uncrossing her bony legs on the back seat between us. 'I don't think I'm going to be very good at this.'

'Right, ladies and gentlemen, here we go.' Victoria gestured at a Morris Minor. 'Easy one. H-O-R.'

'*Horrendous*,' I said excitedly. 'Or *horrified*. No, *horrendous* is better.'

'*Horticulture*,' Victoria countered.

'Oh dear,' Maudie muttered, 'I can't . . .'

'Well, there's a very easy one.' Victoria took her arm. 'Come on. H-O-R. Think of an animal.'

'I can't!'

'An animal – clip clop, clip clop!'

'Oh dear. Oh, I've spoiled the game, I'm sorry.' Maudie wrung her hands in despair.

'*Horse!*' cried Dad suddenly, from the driver's seat. '*Horse*! *Horse!*'

'Oh, God, *horse*. Yes. Oh dear.' Maudie had flushed red and was looking past me out of the window in absolute dejection. 'Oh, I'm useless,' she muttered.

There was an uncomfortable silence in the car, broken only by the groan of the engine. 'Well, it's a silly game, really,' said Mum. 'It's just to pass the time.' Victoria and I made wry faces at each other behind Maudie's head. Perhaps we were a bad family to go on holiday with, I thought.

But as we passed the familiar landmarks – a monkey-puzzle tree looming over a pub, a sign for FRESHLY PICKED VEGETABLES – everyone began to cheer up. Southwold was an unassuming place then, its high street dominated by the Swan Hotel. Wide and many-windowed, announced by an iron swan perched on a latticework of wrought iron, it presided over the high street like some fat eccentric old mayor. As well as the caravan owned by our parents' friends, we had use of a beach hut, painted in yellow and blue stripes some years ago. Mum would sit outside reading her romantic paperbacks about ladies-in-waiting who bedded princes in the Napoleonic War. Once I picked one up and browsed with interest. *He held her so tightly, she was a leaf in his arms; she wanted nothing more than to be* . . . that was all I read before it was whisked away.

The seaside always turned Dad into a one-man amusement arcade: no sooner had he got his shoes off and rolled up his trousers than he began skimming stones, making sandcastles, going back and forth for ice creams. When I was small he offered donkey rides which involved cantering up and down with me on his shoulders – 'He'll break his back,' Mum fretted – and stopping for me to feed him imaginary hay and apples. As I got older and showed no interest in playing cricket with Max and Victoria, he would paddle in the sea with me, squinting short-sightedly into the sun. 'It's never dull with all these gulls!'

All this had been the same since I could remember, but without Max things were different, particularly when evening came. Victoria and Maudie went back out to the beach to smoke and raided the chip shop for late-night feasts. Before much of the week had gone by I was in with this gang, walking arm-in-arm with the two girls up the beach and through the narrow streets. Victoria had bought a cheap camera and kept making a reluctant Maudie take pictures of the two of us.

'I can't see anything through the little hole.'

'You've still got the lens cap on, Maudie. Slide it across, look. And remember to wind it on.'

'Oh, I'm hopeless. I'm spoiling it.'

'Stop snivelling and concentrate, woman. Film's expensive.'

The chip shop was run by a fat whiskery man who wore a monocle. His wife did all the work of shovelling the chips and wrapping them in newspaper. As she toiled above the trays, sweating and shaking the hair out of her eyes, the fat man leaned in the corner with his arms folded across his belly, conversing with customers in the tone of a major-general. 'Haddock again, old boy?' 'Now, old girl, would you like salt on your chips?' Like anything else on a holiday, all this seemed much funnier to us than it probably was.

'Let's get this back to the beach before it gets cold, then, old boy!' said Victoria as we left one night. The three of us screamed with laughter, especially me: it was intoxicating to be in at the invention of a joke, when so many had begun before my time. From that moment on Victoria and I were to address each other as 'old boy' and 'old girl': a tradition which would endure long after that Southwold trip, and indeed long after our final, much less carefree, visit to the beach.

On the last evening of the holiday, our parents set off as ever for a long walk, Mum singing jauntily as they left. '*You must remember this: a* something-something *kiss.*' I had high hopes for the evening now they were out of the way, especially when Victoria sidled confidentially up to me.

'Can I trust you with a secret, old boy?'

'You certainly can!'

'Right. Maudie and I are going to a pub to have one or two whiskies. I'm not meant to leave you on your own here. But I think you can repel any enemies that might come by, can't you?'

'Of course,' I said, my stomach sinking.

I watched them go, arm-in-arm like my promenading parents. It occurred to me that quite possibly Mum and Dad had also gone to a pub, and I was the only one of the party to miss out on whatever magic went on in these dark, sour-smelling buildings. I lay on the patchy grass outside the caravan, watching seabirds circle far above, their silhouettes dark like liquorice strands against the maroon of the sky. Not far from my feet two dirty seagulls landed together and tussled over some morsel, neither quite getting it away from the other. The two of them were so symmetrically placed as they wrestled over the scrap that they almost begged to be photographed. I wandered into the caravan, easily finding the camera which Victoria had thrown down carelessly next to the little gas stove. I came back out and crouched down next to the birds. The button sank with a satisfying click under my finger; it was like some grown-up toy. I grabbed the lever, wound it on and felt the click again.

I expected Mum and Dad to be angry when they returned to find me alone, but they were in a holiday mood; this week in summer was the only time they drank. Mum murmured a couple of half-hearted remarks about how Victoria could hardly be trusted to look after a tortoise, and giggled indulgently as Dad upset the stove coming out of the tiny bathroom. The lights went out. Dad's familiar snore, the sound of someone continually inflating a balloon and then letting it go down again, began to sound in the half-dark. This was one of the signature noises of my childhood. I had drifted into a half-sleep when there was a sharp prick of light. I sat upright and saw Victoria, torch-beam over half her face, peering in. She beckoned me with a single finger. I pulled a jumper on over my pyjamas and tiptoed out.

'Will you accompany us on a jaunt to the beach, old boy?'

Midnight, normally out of my reach, seemed charged with some special energy. The moon hung plump over the dark nothing of the sea, there was a salty tang to the air, and the occasional cries of birds were unnerving. It was as if everything had been tuned up to a high, jittery pitch. Victoria and Maudie were noisy and unsteady from the drink. Maudie almost turned her ankle over as she misjudged the hop down from the wall onto the beach, and Victoria had to reach out and take her by the wrist, the two of them giggling hysterically.

'You must forgive us, old boy,' said Victoria, ushering us to a little clump of weed-covered rocks. 'We've had one or two, as they say in the Army. What did you get up to while we were away?'

'I took photos,' I said proudly. 'Got a couple of nice ones, I think.'

'Did you put the flash on?'

It was my first taste of professional disappointment. 'No.'

Victoria ruffled my hair. 'Maybe they'll still come out.'

'I can't believe how cheap it is to drink here,' said Maudie. The two of them sat either side of me, their legs drawn up in front of them, and Maudie began to roll a cigarette. Victoria opened a packet of digestive biscuits and unwrapped a chunk of cheese, both of which she had, as usual, produced from thin air.

'Yes, they know how to live up here. For what we spent on drinks tonight we'd have been lucky to get a glass of milk at the Red Rose.'

'Well, we're not going to get any richer,' Maudie reflected, 'now we're teachers.'

'Speak for yourself.' Victoria laughed. 'My brother's at Oxford, you know. You're lucky I even speak to the likes of you.'

Maudie sighed. 'I'm just going to have to marry a rich man.'

From whichever pocket had yielded the biscuits Victoria now brought a little hip-flask. She threw back her head – for once, she was not wearing a hat – and took an energetic swig. Then she wiped her mouth and handed the flask to me.

'All yours, Dom.'

I sniffed suspiciously at the flask, which made both of them laugh. 'You remind me of Hercules!' said Maudie.

'You have to start on the booze sooner or later, old boy,' she said, patting my hand.

I tipped the flask tentatively back; for a while nothing came out, and then too much, making me gag and splutter. This made them laugh more and I joined in, my head swimming after its first collision with drink. The flask went round between the three of us and they continued their conversation, while I grasped eagerly for whatever I could understand.

'Marrying a rich man is for those poor cows in the past,' said Victoria, watching the reflection of the moon as it bobbed gently on the black sea. 'These days you can just get someone to knock you up, then make him pay you off.'

'Victoria!' said Maudie, sounding genuinely shocked.

'Don't worry, I'm joking.' Victoria handed me the bottle for the third or fourth time. 'You won't catch me getting pregnant any time soon, thanks to the dear old Pill.'

'Are you . . .?' Again, Maudie's eyebrows arched in surprise. 'Do you . . .?'

'My dear girl, I certainly do, and soon, every woman in the world will, you mark my words.' Victoria made a show of covering my ears, though not well enough to stop me hearing everything. 'What else am I going to do? Have a baby with every clot I may, through no fault of my own, end up sleeping with?'

The two of them erupted in cackles again at this. It was astonishing to think that every time I was in bed, or for that matter in school or in the various other confinements that made up a thirteen-year-old's life, there were always people enjoying themselves like this, people laughing crazily somewhere. The world seemed dizzyingly full of possibilities, all of them inches closer to my grasp than ever before.

Then Maudie broke into coughs after trying to take a double helping from the hip-flask, and it seemed to subdue the mood. 'I do worry about you, Victoria,' she said.

Victoria cleared her throat and gestured up into the vast, star-dappled sky. 'You know,' she said, 'any time now, the Americans could launch a big fat nuclear bomb towards Russia, and from here, we would have a lovely view of it going whoosh across the sky.' She drained the remainder of the whisky and let the flask fall next to her bare feet. 'And then, well, that would be that.'

'You'll scare Dominic, talking like this,' said Maudie unconvincingly.

'They won't get Dom,' Victoria said. 'I'll throw myself between him and the bomb.'

Hairs stood up on the back of my neck at these words, but almost before I could register them, my sister had got to her feet. 'What I'm saying is, they could kill us all any time, so I'm bloody well going to do whatever I can until then,' she announced loudly to the night. 'And on that note, I propose that we all go for a dip in the North Sea.'

Maudie gaped at her. 'What, just . . .? But you haven't – we haven't costumes with us!'

'Good Lord,' said Victoria, 'where's your sense of adventure?'

She had stepped out of her dress already, and was standing in her underwear on the sand, prodding the water's edge with her toe. 'It's fucking cold! Come on!'

Maudie was still protesting, but got to her feet. 'Are you completely off your head?'

She threw off her dress, though, and I could see the outline of her bony frame in the moonlight. Victoria tossed her bra back towards me and kicked her knickers off; they lay on the sand, looking suddenly like doll's clothes. I hastily averted my eyes as, with a yell of joy, she disappeared into the water, followed by her friend.

Everything had happened so quickly. Now I could see neither of them, only hear their squeals as they splashed each other. 'Come on, Dom!' Victoria shouted. 'Come on!'

'I'm fine here,' I called back.

'Stick-in-the-mud!' called Victoria. I did indeed feel stuck to the spot. My heart was beating very quickly.

'There are towels in the beach hut,' I called, 'I'll go and get them for you.'

Their voices receded as I walked up the beach towards the hut. It was surprisingly eerie in the dark. I fetched two towels and tried to trace a straight path back down towards the sea, feeling rather nauseous as the whisky took hold. I had a sudden, violent feeling that my sister and her friend would be gone, that I would be alone on the beach with no idea of how to get back. For a second I thought I would be sick. But the moment passed and soon I could hear the girls again.

'Dom, is that you?'

Maudie was first out of the water; dropping my gaze once more, I threw down the towels a few paces away from her. When I looked up briefly again, Victoria, naked, was bending to claim one of them. I glimpsed the swing of her breasts as she stooped, and for a second my eye rested on the spot where she had shown me the tortoise tattoo, and crept upwards towards the tangle of hair which was then, to my relief, obscured by the towel.

We walked slowly back to our base, the two of them lowering their voices as we wove between other caravans. My brain felt like a ball of wool and the whisky had left me with a hard, sour pain in my stomach, as if I were being prodded by two thin fingers. But there was something else creeping through my guts, less a pain than a strange clenching, like the anticipatory cramps I felt before a dentist's appointment or a test at school. I felt as if all my insides had been tied into a single knot.

Now that I had seen the night-world I normally slept through, the darkness in the caravan seemed greyer and bittier than usual. I lay listening to Victoria and Maudie's drink-sodden snores, waiting for the various little mutinies of my body to subside, for the knot to loosen. When I closed my eyes I could see the moon's soft torchlight on Maudie's skin, and my sister reaching for the towel. I was young enough not to have had feelings quite like these before. I lay there waiting to fall asleep and wake up with everything back to normal.

III

Although I was still only thirteen, the next few months would be crucial in setting the course of my life, and as usual Victoria was the one who provided the push. On the afternoon of Christmas Day 1963, after the usual exchanges of trinkets wrapped like groceries, she handed me a box covered in a red-and-green paper.

'Merry Christmas, old boy.'

I tore at the wrapping. The box inside was white, heavy like a brick, and inside it was a rectangular object. I cried out in amazement.

'A camera!'

'It's an Instamatic. You can't even buy this model in this country yet,' said Victoria. 'Someone at school got their hands on it for me.'

I turned it over in my hands, running my fingers over the cold metal sides, opening and closing the hatch where you loaded the film.

'It must have been expensive, Victoria,' said our mother in the tone she always used for remarks about money: alarmed, but very faintly excited.

'Not as expensive as you'd think.' Victoria shook her head; she was wearing a red paper hat over her beret. 'In a little while everyone will have one. And *this* goes with it.' It was a book, *The Art of Photography*.

'Oh, Victoria . . .' Mum began.

'Don't worry, this one didn't cost a penny. I stole it from school. Goodwill to all men!'

I kissed my sister on the cheek and went upstairs to stash the Instamatic safely in its box under my bed. From the same place I brought out my present for her: a map of the world with all the *Victorias* circled in red pen. For the rest of the day I went every few minutes to check the camera was still there.

Over the coming months very little activity in our household escaped the Instamatic. All my pocket money went on films. I captured Victoria marking books at the kitchen table, cigarette in her mouth and plate of toasted cheese at her elbow; Dad studying the chessboard keenly through his specs ('That's a rather distracting tactic, Dom, but all the same – checkmate, I think'). Mum in her blue oven gloves, shoulders hunched at the sight of the camera, smiling awkwardly.

The summer holiday came round again, and with no Max or Maudie this time, I had Victoria to myself for several long evenings. We walked on the beach and she let me try my first cigarette, sighing patiently as I broke into coughs. We drew a giant grid and played endless noughts-and-crosses across the sand. I had saved up for three 24-exposure films and pursued her incessantly with my finger on the button.

On the last night we headed for the beach as soon as my parents had set off on their walk. The heat of the day had curdled into a stifling mugginess; the sky hung low over the water. We sat there passing a bottle of gin between us. Thanks to Victoria I had become the authority on alcohol at my school that year. She lit a cigarette, gave me a drag, then plucked it from my lips and placed it between her own.

'Fancy another one of my secrets?'

'I certainly do.'

'I hate being a teacher. I'm really no good at it.'

I was caught by surprise. 'You *must* be good at it.'

'No, old boy. I can't control the children. They don't seem to like me.'

'How can they not like you?'

She patted me on the head. 'Some people do manage it, I'm afraid.'

'Well, they're only children.'

'A lot of the parents don't like me either.' Victoria looked away, out to sea. She took off her hat and held it in front of her. 'This woman shouted at me at a parents' evening, you know. *You're not fit to teach!*'

Her face was still turned away, and there was an unusual delicacy in her voice which left me at a loss.

'How dare someone say that!'

Victoria laughed very softly. 'She dared, all right.'

'So are you going to get a different job?'

The laugh this time was rather bitter. 'I wish it were that simple, Dom. But I've trained to be a teacher. It's now understood that I'll spend the rest of my life being a teacher. This is what people do. You have your lot and you – you get on with it.'

She swigged from the gin bottle; a black-headed gull almost grazed our heads as it came in to land on the shore. 'But, you know, in a couple of generations, most of what we do will seem stupid. If you give it long enough, all the assumptions of a particular time seem . . .'

She broke off as both of us recoiled from a flash on the horizon. It was followed by an angry bark of thunder. I felt fat, cold raindrops on my neck. There was another flash and within seconds the rain was falling hard around us. Victoria grabbed my hand. 'Come on.'

We ran up the beach to the hut, the sound of thunder at our backs. She shut the door behind us and we sat on the floor in the dark, our knees just touching. The only light was the pale flicker of Victoria's match and, at intervals, the flaring of the sky outside. My hand shook a little as I passed the bottle of gin to her.

'This'll soon pass, Dom.'

She slipped her hand into mine and we sat there in silence listening to the rain pummelling the old wood. 'It's getting bored, now,' Victoria murmured after a while.

Sure enough, the rain, still heavy on the roof, had lost something of its urgency. When we came out of the hut, the rain had thinned to fine drizzle. The air was cold. We walked arm-in-arm back to the caravan. Victoria smelled of peach perfume and the tang of sea air. As she swung my arm to and fro I felt a brief return of that clenching of the guts which had struck me the year before, after seeing her and Maudie swim naked in the sea. I could not quite account for it, and tried not to think about it any more.

A couple of weeks later I met Victoria from school and the two of us went to the photo shop to collect our records of the holiday. When we went in, the Irish owner Roger Daley had the receiver of a phone balanced under his chin. He nodded genially, as always; he had a large, kindly face which reminded me of the moon depicted in a children's book. He had known Victoria for years, and always developed my films for free.

Daley pushed the three yellow packets across the counter towards us with a wink and continued his conversation. 'That's right. 24 Smedley Street. Yes – I did say *one hundred*.' Daley chuckled; he had a naturally jolly way about him, belying his imposing physique. He was built like a rugby player, though I'd once been delighted to hear him tell Victoria that sport was a God-awful waste of time. 'Well, don't you worry about that. You get a hundred bath buns to Smedley Street and I guarantee they'll pay on delivery.'

My fingernails were too stubby to prise up the tape which fastened the packets shut. I passed them to Victoria and watched as she worked on them, feeling the nervous frisk of my heart as she brought out the shiny pictures: that thrill of the payoff almost lost to photographers nowadays, in the age of the instant image. The scenes had a hazily nostalgic quality already; it always felt like Southwold vanished for another year as we drove back past the monkey-puzzle tree. Holding them carefully by the edges, she passed me the snaps one at a time. There was Victoria pelting along the shoreline in her red-and-white swimsuit, picnic basket in hand; leaning back against the monocle man's chip shop with its handwritten signs and rusting advertisement plates. *CRAVEN 'A' WILL NOT AFFECT YOUR THROAT.*

'Did I just hear you ordering a hundred buns?' Victoria asked as Daley thumped the receiver back into its cradle with a satisfied grin. We'd been taught at home that it was rude to enquire into someone else's business like this, but as usual she seemed to be in possession of another set of rules.

'On behalf of a customer of mine,' said Daley. 'Lady I did some baby photos for.'

'What does she want all those buns for?'

'Oh, she doesn't. She doesn't even know they're coming. But that'll teach her to pay me on time.'

Victoria and Daley laughed loudly. 'God, you and your practical jokes,' said Victoria. 'How does your wife put up with you?'

'The Authorities,' Daley said, referring presumably to his wife, 'always says she doesn't mind what I do, as long as nobody dies and I don't go to jail. I've only let her down once on each count.'

This time their laughter only half reached me. I had brought out the third set of pictures and was looking in bafflement at the top one. It showed a couple, both with long golden hair, standing naked in a field.

'This isn't ours,' I said.

Daley reached out for the picture. The next in the film depicted the woman in the same field, reaching up to pick an apple from a tree. I pushed the film away. Victoria and Daley were hooting with mirth. 'Ah,' said Daley, 'I've made a bit of a bollocks. Mixed your film up with someone else's. Sorry, Dominic.'

Red-faced, I handed him back the stranger's pictures. He delved under the desk and brought out two huge handfuls of identical yellow packets. 'It'll be one of these. Ah, I'm all over the place since Ronnie left.' He grimaced at Victoria. 'You're not wanting any extra work, are you? Just at weekends, or . . .?'

'I honestly couldn't, Roger.' Victoria made a regretful gesture. 'There's all the marking and stuff, and I also have to get drunk and so on, you know.'

'I could do it,' I piped up.

Daley raised his eyebrows. 'How old are you, Dominic?'

'Fifteen,' I said, 'more or less.'

'Less,' Victoria ruled.

'I like your spirit.' Daley grinned. 'You're hired.'

'Is it legal for him to work?' asked my sister.

Daley's eyebrows went up again. 'I believe so. It may just not be legal for me to pay him.' The two of them laughed again and he extended his inky hand across the counter for me to shake.

When I reported for duty the following Saturday, Daley was in the darkroom, sporting the grey jumper he would wear almost every time I saw him over the next thirty years. His hair was greying too, though he was barely thirty at this time. Daley poked his head out and the room's strange chemical smell drifted towards me. He was perspiring as if he had physically fought with a camera to give up the photos.

'Ah, Dominic. Now, your first duty. This is an important part of photo development. Go to the fridge.'

Nobody else at school had any sort of a job, let alone something like this. 'OK.'

'Get out the milk.'

'Sorry?'

'Get out the pint of milk, and pour some into a saucer.'

I thought this was one of his jokes, but it turned out that he had struck up a friendship with a crumpled hedgehog he found at the back of the shop, and fed it all through the past twelve months. Before I had been with him long he noticed a stray cat lapping at the milk, and after that I was charged with leaving two saucers.

'Let's hope there's no bloody badgers about or I might as well just start up a soup kitchen.'

Over the school months to come I half-consciously withdrew from my studies and waited impatiently for the weekend to come, so I could get back to thumbing through pictures fresh from the darkroom. Most were in black-and-white, but almost week by week there were more in sickly, streaky colour. I saw the highlights of holidays and expeditions: the Eiffel Tower, the Statue of Liberty, locked up in six-inch-by-four-inch cubes with grinning tourists in the foreground. There were odd extracts from strangers' lives: a woman posing with a cow, a group of thirty people proudly holding up what looked like a Yorkshire pudding big enough to fill a football field, a series of twenty shots of a man in a butterfly costume, pulling a ridiculous face to the camera. When he came to collect the photos he gave me a long look as if daring me to ask a question.

Now and again there would be a picture like the one I found by accident that time, a lovers' snap: the strange frank sight of pink flesh. These always gave me a brief qualm, the muscle memory of what happened on the beach, but the instinct was dulling as I became a little worldlier. I had started going to discos and the pictures on Saturday nights. I read Daley's photography magazines and snapped everything I came across. It was never quite clear why I had chosen this as my mission, but taking pictures was now all I was ever likely to devote myself to.

One Saturday I came home from work in good spirits after being left to mind the shop on my own, and challenged Dad to a game of chess. He put his work to one side and watched approvingly as I set up the board as he taught me: white square on the right, king next to queen. We played for half an hour, forty-five minutes, in attentive silence. The only sound was Mum's singing in the kitchen – *'I'll be seeing you, in all the* something-something *places'* – and a couple of times her footsteps in the corridor as she made fruitless phone calls to Max. My brother had finished at Oxford and was now working for some firm in London and living in a shared flat with friends. He never seemed to be in when they rang him. It dawned on me after a little while that I had held out far longer than I managed in most games; in fact we were pretty much on level terms. A little later I realized I was winning, and eventually the unthinkable: 'Checkmate!'

Dad took off his glasses, rubbed his eyes and put them back on. 'Goodness. Is it?'

'It is. Look. There's nothing you can do.'

'Ah. Yes.'

It was a historic moment in my brief life, but there was something odd in Dad's failure to acknowledge it. His muted reaction suggested that he hadn't quite been concentrating on the game; or even worse, had let me win. As I was leaving the room in an oddly mixed frame of mind, I glanced back to see him packing the pieces away, still with a distracted expression.

I went upstairs to report back to Victoria, but she had some news of her own.

'You know, Max has been promoted. He's got a big job now with his friend's dad.'

'The one he was at university with?'

'Yes, the one he's always waffling on about; the one who's going to play cricket for England, or for Earth against Outer Space, or whatever it is.' She signalled for me to pass her a pair of tights, from a slagheap of items tumbling out of the wardrobe. 'His old man runs some sort of shifty company managing sportspeople. Max is going to be his second-in-command.'

I remember my first emotion was relief. I had always imagined that when Max became an adult he would be, at the very least, a famous mathematician, and at worst Prime Minister or one of the people on television. Instead he was going to become a mere office worker. Perhaps he would not after all continue to loom over my life.

Victoria may have been thinking something similar, because she said, after a reflective pause, 'No doubt he'll still make a fucking enormous great success of it, though.'

He could make as much of a success of it as he liked, I wanted to burst out. He would never be half the person she was, in her grotty little junior school. I had just enough sense to realize that all this would make me sound like a sap, and kept quiet, watching as she pulled on the tights and turned to the mirror with a hat in each hand.

Maudie, Hercules' owner, had been ill recently, and Victoria had taken charge of the tortoise for weeks at a time; she'd even bought a little glass vivarium and installed it in the garden. Today she had a soft-boiled egg and a plate of buttered soldiers by her side, and was alternately feeding Hercules and herself. 'One for me, one for you.' She pulled a couple of leaves off a lettuce, fed them into the tiny, flapping mouth, then dipped a soldier into the egg.

'Hey. We've been invited to a big party by Max's friend and his rich dad. The Shillingworths.'

'Am I going?'

'You'll bloody well have to. I'm not spending all night with some ghastly cricketer and his snub-nosed parents without you.'

I felt the usual swell of pride at the notion of being her accomplice. 'Good. All right.'

'We'll have a code. If I tap my nose, you interrupt and say you're sorry, but we have to go outside and see to something. If I take my hat off, you are to say you're *dreadfully* sorry, but someone has died and we have to go home.'

I laughed. 'What if they ask who?'

'Then you get angry and say it's none of their business.'

'Can't I invent another brother?'

'All right. Our other brother, Kevin, has died.'

The laughter was cut off by the neighbour Mrs Linus, the usual bundle of laundry in her red arms. 'Nice evening, ain't it!' she boomed, panting slightly as she steadied herself against the fence.

Victoria agreed politely that it was.

'Max got 'imself something good lined up, 'as 'e?'

Mrs Linus had had this same conversation with Mum only that day, but Victoria indulged her. 'He has.'

'Brainy one, i'n' 'e!'

'He is indeed.'

Mrs Linus then gave a quick look left and right and spoke in what she probably imagined was a confidential whisper, though in fact she could have been heard in any of the dozen parallel gardens. ''Ow's your dad?'

'He's very well, thanks,' said Victoria stiffly.

Mrs Linus looked as if she would pursue the subject, but was put off by Victoria's expression. She nodded and shuffled away to the washing line.

'What did she mean, asking that?' I asked eventually.

My sister shook her head. 'That woman's gone batty since her husband went off. She doesn't know what she's on about.'

She picked up the tortoise to return him to his pen and then drew her cardigan around her shoulders and went inside. I followed her at a distance, not wanting to ask any more questions.

The Shillingworths' party was to begin at Saturday lunchtime, and go on – by the sound of it – indefinitely. This caused some consternation to my parents, who were used to parties which began at seven sharp and were out of the way by ten.

The car was quiet. It was odd, going to a rich family's house on the other side of London to meet Max: as if he had been promoted to better things, and we were his old, slightly shabby friends. We chugged our way west along the Chelsea Embankment. Dad smoothed his hair with one hand. Victoria and I played the number-plate game.

'E-T-L. Your time starts now.'

'Eternal.'

'Excremental.'

'What does that mean?'

'It means pertaining to excrement.'

'I think that's probably enough of that,' Mum said.

'We're here,' said Dad suddenly, and the car fell silent.

The house was grand, ivy-covered, and situated on its own at the end of a narrow mews. There was a huge driveway in which twenty or so cars were already parked. It was the sort of house that gives the impression you are only seeing a little of it; it has far more up its sleeve if you are lucky enough to get close. People were swarming around the front door, holding champagne flutes. At the back of the house was a large walled garden presided over by a trio of giant cedar trees. Max was waiting for us, his hair long and fashionably dishevelled; he had flared trousers on, and a cricket jumper. He shook hands with our parents.

'Didn't know you were bringing Dominic.'

'He's here as my chaperone,' said Victoria.

Max led us to a long table. I wondered whether it had been moved out here for the party, or whether rich people always had furniture in their gardens.

'This is George Shillingworth, the head of Shillingworth Enterprises – my new boss,' said Max proudly. He indicated a tanned man with bright white hair, who nodded at Dad.

'You're a pen-pusher, I hear?'

My father fiddled with his top button. 'I cover Arsenal matches, yes, for the—'

'Pretty useless shower, the Arsenal, aren't they?'

'He writes about a lot of other things, as well,' said Victoria hotly.

Max, talking over her, drew our attention to the other person at the table. 'And this is Tom Shillingworth.'

He was at least six feet tall, sandy-haired with an eager, good-natured face; he could not have looked more like a sporting hero if he had been transported straight from the pages of a comic.

'Tom, of course, plays cricket for Surrey,' said Max, still talking as if he were presenting *This Is Your Life*, 'and is about to make his debut for England.'

'God willing,' said Tom Shillingworth modestly. His eyes, which had been moving politely over the group of us, came to rest on Victoria. The colour rose in Victoria's cheeks for a second as she shook his hand. Then he kissed her on the cheek, and did the same to my mother.

'Well, if Max got the brains, it's pretty obvious who got the looks!' said Tom Shillingworth. I thought this was a stupid remark, but Victoria and Mum laughed like school-girls and Mum began to ask Tom about his cricket. He answered each question as if he had never been asked it before, and the more my mother apologized for her ignorance of the sport, the more charmingly he sidestepped her apologies.

'Red for me, red for Victoria, white for both of them, thank you,' said Max, as someone came round with wine. 'And have you got any juice for him?' I realized uncomfortably I was being talked about and looked again for Victoria's eye, but it was on the Cricketer.

I sat for an hour or so with conversations weaving around me. Mr Shillingworth talked about the money to be made once sport got its act together. Max agreed with everything he said. Dad was trying to get into the conversation, but Max cut him off again and again; only I seemed to notice. The sun had moved around: it felt as if it were boring straight through the top of my head. I wished we could go home. Before long Dad made an effort to deliver an anecdote.

'I remember one match I did for *The Times*,' said Dad, 'this is back when I was at *The Times*. Now, the referee for this particular game. This is a funny story, actually, if I can just remember the fellow's name. Now, what was his name?'

'I think Tom and George can probably live without this story, Dad,' said Max.

'No, no, now, let me finish it, let me finish it,' said Dad. 'The referee for this game . . .'

'Dad, shut up, for God's sake,' said Max.

Dad winced as if he'd been slapped and fell silent. I saw him cast about in vain for something to say; in the end he pretended to polish his glasses. I stared appalled at Max, who had already moved the conversation on. Victoria and my mother were pretending not to have noticed what happened: they were listening to the Cricketer talking about India.

I left the table and went off with my Instamatic in my hands. I made for the far edge of the garden, where the three cedar trees stood like observation towers. There was nobody around here, and I leaned against a tree, looking back at the party spread over the vast lawn. I felt very strongly, and with that knotting of my insides which came from time to time, that it was a bad thing we'd ever fallen in with these people. I've made many mistakes in my life, but I was right about that.

Part Two

IV

Victoria and the Cricketer got married three years later.

She had long since moved into the Cricketer's flat in St John's Wood, next to Lord's where he did a lot of his important business of propelling a little ball around a field. She had given up the teaching job and now trailed around with the Cricketer to Test matches and television studios and black-tie sportsmen's dinners. He took her on his tours to New Zealand and Australia, India and Pakistan.

I mooched around the empty-feeling house on Park Street with my patchy first-time moustache and leather jacket, taking photographs and waiting for postcards to arrive from all corners of the globe.

Old boy – I'm in India! The heat is astonishing. It's so hot that I had to take a break in the middle of writing the word 'astonishing'. I'm only just managing to keep up my smoking. Damn, now I've left no space to tell you about the

OB – Down Under! Hope you like the BEAUTIFUL VICTORIA on the front. I'm having to write this upside down, so forgive me if the postman looks at you oddly. Heavenly down here. Tom made a century today and we danced on the balcony of our hotel room. He's an excellent dancer. I'm rather drunk. Over and out.

Sir Dominic of London – bought six hats today and ate a cheese only just smaller than my head. Hope you are keeping an eye on the parents while I swan around with my fiancé. I remain, + c, Victoria Kitchen (the future Mrs S).

Yes, she was in love all right, and although marriage was meant to be about joining two families together, it felt as if she were becoming part of the Shillingworths much faster than the Cricketer was becoming one of us. Given his sporting commitments, he rarely set foot in our house. When he did favour us with his presence, we all had to tidy up beforehand. He would chat about Arsenal with Dad, charm Mum by admiring a vase. Undaunted by my dislike of sport, he astutely quizzed me about my camera. You could not fault him.

At a quarter to two on the wedding afternoon I caught Victoria pacing behind the church in Marylebone. She was anxiously holding up her big lampshade of a dress to stop it trailing in the dry grass. The dress was accompanied by a garland of purple-blue flowers which almost swamped her short hair entirely: it was the closest she could get, I thought, to being married in a hat. Mum had lobbied in vain for her to grow her hair. 'Just this once, Victoria, you only get married once.'

'We shall see about that,' Victoria had replied. 'If I don't like him, I may give it another go.' Our mother spluttered quietly at the dinner table and the subject was closed.

This sort of bravado was missing from Victoria's bearing as I approached. She looked up and grinned wanly.

'OB! What are you doing here?'

'Said I was going to take some snaps. Everyone's still blathering away outside the church. What are *you* doing here? Shouldn't you be . . . aren't you meant to be late for the wedding?'

'Collywobbles. Got the driver to drop me off.' She wrinkled her nose. 'I'm hungry. You haven't got any cheese, by any chance?'

'Of course I haven't got any cheese. Do you think I carry cheese around in my pockets?'

'I assume everyone does.'

I took a fag from my jacket pocket. 'You can have one of these.'

'You're the best brother ever.'

I lit it with a match and put it in her mouth. She took a drag and held it out gingerly at arm's length. 'Mustn't get it anywhere near the dress.'

'I've never seen you wear anything so . . . big.'

'It's the done thing.' She shifted her weight uneasily from one foot to the other.

'Why the collywobbles?'

She picked at the garland on her head, teasing a purplish flower from its stem. 'Just all a bit much, isn't it, as Mum would say. I'm really only a kid, Domkins, like you. But now – a wife! Babies, cooking!'

'You won't be just his wife,' I said. 'You'll still be . . . you know. What you are.'

'What am I?'

'You're larger than life.'

She beamed at the memory of this earnest phrase. 'Ah yes. So what are you, anyway? Smaller than life?'

'I think,' I said, after considering it, 'I'm about the same size as life.'

She laughed. The two of us stood in silence for a moment. The bells of another church were clanging on the breeze.

'Anyway,' I ventured, feeling rather unequal to the conversational territory, 'you must, er, love him.'

'Oh, I do, I do,' said Victoria. 'He's a wonderful man, and he makes me laugh ever so much, more than anyone. And he's so talented . . .'

She bit her lip and I thought she was about to say something else. But then we heard voices on the other side of the wall, and she hastily dropped the cigarette and speared the butt on the heel of her shoe. 'You ought to get back in there,' she said.

It occurred to me as I walked away that it might be a long, long time before I got a few minutes alone with her again, that in only a couple of hours she would belong to someone else. In truth, of course, the transition had taken place some time before.

*   *   *

Not allowed to take pictures in the church, I watched the first of what would be thousands of weddings. It did not feel as if the garlanded Victoria at the altar were the same Victoria I had drunk gin and played the number-plate game with. We sang 'Love Divine, All Loves Excelling', led by a squad of blue-clad choirboys, their starched collars and expressions so earnest they almost seemed in pain as their mouths opened in perfect Os. The dusty antique phrases came and went: *'Till death us do part.' 'With my body I thee worship.'* I flinched slightly at the thought of what this meant. *'If any man can show any just cause why they may not lawfully be joined together . . .'* Dad reached for Mum's hand at this moment and the two of them anxiously surveyed the congregation. I had seen *The Graduate* not long ago, and for a second the idea of a dramatic intervention fluttered at the back of my neck. Of course, there was no such excitement, and before long the two of them swept back down the aisle. As they passed me, I tried to catch Victoria's eye and give her a wink, but someone leaned across my field of vision to kiss her on the cheek, and then they were gone.

The reception was held in a marquee erected in the Shillingworths' garden, and it was here that Dad gave the father-of-the-bride speech. There had already been a speech by the Cricketer himself – he called Victoria the most beautiful girl in the world – and one by Max, who made all sorts of cracks about cricket and sex, lost on me as I knew very little about either.

Dad had his words written on a series of postcards. As he walked up to the stage, he seemed to be shuffling them around as if they had only just been handed to him by a scriptwriter. Mum's face was frozen in the tidy smile she had worn all day, but she was holding the edge of the table, I suddenly noticed, as if braced for a physical shock. When he got to the stage, there was a long wait as he continued to fiddle with the notes. I felt very hot in my starchy shirt and was horribly conscious of the hundreds of eyes on my father.

'And so, on this happy day . . .' he began at last, after clearing his throat, 'I can only say: well, I can only say that this is a happy day!'

'Great start,' muttered a Shillingworth at my right elbow. I could feel my cheeks prickling.

'Victoria Shuttleworth,' said Dad. 'It has a very nice ring to it, hasn't it!' There was a pause while everyone waited to see whether he had got the name wrong on purpose, to set up a joke; then another pause as it became clear that he hadn't. 'I'm sorry . . .' he began, backtracking. 'I meant, of course, Shillingworth . . .'

'Shouldn't be that hard to get it right,' called Old Man Shillingworth, from his pride-of-place spot next to Victoria, 'just look at the name on the cheque that paid for this!'

Mum's hands on the table-edge tensed even more, but a number of people laughed, among them Max, who slapped Old Man Shillingworth on the back and began to top up his glass.

Dad's speech tottered on. He referred to Hercules without explaining that it was a tortoise, baffling everyone. There was an embarrassed laugh when, rather than referring to Victoria as the best daughter he and Mum could have had, he simply read out 'the best daughter we have had'. He continued to rearrange his notes every now and then with a puzzled frown. What goodwill there had been at the start of his speech very quickly gave way to a sticky silence, threaded with coughs and shuffles and the creaks of chairs as people slipped out.

'Oh, I wish he would stop,' Mum muttered. Not knowing what to do, I lightly patted the hand which lay white on the table.

'Victoria,' said Dad, 'is not just one in a million, but . . .' and then stopped dead. He fiddled once more with the pages and raised his eyebrows regretfully. 'I'm afraid I have completely forgotten what I was going to say.'

'Good thing, too!' piped up Old Man Shillingworth. 'Wrap it up, man! Let's have a toast to the bride, before we all die of old age!'

There were cries of 'Hear, hear' and everyone was suddenly on their feet except Mum, who didn't join in the toast at all; she watched as Dad tucked the postcards into a pocket and came back to the table. As he wriggled back into his seat, she turned her eyes away.

'Shame,' he said, 'made a bit of a hash of that.'

She said nothing, but for a second I saw tears bloom in her eyes, and the sight was so peculiar that I had to look the other way. I saw Victoria in discreet conversation with the Cricketer, the two faces warmed by a quiet, shared joke; she didn't seem to have been upset by our father's humiliation, or even really to be conscious that it had happened.

The afternoon wore on, another long day in the Shillingworth garden much like the one that had started all this three years before. Hired waiters circulated with trays; a jazz band appeared from nowhere as the shadows lengthened. Every conversation I overheard was about sport or money. I was offered a glass of wine, helped myself to a couple more, and began to forget the dreadful speech and all the other aspects of the day I didn't care to think about too much.

The sun hung over the garden for so long that it was as if the Shillingworths had hired it especially for the occasion. I was surprised, as I had been at that party three years ago, by the sheer inexhaustibility of festivities. Victoria and I had watched Churchill's state funeral a couple of years before on her fuzzy little television, and that had seemed to go on all day – 'Will they ever get the bugger into the ground?' I remembered her asking in despair – but weddings, in my imagination, had always been brief affairs. I'd assumed they were all over when you saw people spilling out of churches in the early afternoon; it was becoming clear now that they were really all about what happened afterwards.

I began to wander around with the camera, racking up shots of people I didn't know: a grandmother lifting a three-year-old onto her lap, a couple of oiks beginning a game of cricket with a champagne cork. It felt good to be capturing these instants: not for posterity, more as a sort of small victory, the kind felt by a spy. There was a quiet power in moving between these much older people, breaking off a crumb of their lives for myself. I much preferred it to trying to make conversation.

In the marquee, the shuffling tones of the jazz band had given way to livelier fare as a friend of the Shillingworths spun Stones 45s. But the real action was on the other side of the party, beyond the great trio of trees. A slip of a river, one of the Thames' muddy little tributaries, dipped in and out of the grounds here. About twenty revellers had set up camp with magnums of champagne carried off like warriors' spoils. Girls slumped on the yellow-green grass, dresses spread around them and hair streaming loose as they swigged from bottles. A few men in rolled-up shirtsleeves were booting a football about with the usual exclamations.

In the middle of it all, a photographer was cajoling Victoria and the Cricketer into a series of late-wedding-day poses: head resting on shoulder, laughing, arms linked with friends and so on. This was often the most fruitful time of day for bride-and-groom shots, I would later learn, away from the stilted gestures of the church-yard and the pressures of the day. These were the photos that ended up being enlarged and frame-mounted in the new couple's bedroom. The photographer was a willowy figure with a long nose; he wore a waistcoat and tie and had a huge accordion of a camera set up on a tripod. As I approached with my more basic equipment he glanced up for a second and then continued what he was doing. 'And another of those lovely smiles, please, Vicky!' *Vicky*, I thought in disgust.

The ball came to rest a few feet from the photographer. 'Over here!' yelled someone, but he ignored the game altogether and bent over his tripod again. He was side-on to the water and had framed Victoria and the Cricketer beautifully, with the river curving behind their left shoulders and a bashful willow batting its lashes in the distance. I took a bootleg picture over his shoulder. 'And just one more with that little laugh,' commanded the snapper, fiddling again with his lens.

'Hey, kick it back!' yelled a drunken guest. The photographer ignored them again, and this time it was a mistake. I turned around to see an ugly tangle of men roaring and bantering as they wrestled to get the ball. Like a single multi-legged creature, suit-tails and shirt-ends flapping and leather shoes skidding, the jumble hurtled down towards the river. I jammed down the button and got a blurry image of mayhem and motion which I'd keep for many years. 'Jesus! Watch out!' yelled the Cricketer, but for once nobody was listening to him. Victoria let out a thrilled, horrified shriek. The glued-together men, at the mercy of their own momentum, went careering past the photographer and with a tremendous splash plunged into the river, taking the camera with them.

There was a stunned silence, broken after twenty seconds as heads bobbed above the surface and laughter tore the air. The first of the miscreants rose up like a sea-monster, his sodden jacket weeping river-water. Victoria's face looked both aghast and amused. The photographer had become ghostly. I was not quite brave enough to steal a picture of him. His Adam's apple bulged; all he could manage for a while was a series of clicks as if he himself were a camera. Then he yelled, 'You utter fucking bastards!'

The words sounded ridiculous in the placid evening, and in the mouth of someone plainly not used to swearing. I had never seen an adult lose his temper quite like this. 'You absolute stupid bastards, you fucking – terrible animals!' bleated the photographer incoherently. 'You will have to pay a lot of money for that! A lot of money!'

This scrubbed some of the glee from the culprits' faces. The Cricketer was raising his hands in an emollient gesture, like the fine sportsman he was meant to be. 'We'll take care of all that.'

'Well, I don't know who's going to sort out your pictures!' snapped the photographer, seemingly only further inflamed by the Cricketer's efforts. 'Those are gone, sir!' He cocked a thumb towards the river. 'Those are bloody well gone!'

Victoria bit her lip. The Cricketer began a confident rejoinder, which died in his mouth. The various soggy offenders stood hands on hips, avoiding his eyes.

'I've got some good ones,' I said, so quietly that nobody heard it, but with a rising feeling of triumph.

Daley developed my films, enlarged about a dozen shots and had his assistant Lauren arrange them in a hide-bound album with patterns of psychedelic hearts and jagged suns fringing the pages. He gave it to Victoria and the Cricketer as a gift. Then he waited for the orders to come in. The

Shillingworths purchased an album (with more traditional floral piping) and so did my parents. Another dozen relatives bought a set, and then came the requests for enlargements. My pirate photo of the newlyweds by the river, moments before the accident, emerged again and again from the darkroom; there was plenty of demand too for a hijacked shot of the whole wedding party on the church steps which, again, I had taken over the real photographer's shoulder. The quality of the pictures was nothing special, but since people had thought there were no pictures at all – except a couple of casual snaps by relatives – they were received like masterworks. Word got around that a kid's private photo collection had saved the big day from obscurity. Daley had long been photographing weddings as a sideline to his main business, but this was the moment he realized fully how lucrative it could be.

As for me, I left school and began a night-school course in advanced photography, worked full-time in the shop, and within the year would be Daley's business partner. The legacy of my work at Victoria's wedding would be that people continued to ask me about it in the shop for years to come. I soon tired of the subject, because for all the fuss in the aftermath, there was only one person whose admiration I really craved. But she and the Cricketer had taken off for a two-month honeymoon to coincide with his tour of the West Indies, and all I got were a few postcards, more widely spaced than before. *OB – sky is even bluer than it looks in the picture!* In the world she had now been initiated into, a world of famous sportsmen and cocktails on beachside balconies, I supposed the topic of my camera-work was pretty small fry.

Daley and I did our first wedding together the following spring. He'd already taken me to school prize-givings and a couple of family portrait sessions. I knew from my course how to fit the different lenses and test the light and handle the unwieldy films. Mum and Dad were pleased to see me working, and there was very little pressure on me to stand out; Max had satisfied their appetite for academic success, and now that Victoria had provided the surprise bonus of a glamorous marriage, Mum had more than enough garden-fence ammunition to keep Mrs Linus in check for the rest of her days.

The age difference between Daley and me – around fifteen years, though I never found out exactly – ought to have meant we always felt like master and apprentice, but from that first car journey onwards we felt like colleagues, partly because Daley was so appealingly childish. He took immediately to the number-plate game.

'Wispification.'

'What?'

'Wispification. The process whereby something becomes wispy.'

'That's not a word!'

'You haven't a dictionary with you, I see. So I think it stands.'

On the way down to Sussex we got caught in foot-ball traffic and to my alarm Daley began to bait the match-bound fans as we drew up alongside them, bringing a blue scarf out of the glove compartment and shaking it at a carload of men dressed top to toe in red. Their faces twisted in contempt and the man by the rear right-hand door stuck his finger up and began shouting at us. I found myself gripping the sides of my seat as we jolted away. Daley handed me the scarf to put back in its place, and as I replaced it I saw that he kept a red one there too.

'It's a little bit of fun I like to have on Saturdays. If a fellow likes a team in red, there'll be a blue team he hates. They really are that simple, football people.'

'Aren't you scared they'll come after you?'

'I've seen some bad things,' Daley replied with a proud jut of his head. 'It takes more than kids to scare me. What are they going to do? Honk me to death with their car horn?'

'Who *are* you scared of, then?'

'There's only one person, and I don't expect to meet Him any time soon.'

'Are these people honking at you because of the scarf, too?'

'No. They're honking because they think I'm a bad driver.'

'And are you?'

'Oh, yes.' He cackled. 'I'm a terrible driver. Don't tell your mam.'

I was almost sorry when we got to the church, a pile of late-medieval stone with a proud spire like an antenna scouring the sky for God. I unloaded our bags from the boot and set up the tripod for Daley, watching as he clicked and wound and clicked his way through the arriving congregation. The atmosphere outside the church was more subdued than at Victoria's wedding, and the general style more like the forties than the sixties in appearance: the men wore carnations, the women pastel dresses, and the train on the bride's dress looked longer than the nave of the church.

We weren't allowed in to take pictures. 'I have to ask you to respect the sanctity of the service,' the vicar said, with a bow of the head. People always talked about 'respect', I had already noticed, when they were trying to stop you from taking pictures. Daley lit a couple of fags on the church steps. I took one and puffed it, feeling twice my age. The organist ground the pipes into a wobbly hymn, which I recognized from Victoria's wedding. *'Love divine, all lo-o-oves ex-CELL-ing . . .'* The singing came like faint smoke out of the church: the nasal top-notes of middle-aged women, the non-committal mumbles of the unbelievers, the clanking organ holding it all together.

'Why don't they allow pictures?'

Daley glanced up at the heavens. 'Something to do with it being a holy place, or what-not.'

'Did you have them at your wedding?'

He shook his large head slowly. 'We had a proper Catholic wedding. Lot of words. Lot of ceremony. Went on half the day. I was nineteen. Did what I was told.'

'You've been married for ages, then.'

'Certainly feels like it,' said Daley, but there was a knowing softness in his smile.

'I'm definitely going to let them take pictures at my wedding,' I said.

'I didn't know you were getting married.' Daley gave me a wry grin.

'Well, everyone does, don't they?'

'It's better than being alone,' he said, 'I think most people agree on that.'

We heard snatches of the liturgy through the walls, intoned by the vicar and repeated at a higher pitch by the couple. '*To love, cherish, and to obey,*' he prompted. '*To love, cherish, and to obey,*' said the bride. At her wedding I'd noticed that Victoria had had to say 'obey' but the Cricketer hadn't; I asked Mum why, but she said she didn't know. We heard snatches of liturgy through the walls. There was the appeal to anyone who knew just cause, and that moment of pantomime suspense. The vows were intoned by the vicar and repeated at a pitch often by the couple. Then the organ began to groan into another hymn. I knew this one from school: 'Jerusalem'.

'*I will not cease from mental fight,*' said Daley. 'Perfect for a wedding. Now, they'll be out in a minute. Take the Pentax and just snap away and see what you get.'

Through the horizontal spyhole I glimpsed one face after another as they surfaced on the steps: some dabbing at moist eyes with handkerchiefs, others seeming cheerful to have got out. Daley arranged the new couple against the stonework for the first, carefree pictures and then began to coax the motley guests into formation on the steps. 'Tall at the back, please! That's you, sir! Here's a little tip: you can tell you're the tall one if your face is higher up than the others'. And now smile, those of you who have the necessary muscles . . .'

We drank a couple of glasses of the gassy, slightly sour champagne which I would come to associate with Saturday afternoons, and Daley clattered us back towards town, the dusk swallowing the motorway one piece at a time. Our next wedding was the following Saturday and already I couldn't wait for the week to roll away.

A couple of months later Daley and I were crouching in the organ loft of a much grander church around an hour before formalities began. I had seen, in the intervening period, a synagogue, a Methodist chapel, and a registry office for the wedding of two divorcees at which all the guests seemed slightly embarrassed. This latest appointment was the first of a June and July which saw us in high demand. The couple wanted some atmospheric shots of the church. The organ loft was obscured from the congregation's sight by a pair of stone columns, and gave a fine aerial view of the pews and the stained glass, which gleamed almost gaudy green and blue in the sunlight. Daley was perched on the organist's stool peering through his viewfinder. The organ's pipes gave off a strong coppery smell; the white stops were like the dials of some time-travelling machine. As Daley was about to take the shot, two ushers came clumping down the aisle, their footsteps and words ricocheting up to us with perfect clarity. I'd come to be fond of it already, all the antiquated terminology: *groom, usher, page-boy.*

'I'll be glad when it's over, to be honest.'

'Me too. All the standing around. I mean, this church stuff is not really my thing. I guess it's for Megan's family.'

'Are they churchy?'

'Oh, awfully. Proper High Church. They really go for all that guff.'

'I WILL STRIKE YOU DOWN!' boomed Daley suddenly from our high perch. The two unsuspecting men leapt in shock and one gave a cry like a sheep's bleat. A cackle nearly escaped from me, but Daley clamped a finger to his lips and yanked me down and out of sight. The two of us burrowed there, watching as the ushers looked around in bewilderment. My stomach was clenching with suppressed laughter. We waited for them to turn, unnerved, and leave the church before we stuck our heads out again and howled with laughter.

'Listen, Dom,' said Daley, as the laugh melted slowly away, 'you're very good at this already. You can take the main pictures today.'

'What?'

'There's really nothing to it. Line them up. Tell 'em what to do.'

My hands gripped the camera as if it were there to keep them steady rather than the other way around. Even in this church, which had a more liberal vicar, we were only allowed to take pictures during the signing of the register.

I came forward nervously from my nook at the back of the choir-stalls and stood in the vestry door. The bride and groom, a good-looking pair named Megan and Hamish, were exchanging quiet words as the organist began an incidental score. The relatives clustered around to sign; I could hear the fountain pen scratching across the stiff paper. This was always a lull in proceedings. I fixed them in view and snapped away. The bride's blue eyes sparkled and her mouth twitched into a sudden brilliant smile.

'That's all,' I mouthed at them.

I lowered the camera and the bride leaned across and grabbed both her new husband's hands. 'Thank you,' she whispered, just audibly.

'Thank *you*,' he replied, and they looked at each other with a cocktail of affection and lust, and a sort of awe of the occasion, which made me yearn to feel something of what was in them now. I quickly clicked the button and froze this extraordinary look onto the film like someone encasing an insect in amber. I had inadvertently learned an important rule: the best pictures come when people think you aren't taking them. I slunk back to my choir-stall and waited for the Mendelssohn with a pang of anticipation.

This time we were also taking pictures at the reception, in a hotel ten miles down the road. They laid out extra places at the table and we laughed gamely at the speeches and toasted one stranger after another. I was light-headed as I followed a little crowd outside to watch the tossing of the bouquet.

'I've got no chance,' said the girl next to me, rocking onto her tiptoes. 'I can hardly see her.'

'I'll get it for you.'

She had her hair in a long ponytail which made her face appear very round, and her eyes were large and startled; she looked a bit like a cartoon animal. 'You won't.'

'I bloody will.' I was so buoyed up by the day, anything seemed possible. 'I've got the element of surprise. They won't be expecting a man.'

The bouquet came thudding through the air like a grenade, faster than I expected or hoped: after all, I had spent years on the sports field trying to dodge catching duties. I shouldered someone out of the way and hoisted myself up at the same time as a lanky girl with very straight hair like spaghetti. The two of us clashed elbows in the air and the prize eluded us both and fell to earth. The scared-eyed girl was first to react and went darting for the bouquet. As she held it aloft I went rather sheepishly back to her side.

'Well, I *sort of* got it for you.'

'Close enough,' she said. 'How can I repay you?'

The hotel had a little private garden for guests. She led me over the low wall and put out her arms. I drew her towards me and she took hold of my hands and placed them with a surprising decisiveness under her skirt. She was twenty-four; I was only nineteen. In a sense I had been waiting for this moment ever since those uneasy whispers on the beach at Southwold. After the success of the wedding itself, now this: it was as if my life were starting for real. I would never see her again, but then, many of the guests would never see each other again. This was a wedding: behind the main action, a brief convergence of a hundred lives where any number of smaller stories could be written.

In the car I could hardly get the grin off my face.

'Enjoy the day?' asked Daley with a sidelong glance.

'I think it all went very well,' I said, deadpan.

He wrinkled his nose in amusement. 'Just be a little bit careful, Dom. Now. R-D-U.'

I was having difficulty focusing on the game. '*Reduction*.'

'*Rodulation*.'

'What?'

'Rodulation. The process whereby rods are made.'

'That's not even close to being a real word.'

'Unfortunately, Dom, you still don't have a dictionary. Besides which, I think you've probably had enough luck today, don't you?'

There were a couple of years of this: weddings every weekend and sometimes even midweek; albums, enlargements, duplicate sets. Portraits and special events. The occasional trip to a country house and a weekend in Brittany. At the beginning of the seventies, Daley and I had stolen a march on a market which would be far more competitive by the eighties: the memory business. Sometimes I went alone in my new Ford Capri, and then I would stay late, dance, and perhaps steal a fumble with someone in a hotel room or car park. Saturdays blurred into one long heady party. I enjoyed the ceremonies, which I could now follow word-for-word in my head; I enjoyed the rampaging hormones of the reception even more. It was hard to believe that I had depended so heavily upon Victoria for my understanding of the opposite sex.

For the first time ever I found I didn't really want to see Victoria, because it would mean seeing the Cricketer, and that in turn would unfortunately mean cricket.

They once invited my parents and me to a match at Lord's. The Cricketer was playing, but the match itself was only part of the story: Old Man Shillingworth was putting on a lunch in some private box, and Max, his lackey, would be in charge of running it. I had little appetite for all this, but Mum was longing to see her daughter, and Dad had wanted to be in a private box at Lord's his whole life. I drove them in the Capri.

When we got there, the box was already over-full; under Max's supervision an Indian waiter was serving cocktails, although it was only half past eleven in the morning, and endless people in white jackets were milling noisily around tables. The Cricketer was batting for England on the field, but few of the people there seemed to care about the game. I went out to find Victoria on the balcony, smoking a cigarette and watching intently. She had on a peculiar purple hat; very flat, almost like a mortar board. Her hair was short as ever, barely reaching her ears. She acknowledged me without taking her eyes off the game.

'Dominic!'

'You're quite the cricket fan these days,' I observed as neutrally as I could.

'He's made 48. Two more runs and it's a half-century.'

'Let's all hope he makes it.'

She winced slightly at the sarcasm in my voice.

'Sorry.'

'It's nice to see you, Dom. How's the photography?'

The question seemed pat and ordinary, like something a distant relative would ask, and I felt a rising disappointment.

'It's fine, thank you.'

She cried out in delight as, far below us, her husband whacked the ball and the umpire waggled his hand as if tracing the line of an invisible river.

'That's a 4!' She raised her arms above her head to applaud. Down on the pitch, the Cricketer removed his helmet and raised his bat to acknowledge the crowd. Even some of the freeloaders from the private box had come out to join us on the balcony, and as he continued to bat, they made all sorts of fawning remarks.

'On the front foot, he's as good as anyone in the country.'

There was a lunch break, during which I tried to corner Victoria, but she was busy chatting to Max and Old Man Shillingworth; then, in the remorseless way cricket matches have, it all started up again.

When I next went outside, two men were leaning over the balcony either side of Victoria, languidly watching the game with drinks in their hands. In its accidental symmetry, the scene begged to be photographed. I clicked the lens cap off. Pointless as the whole thing seemed to me, there was no denying that cricket had an aesthetic appeal: the white-clad fielders dotted in their neat patterns around the huge green sea, the grey stand climbing into the low London sky. I took half a dozen pictures before someone tapped my elbow.

'Excuse me. Can you not do that.'

'Sorry?'

I turned to see a small bald man in a blazer; he pointed gravely to the camera. 'Can you kindly not take photographs, please.'

'I'm not using a flash or anything.'

'No, but even so.' The official looked at the camera as if at a device whose precise powers were unknown. 'You're right behind the bowler's arm here, and if you were to distract the batsman . . .'

I was about to say something sarcastic, but Victoria had half turned to follow the conversation, and I felt that by staying in it at all I would look petty. I lifted the camera from around my neck. Once more I marvelled at the presumption of the game, of all sports: you could be told off for the tiniest act which might throw them off their course.

Late in the day the Cricketer was finally bowled out. He received a huge ovation as he trooped off, and within half an hour was in the box with us, being congratulated by so many people that it was hard to make him out at all. Max, by now midway through a campaign of flirtation with a thin and loudly-laughing girl, clapped the Cricketer on the back and reeled off a series of in-jokes to demonstrate what good buddies they were.

But the Cricketer was only interested in one person. She took off her hat in mocking subservience, then grabbed him in a way that was anything but playful. Right in front of me she kissed him, her hands digging in to the back of his cricket whites with the hunger of little animals after prey. I looked away.

Before I left there was a comic turn by Old Man Shillingworth. The Indian waiter, who had been at his post now for nine or ten hours, came round to ask if anyone wanted a brandy or cognac. He pronounced the word as if it were English, with 'cog' and 'nac' as the two syllables. Shillingworth was delighted. He made a big show of shushing everyone and getting the waiter to repeat what he had said.

'I was just asking, sir, if anyone was requiring a brandy or a cognac.'

'Cog-nac!' Old Man Shillingworth clapped his hands vigorously. 'That's a classic! Say it one more time for me!'

With a confused smile, the waiter said 'Cog-nac' a third time. A number of people were in on the laugh this time, and when I glanced around I saw that Victoria was among them.

She sat there blithely with her hand on the Cricketer's knee, laughing and fluttering her eyelashes. It was hard to blame her, I supposed. She was with a handsome man she loved, she had been promoted to an entirely different social sphere from the one we grew up in; and she had a glass of champagne in her hand and a cheese platter in front of her. It was much easier to blame myself, for the acid dislike I felt for everyone there, and for the chastening hollowness in my stomach as I left the gathering, barely noticed by Victoria or by anyone else.

V

The trouble with rich, powerful people isn't merely that they always insist their way is the right way, but that they very often have a point.

When Dad's sixtieth birthday came round, the year after that wretched day at the cricket, nobody quite knew how to celebrate it. Victoria, for so many years the family's motivator, had been away most of the year watching the Cricketer swat balls around the lawns of Bombay and Barbados. Max was too immersed in money-making to think much about birthdays. Mum might have liked the idea of marking the occasion, but would never go out on the financial limb of booking a restaurant. Which just left me; but although I was now well into my twenties, it had never been me who told the rest of the family what to do.

But Old Man Shillingworth had a plan: why didn't we come round to the mansion for dinner? Victoria and Max loved the idea, of course. Mum was still sneakily attached to the novelty of being connected with a rich family, and Dad with the idea of being in with the sporting crowd. And so we piled into the old Fiat as a family for the first time in years.

Unusually, Mum was driving, presumably in case Dad wanted to drink; or because he already had. Under pressure from Victoria, she had bought herself a blue floral dress from Marks & Spencer for the occasion. It sat rather awkwardly on her: so rarely did she allow herself new clothes that, when she did have a new dress, she wore it as if she were bluffing and might be found out any minute. Dad sat whistling in the passenger seat. 'Not too far to go,' he said several times, and, 'This is all very pleasant,' as if the car trip were a celebration in itself. Once he started up singing, seemingly out of nowhere – *'For he's a jolly good fellow . . .* and something-something-something.' I assumed this was a whimsical parody of our mother, but she didn't respond: she seemed to be concentrating hard on the road.

Despite being well acquainted with the Shillingworths' sprawling grounds, my parents and I had hardly set foot in the house itself until now. Old Man Shillingworth set about giving us a tour while Max and Victoria piled into the kitchen and began to help with setting the table, chatting and chuckling with Mrs Shillingworth as if this were their home now.

It was a seventeenth-century farmhouse converted into a four-floor Victorian abode, with what estate agents these days would call 'charming original features': the fireplace, the low oak beams, that woody, venerable old-house smell.

Its owner informed us of the price of everything. 'That's a £14,000 painting, up there.' 'Those rugs don't come cheap, I can tell you. Three grand apiece.' My mother laboured gamely to reply each time. I wondered as usual whether she was revolted by this sort of talk, or yearned deep down to be able to join in with it.

There were seemingly dozens of guest rooms; there was a drawing room, a scullery, a games room, and one labelled *Trophy Room*.

This was Old Man Shillingworth's favourite. He opened the door slowly, coaxing an ostentatious creak from it, and dropped his voice slightly like a museum guide coming to a world-renowned landmark. 'Now, in here,' he said, in a tone that was almost sentimental, 'is a hundred years of history and untold thousands' worth of treasures.'

Shelves and cabinets ran all the way around the room, piled with trophies and curiosities. There were marble busts and photos and a procession of weathered cricket bats. There were odder things too – African masks, an antique harpsichord – and numerous drawers packed with smaller valuables.

'All Tom's trophies, right back from school,' said Old Man Shillingworth, 'and all the things I've picked up along the way, and some of the things that belonged to *my* father, and even *his* father who killed a lot of Zulus.' He browsed our faces briefly and chuckled. 'This family,' he said, as if reciting a motto, 'has always been able to win things, and what we've not been able to win, we've bought, and what we couldn't buy, we got by other means.'

'How lovely!' said our mother faintly.

And here, I saw, was the crux of the Shillingworths. There was no contradiction in hoarding sporting honours alongside things they had bought at auction, or stolen from other continents, because to them everything you owned was a trophy. Whether it was given to you for outstanding batsmanship, or left to you by your grandfather who shot someone for it, it was all the same. The whole of life was a sport, like cricket, whose winners were measured by the sheer number of things they had.

For the first time I realized fully the gap between us and the Shillingworths. The Kitchens had always successfully convinced themselves that having more than you strictly needed was somehow undignified, almost shameful. Here was a world where the opposite was true – it was shameful *not* to be rich.

As Old Man Shillingworth ushered us out and creaked the door shut, I tried to feel appropriately offended by the decadence of it, the shamelessness. But a horrible sort of thrill had crept around my heart. I could see why Victoria, who would have disapproved so strongly of all this, was also guiltily attracted to it; and I could see how easily I could lose her to this other world altogether.

There were four courses, each accompanied by a different wine. 'You've excelled yourself, Maria,' said Max to Mrs Shillingworth with a jarring familiarity. I suspected that the bulk of the cooking had actually been done by their maid, a Spanish girl. We'd bumped into her as we toured the house; she had scuttled away like a mouse disturbed from its nook. Victoria said very little, but attacked the food with her customary zeal, shovelling a second helping onto her plate before most people were halfway through their first.

'It's a wonder she doesn't put on weight, that girl,' our mother murmured to Dad.

'What . . .? Who?' he asked.

'Oh, Harry, who do you think? Victoria.'

'Ah! Yes. Yes, indeed.' He peered through his glasses for a moment at his daughter, nodded thoughtfully and returned to the lamb.

Given that the dinner was meant to be in Dad's honour, he was hardly involved in the conversation, which was not really a conversation but a monologue delivered by Old Man Shillingworth. He talked about the vast sums that Tom would make when he retired, from 'endorsing' products, after-dinner speaking, and so on. He spoke about some of his other clients – footballers, boxers – who now made as much money from what he called 'after-hours stuff' as they did from actually playing the game. As the evening went by the Old Man's observations became more controversial. He declared that, unless something was done, we would soon be a nation of mongrels.

'They talk a lot of guff about society, but there are certain people here who would be better off back home. Great Britain was called Great for a reason. It ought to stay that way.'

As usual, all this talk was indulged by everyone. A couple of times Victoria tut-tutted good-naturedly and said, 'Oh, George!' What had happened to my sister, I wondered bitterly; how had she been brainwashed like this? Or was this the real world, and our childhood merely a prelude which I should resign myself to letting go of?

'. . . and that is why women,' I heard him say around nine o'clock, 'should be realistic about what they can achieve. They weren't designed to do the same things as men, any more than dogs were meant to fly aeroplanes.'

I thought that this time Victoria would surely intervene. But when I looked up hopefully I saw that her eyes were on the door.

'Where's Dad?'

He had excused himself some twenty minutes ago. 'I'm sure . . . I'm sure everything is all right,' said Mum awkwardly. 'George, what were you saying?'

'*I'm* not sure everything is all right,' said Victoria, 'he's been gone too long.'

'He's probably got lost,' said Max. 'This is the sort of house people do get lost in,' he added approvingly. 'Remember when that French guy was here and he couldn't for the life of him . . .!'

Everyone seemed to remember this incident, whatever it was, and find it hilarious. Old Man Shillingworth snorted. 'I said to him: next time, go forward! I know you people like to retreat, but try walking forwards!' He gave his own joke a generous laugh.

Victoria still looked anxious. 'I might just go and call to see if he's all right.'

'I'll come,' I said quickly.

My stomach was sinking at the thought of Dad embarrassing himself again, locking himself in one of the bathrooms, perhaps, or blundering hopelessly between bedrooms. 'Where do you think he might . . .?'

But Victoria had already paused by a huge picture window at the halfway point of the staircase. 'Shit.'

She pointed out into the dark garden. Between the dots of fuzzy light reflected in the window, our father could be seen standing motionless between two towering conifers.

'Come on, old boy.'

We stole out of the door and around the back. Victoria moved in long, purposeful strides; when her hat slipped off, she stooped to pick it up and replaced it without missing a step. Just as in the old days I tumbled after her, feeling the ominousness of the situation compete for my heart with a covert excitement, a thrill at having an adventure together again.

When we got close to Dad he looked exactly as he had from the window: he was standing quite still, gazing up into the cloudy night sky. Victoria gently advanced towards him and put an arm around his shoulders.

'What on earth are you doing out here?'

'Well, the fact of the matter . . .' he began. He rubbed his nose. 'The fact is, it's hard to say, really.'

In the dusk I caught for a second a liquid fear in Victoria's eyes. They widened and moistened momentarily in a way I had never seen before.

'Righto, well, it's getting chilly. Let's get you inside.'

We arrived back in the banquet room – which suddenly felt clammy and overheated – to an ironic welcome from Old Man Shillingworth. 'Fancied a spin in the garden, did you, Harry!'

'Very pleasant. Breath of fresh air,' said my father softly.

Our mother couldn't look at him as he sat down beside her; she had turned her eyes away as if examining one of the many knick-knacks on the walls. But when eventually the conversation was dropped and she swivelled back to face the rest of the party, I could see a gloss around her eyes that was the same as Victoria's a few moments ago.

I couldn't be sure if we were all discovering at the same time that something was wrong with Dad, or if everyone but me had known it all along.

Some time after ten everyone sang 'Happy Birthday' with a vigour which only emphasized the awkwardness of what had happened earlier. Shortly after, our mother rose with strained dignity. 'This has been a really lovely evening, but Harry and I had better be going.'

'Oh, no, no, stay longer,' Shillingworth urged. 'There's whisky, or coffee. I've a whisky in the library which is older than I am.'

'No, we really ought to go,' she said firmly.

'Sure you don't want to take another turn around the garden? Climb a tree?'

The Old Man laughed nastily; not even Max joined in this time. Dad thanked Mrs Shillingworth, who was watching sharply as the Spanish girl began to gather up plates.

'You don't have to come home with us,' Mum said suddenly to the three of us. 'You children should stay and have fun.'

We looked uncertainly at each other. It was impossible, as usual, to tell what she really wanted.

'No, no, we'll come,' said Victoria.

'Stay, for Christ's sake!' barked the Old Man. 'We've got eighteen spare rooms! Haven't we, Max!'

'Maybe . . .' said Max, uncharacteristically hesitant. 'Maybe we *should* stay and give Mum and Dad a bit of peace. Let them enjoy the last bit of the birthday together.'

Victoria looked at me. I suddenly knew that I desperately did not want to be back in the car, chugging in silence back to our little house.

'It might be fun to stay,' I mumbled.

'The mouse speaks! Well, that settles it,' crowed Old Man Shillingworth. 'Conchita, make up some rooms.' The Spanish girl, who was carrying nine plates in a stack like a circus performer, nodded meekly. I felt for a second as if I were betraying my parents, but the look on Mum's drawn face was now unmistakably one of relief.

Between them Max and Victoria somehow made the Old Man understand that we would like to be alone, and we retired to one of the numerous rooms in the Shillingworths' house where private business could be done: a magnificent library, mahogany-panelled, the walls covered in antique maps. We sat in leather armchairs. A fully stocked cocktail cabinet looked as if it had not been disturbed in thirty years, and the same was certainly true of most of the books above my head. Max pensively filled our glasses with claret.

Victoria took a long gulp of her wine, almost downing it in one mouthful, and replenished the huge bulb-shaped glass at once.

'So,' she said, breaking the silence, 'is he ill?'

'It may not be anything as, as dramatic as that,' said Max quickly. 'He's always been a bit eccentric.'

'Not like that. Wandering out into the garden. And . . . well, there have been a lot of signs, if you think about it. He was always vague, but this is different.'

'Dominic, you've been living there. Has he been doing this sort of thing a lot?'

I was startled to have my opinion sought by Max, more or less for the first time. A vestige of the ancient longing to impress him flared up in my chest and I found myself deliberating.

'Not . . . not really. I mean . . . The thing is, although I do live there, you know, I don't necessarily really see them all that much.'

'But Mum must have said something.'

'Mum never says anything,' I pointed out.

'Mum never *will* say anything,' Victoria agreed. 'You know what she's like. Jack the fucking Ripper could come round and she wouldn't bat an eyelid. That's how she was brought up. That's our family, that's how people like us . . .'

Max interrupted her. 'Would you mind awfully, just *once*, having a conversation without making everything into some sort of flimsy point about society?' His lips curled into their mocking grin. 'Can we not discuss Dad without you trying to be the scholar that you tragically never became?'

'I'm just trying to work out,' said Victoria in an unusually high, wavering voice, 'how it is that if, if there is some problem, we've let this develop in front of us . . .'

'In front of us!' echoed Max. 'It's hardly been in front of *you*, has it! You've been swanning all around the world for the past three or four years! I'm surprised you can remember where they live!'

'Oh, and you've been a model son, I suppose,' snapped Victoria. 'Call the parents every night, do you? Check up on them?'

'It's a fair point,' I said, seizing the rare chance to fight Victoria's corner. 'She's been in Australia. You're only up the road.'

'Ah, the runt of the litter joins in,' spat Max. I wondered if he was drunk, but there was the usual precision to his spite. He had never been able to stand even the mildest opposition to his opinions.

'Max . . .' Victoria warned.

'Well, for fuck's sake! So you've been actually living in their house, and yet it's everyone else's fault?'

'*It's all our faults!*' screamed Victoria.

Max hissed at her. 'Keep your bloody voice down.'

I could see a vein throbbing in Victoria's neck, and could feel the juddering pulse in my own. The atmosphere was both horrible and somehow exciting.

There was a long silence. Max rose to his feet.

'I don't think we're going to agree on this for now,' he said, as if he had been chairing a perfectly civil debate, 'so I am going to have a bath, and then I am going to bed, and I strongly suggest you do the same. Goodnight.'

Victoria and I sat, not looking at one another, for some minutes. The heavy hands of a clock were shunting themselves around the hour, clunk-CLONK, clunk-CLONK. It was nearly midnight.

Eventually Victoria refilled our glasses. I could see that her hand was shaking.

'Do you want me to do that, old girl?'

She smiled weakly. 'You shouldn't even be drinking. You're a mere boy.'

'I'm twenty-two.'

'I suppose you are.'

Clunk-CLONK. The ticking of the clock was disconcerting; it sounded as if it were forever tripping over itself, like someone emphasizing the wrong syllable in every word. Victoria rose and stumbled out. I looked at the wall of solid dark books. I heard the toilet flush and she was back, steadying herself with a hand on each side of the door-frame.

'Come here.'

I patted the armchair and she came and sat at the foot of it. It was exhilarating to be taking the lead for once. I put my hands on her shoulders. She leaned her head back against my knees.

'He was right, you know,' she said in the end, still facing away from me, out at the plushly appointed room.

'What?'

'He's right. I *haven't* been here. I *have* just been gallivanting around the world.'

'Of course you have. You're married to a famous cricket star.'

'So that gives me the right to stop caring about anyone else, does it?'

'You haven't done that.' I put my hand on her head, felt my fingers in the tightly cut layers of hair.

'You remember Maudie?'

'I remember her all right. I seem to remember her naked on a beach, in fact.'

But Victoria didn't laugh at this. She stared at the clock. 'Well, she's pretty ill, now. I didn't know. I hadn't been . . . I've just been sending her the odd postcard and not hearing back, and then carrying on with my jolly life.'

'So what's wrong with her?'

'She has an eating disorder.'

'What does that mean?'

'Not eating enough. Starving herself.'

'Do people do that?'

'Yes. It's an illness.'

'So is she . . . how do they cure it?'

'She's gone into a place to be looked after.'

'Like a mental home?'

She straightened up, pulling away from my grasp.

'I'm sorry. I didn't mean . . .'

'No, it's all right. A mental home is precisely what it is. It's just . . .' Her voice was breaking up at the edges, like paper dipped in water. 'It's just with that, and Dad, and meanwhile I'm just enjoying myself . . .'

I squeezed her shoulders again. 'Dad will be OK. We just need to try and get him to see someone.'

I felt like an adult, dealing with this unpleasant family business. We sat in silence as the clock paced out another staggering minute.

'Anyhow,' she said, 'I'm taking care of Hercules.'

'The tortoise?'

'Yes,' said Victoria, 'apparently we can get him quarantined and take him out to Australia, when we're over there for the winter.'

'You're going to Australia for the winter?'

'It'll be summer there. Tom's playing for a club in New South Wales.'

'Right.'

'I'll have a tortoise at last. So some good has come out of it, at least.'

I began to laugh, but she flinched violently. 'Christ. What an awful thing to say. What a horrible fucking joke.'

She tried to squirm away, but I had her tight by the shoulders. 'It was only a joke.'

'I'm just a really horrible person,' she said, her face burning; I could feel the heat on the back of her neck. 'I'm just . . .'

'You are not *just* anything,' I said.

She gave a flat laugh. I took her left arm and turned her around gently. She shifted her weight so that she was kneeling at my feet, and our eyes met. Hers were glossy and frightened. 'I mean it, Victoria.'

'You're delightfully partisan, old boy.'

'I'm not saying it because I'm your brother. I mean it. You're extraordinary.'

I held her face in my hands and felt my insides knotting suddenly and violently. She started to say something, drew back from it, and swallowed hard. Our lips met and brushed together, parted, then met again. This time it was a kiss.

It lasted three seconds. Then she tore her face away, stood up and stared at me as if we had never met. She brushed her hands furiously on her skirt. I said her name, but she began to back away, almost tripping over the armchair Max had been sitting in. I said, again, 'Victoria!' but she was gone. I heard her rapid steps on the staircase and then another door shutting behind her.

The silence in the huge house was so complete that the clunking of the clock and the faint stirring of the wind outside only made it thicker and more real. I walked shakily over to the wine bottle and, trembling, filled up my glass with the last of it. A few red drops spilled onto the gnarled wood and seemed to dry instantly.

For a long time I sat and drank alone in the library, with the clock lurching through its uneven syllables, and the darkness outside.

VI

By the time I got up in the morning Victoria had left. I had to catch two buses to get home. For the final half-mile, as we trundled past my old school and the Shipmate, my brain played incorrigibly with the idea that she might be there and we could pick up as if nothing had happened. By the time I got the key into the door, the idea had only blossomed from my denials, and I all but expected her to be sitting at the table with a plate of assorted cheeses. The house, though, was dead quiet. At first in fact I thought I was alone, but then I caught sight of Mum pegging washing on the line, chatting patiently to Mrs Linus next door. When our neighbour had waddled away with an effort that was painful to watch, I went out into the garden.

'Oh! Hello, Dominic. Did you have a nice night?'

'It . . . it was fine, yes.' I tried to look as if the question was as trivial as it ought to have been. 'Victoria's not here . . .?'

'No, I haven't seen her.' Mum was holding a peg between her teeth. 'And Dad is at the cricket today.'

This brought my mind back to the confusing episode with Dad, and I felt something between a desire and a duty to ask the question we had all been left with.

'What's happening with Dad? Is he all right?'

She put down the basket and looked at me.

'What do you mean?'

'You know what I mean. Is there something wrong with . . . well, with his memory, or . . .? I mean, why did he . . .?'

Mum folded her arms and gave me a look, amused and exasperated. It was one of her never-to-be-photographed looks, which would one day be impossible to replicate in the memory. She glanced across the fence at the Linuses' house, and then back at me. In recent times, with the development of the photo business, I'd felt older than my years; after everything that had happened last night, I now experienced the uncomfortable flipside of that feeling, the sense that life had a new weight and complexity.

'Dad's had his little episodes all through his life. He's had trouble with his . . . mental composure, on occasion. These sort of things come and go.'

'Really?'

'Well, he doesn't like being under pressure – like at the wedding. He tends to flap a bit. You know. He just needs a bit of peace and quiet.'

'Is his job going all right?'

She smiled ruefully again, and with a hint of reproach, I thought, that I was asking a question like this. 'He's absolutely fine. He's not quite in the same league as Max, of course. But in our own little way, we do all right.'

Although it was difficult to own up mentally to such pettiness, my first impulse was to be unhappy that it was Max and not me who came to mind as her example of success. My photography, however well it might be going, still seemed like a hobby to them. None of this should have been as important as Dad's health, but my attention had wavered just long enough for Mum to collect up the basket. She nodded at the house. 'Better go in and check on the potatoes.'

There was more that needed to be said on both sides, but both of us were happy to let the conversation go.

Victoria went off to Australia, and there were no post-cards: there was no contact at all. I tried not to think about her and what had passed between us. The latter task was quite easy: within weeks it came to seem as if it could not possibly have happened, as if I must have misremem-bered it, something which would have been easy to do on a fraught night. I met girls at weddings or when I was out with my old mates from the course; I took dates to the cinema or the Shipmate. Now and again at a reception I would disappear for an hour with a jealous bridesmaid and return to Daley's mock-wrathful gaze.

'I can't take my eye off you for a moment!'

'I didn't do anything wrong. *She* seduced *me*, if anything.'

'Right, well, we'll be off now. Some of us have wives to get back to.'

The seasons came and went, mapping out the year in photographic assignments. Spring meant baby-blue weddings and football fans winding down the window to spit at the car as Daley taunted them. Summer was high season, of course: sometimes Friday, Saturday and Sunday would bring three consecutive weddings. In autumn we photographed back-to-school groups in the playground, their teachers' shapeless blouses and permed hair making me think of the life Victoria had escaped. Even in winter people kept tying the knot, and as decorations began to appear in windows there were jobs photographing children on the lap of the supermarket's Father Christmas.

Much as I enjoyed weddings, I had little interest in finding a wife, even a steady girlfriend. When the right time came, I would recognize it. Until then, each late afternoon in the clutches of a woman I had only just met, each post-pub kiss in the streetlight only reinforced my belief that I was quite normal after all, and that whatever had happened with my sister could safely be dismissed from memory: if indeed my memory was to be trusted in the first place.

I didn't see Victoria again until months after the incident we never discussed. She spent that Christmas Day with us – the Cricketer in tow, impeccably respectful as usual of our modest home – and we got through Boxing Day at the Shillingworth palace. The Spanish maid cooked a goose as big as a pig. Dad seemed alert and good-humoured, even when asked why he wasn't reporting on the Boxing Day football game, which had never happened before in my memory.

'The paper's skimping, didn't want to send someone up to Leeds. Can't say I'm too sorry!'

'Hard times at the *Gazette*, eh?' Old Man Shillingworth leaned back in his chair, a great chunk of goose speared on the end of his fork. 'Still a three-day week there, is it?'

'I think it's still hard times everywhere,' said Dad mildly.

'I suppose so,' said Shillingworth, plunging the forkful into his mouth and surveying the grand room around him: the table a mess of champagne bottles and antique cutlery, the window with its view out onto the frosty expanses of the lawn.

'Now that dear old Wilson's back in,' said Max, 'I'm sure things will pick up for the poor. They certainly did last time.' Shillingworth laughed at this, and the Cricketer smirked. Victoria was gazing out of the window. I wished I could offer, as she had once offered me, a penny for her thoughts.

I only spoke to her once that whole day. It was late afternoon and a crushing, imperious darkness had descended, which the sprawl of chandeliers did not entirely seem to dispel. I found myself drawn for some reason to the Trophy Room. The door opened with its slow creak; inside, all was just as it had been the last time. The rows of trophies sat quietly; packed into the drawers, invisible treasures nestled like snakes. The vulgarity of it all was as compelling as usual, and I stood for a few moments taking in the scene. I slunk out of the room, thinking nobody would see – the Old Man's honking laughter could be heard from the dining room – but there, outside the door, was my sister.

'Old boy! Snaffling a few things?'

'Of course not.'

'I was joking, Dom.'

'Yes. Sorry.'

You could just hear the clunk-CLONK in the room just along the hall where it had happened. Both of us pretended not to notice.

'Been a tolerable enough day, hasn't it?' said Victoria, who was wearing a red-and-green party hat garlanded with sprigs of holly.

'Not bad. Bet it's warmer in Australia, though.'

'Rather unfestive. Better off here at Christmas.'

'But better off there the rest of the time?' I chided.

'Well, it *is* nice. You should pop down and see us,' she suggested, as if Australia were Dorset. 'Tom would really like to have you visit.'

It all comes back to him, I thought.

'Well, I'll see what I can do,' I said. 'I'm just trying to buy a place at the moment.'

'Wow. Moving out of home?'

'I'll only be round the corner.'

I hated us for talking like this: like teachers at a staff Christmas party. The Cricketer appeared in the hall, and behind him Max in a horrible new brown suede jacket. Max had a cricket bat in his hand and a screwed-up ball of wrapping paper: the three of them started to play a mock game of cricket. I found a room to disappear to and waited till it was time to leave.

The following March, on the weekend before St Patrick's Day, we drove to a wedding in Somerset. It was an Irish friend of Daley's getting hitched to a girl from Wells. Daley was wearing a grey suit which looked as if it had last seen service some time during the war and a preposterous hat, like a baker's cap, with the Irish flag flying from its middle. We'd booked rooms in the hotel where they were having the reception, and were going to make a weekend of it. Daley broke into 'Cockles and Mussels' as we hit the motorway.

'You are going to take that hat off before we get there, aren't you?'

'Ah, no one'll mind the hat. Everyone there's going to be Irish.'

'Who am I going to talk to, once you all start getting drunk and singing your bloody songs?'

'Lauren'll be there. You'll like her. She's not Irish. She's American.'

'Who?'

'Lauren. The girl who makes our albums.'

'Great. You'll get smashed and I'll be left talking about the cost of leather.'

'I can guarantee you're right about the first part. If I'm not roaring drunk by nightfall, I'll eat a brown bowler.'

Outside the church friends and family were drifting about in the tentative early-year sunshine, shaking hands, tossing lively pleasantries about. I shot a roll's worth of pictures very quickly. Inside, as well as the organ with its balding custodian, a string quartet was warming up. The father of the bride shook hands sweatily with each new arrival. Daley, rather than assisting me, was plodding about to dole out wisecracks to old mates. The bridal Rolls-Royce was poised around the corner; I caught a glimpse of the spreading frills of a dress, a pair of hazel eyes dancing with nerves. The last people were herded inside and the bride came shakily down the aisle. A sharp-faced lady materialized like a ghost on the balcony and sang a Celtic refrain over the swell of violins.

This was a rare occasion on which I was allowed to take pictures during the entire service; the vicar was the trendy, bearded sort who said things like 'We're not all about stuffy old readings, here'. My lens roved over the crammed-in congregation. The red-faced father of the bride, a butcher by trade, was grinning and rubbing his podgy hands together. The jolly modernity of proceedings was maintained by the vicar, whose sermon was short and contained a reference to *Top of the Pops*. The two of them made their vows and signed the register, and turned around into a hail of applause and cheering. My camera was following the couple through the forest of backslapping hands when a heavy thud sounded behind me. Somebody shrieked.

'Help! Help!'

It was the father of the bride: he'd collapsed in the front row. A throng immediately gathered around him. His newly married daughter stopped dead at the church door and turned around. I had never seen a bride go back down the aisle before. She broke clear of her new husband and ran back towards her father, shouting piercingly, 'Dad! Dad!' The groom stood motionless, a faint resentment in his eyes. The throng was now shouting for an ambulance and a moment later I saw Daley, looking mightier than ever, sprinting down the nave like someone about to put out a fire.

Confusion spread through the church. The organist began to pitch into Mendelssohn, and then seemed to decide against it. The string players held their instruments uselessly in front of them. The bearded vicar had his hands pressed together, prayer-ready, but nobody was looking at him. Daley had already summoned an ambulance and was now back in the church, looking after the mother of the bride as she sobbed and shook quietly in the corner. He sat her down on a pew and threw a great arm around her shoulder.

Before long the ambulance sounded ominously outside. Two paramedics came in and the crowd around the prone man melted away. They squatted down and strapped him to an orange stretcher with an oxygen mask clamped to his mouth. They carried him down the aisle in what seemed some ghastly mockery of the procession that had taken place only an hour before. Quickly, in small and then larger groups, the friends and family members began to leave the church. I packed my camera into its case. We stood in the chilly air by the door, watching as a paramedic helped the man's wife into the back of the ambulance and slammed the door behind her. The wail of the departing siren might have been the only sound in the world.

At the hotel, the tables had been laid out with a buffet and the champagne was ready in silver buckets. By the time we arrived, most of the guests were already there, standing around dazedly in their finery; the food sat untouched. The bride and groom had gone to the hospital. This standing around continued for half an hour. The afternoon felt as if it would never reach an evening, as if it had escaped time altogether.

Eventually Daley came in, his face a little flushed, and headed for the lectern where the speeches ought to have been made. He tapped one of the microphones to appeal for quiet, but complete silence had already fallen as soon as he entered.

'Ladies and gentlemen, I'm afraid I have to pass on bad news. Roy – Mr Langbourne – I'm afraid he died in the ambulance. The family's asked me to . . . to pass this on, as I say.'

The microphone screeched in the emptiness after these words. In front of me two elderly ladies clung to one another's arms as if they might be pulled away next. Hotel staff around the edges of the room coughed and glanced at one another. I saw one cock a questioning thumb in the direction of the still-untouched food; his colleague shrugged.

It was unbelievable that sixty years' living could be hammered out suddenly into this full stop: an announcement into a malfunctioning microphone, while people stared blankly at rolled-up napkins. Some there had known the dead man intimately, some like me had barely met him, and this also contributed to the queasy atmosphere: everyone felt in danger of reacting either too much or too little. With the strap of the now-useless camera biting heavily into my shoulder I slipped out of the room, glancing back to see Daley's huge hand descending on a man's shoulder in consolation.

I went out for some air, smoked a couple of cigarettes, drank a bottle of beer in the car park with a similarly disconcerted family friend, and was waiting for the lift to take me up to my room when I heard a strange sobbing.

I glanced left and right down the corridors. Nobody was around. The sobbing continued, mixed up with choking and spluttering. It took a few moments to realize that the sound was coming from the lift, and the person responsible for it was descending towards me.

The lift was an old-style one with a heavy grille at the front. I waited as it clanked to the ground. There was a longish pause before the doors juddered apart. Finally, and with difficulty, the grille was wrenched to one side. In the lift stood a blonde woman about the same age as me. Her face was red, her nose streaming. Her eyes were so full of tears it was hard to see what colour they were. At the sight of me she gave a helpless splutter.

'God. Sorry.'

She lowered her face and tried to walk past me, but on instinct I took her lightly by the arm.

'Are you all right?'

'Who are you?' she asked. In the drawled 'are' I caught the spike of an American accent.

'I'm . . . nobody. I'm a photographer. I'm just concerned.'

'Concerned.' She gave a thick sniff that would, with clearer airways, have become a laugh. 'I guess I look like someone you should be concerned about.'

She wiped her eyes, and a whole fat tear fell to the ground. I could see now that her eyes were a strange keen green, like a cat's. Her face was still red, but her neck and arms were very pale, with patches of sudden pink here and there. She reached for a handkerchief with an embroidered 'L' at the corner and I had a recollection. 'Are you Lauren?'

She dabbed her nose and looked up. 'Yes.'

'I'm Dominic. I work with Roger Daley. You do our photo albums.'

'Oh!' She took a big breath and pressed the handkerchief to her nose again. 'Oh, right! It's . . . it would be good to meet you, but it's actually embarrassing.'

'Don't be embarrassed. I think you should blow your nose properly, rather than pressing it like that.'

Her face flickered into a grin; another displaced tear slid wetly onto her cheek. I had never seen anyone harbour so many tears in her eyes. I supposed, thinking about it, I had never seen Victoria cry, or my mother, or really any adult at close quarters. It wasn't the done thing.

She blew her nose hard and gave a rueful smile at the noise. 'There goes the last of my pride.'

'Where were you off to?'

Her tear-jammed eyes narrowed in thought. 'I really didn't have a plan. I've just . . . I was meant to be staying with friends tonight. The bride's a friend of mine. They're all at the hospital now. Or, or wherever he is. Wherever the . . . cadaver is.' I must have winced. 'Sorry. "Cadaver" is a disgusting word.'

'You're right,' I agreed. 'Corpse. Much better.'

She gulped back a laugh. 'I shouldn't find that funny.'

'Well, this whole situation isn't funny, but what are we meant to do?'

Lauren swallowed again and nodded. 'I just got upset because I don't know where I'm staying now, and I don't know anyone here, and it's just so awful that he died, and . . . anyhow, basically I just got myself upset. And then I thought I was stuck in the elevator for a while. It seems ridiculous now.'

'You're being unduly hard on yourself,' I heard myself say.

Her mouth twitched smilewards and afforded me a teasing glimpse of dimples emerging in the corners. She was so beautiful, I realized that I was shaking slightly. 'I like the way you said that. Un-dew-ly,' she mimicked. 'Very English.'

'Well, I am English. Actually, a lot of people are here. We're in England.'

'That explains a lot of things,' she said, and the shared laugh was like a trampoline pitching me into a new sphere of confidence.

'Why don't we get a drink?' I suggested.

'I can't go anywhere looking like this.'

'You look fine. Great, in fact.'

She snorted in amusement. 'This is probably the worst I have looked in my life.'

'Well, I'm looking forward to seeing you when you *do* look good, then.'

This was pretty naff, but she favoured me this time with a sensational smile. Her eyes were wide pools of witch-green light. Her lips parted slightly and then closed bashfully, as if she were swallowing a much bigger smile, of which this was only a prelude. The dimples formed fully at the edges of her mouth.

'Thank you.'

'Here's my room key. Why don't you go up and use my room to get yourself sorted out.'

The colour of her face was extraordinary, somewhere on the road from pink to red.

She laughed a very light, pretty laugh.

'I hope your intentions are honourable.'

Her accent, and the brisk way she picked out her words, made me feel I had been transported into some Woody Allen movie.

'Believe it or not,' I said, 'they are.'

She took the key and went into the lift, grinding the grille back into place. The doors slid across, removing us bit by bit from each other's view. I heard the heavy box begin its unwieldy way back up the shaft.

It seems true to say that everything that was to happen

between Lauren and me was written in those few moments outside the lift. I had met the second of the three women I would love the most in my life.

She'd grown up in Vermont and New York City, with an American father and Irish mother, in a quietly unhappy household. She'd inherited her father's accent, her mother's colouring, and not much of anything else. The parents split up when she was twelve and her mother brought her to England. Her dad was now a psychoanalyst in New York; he had not spoken to her much since she'd grown up, and now she was returning the favour.

'What kind of people does he psychoanalyse?'

'All kinds, I guess. It doesn't really matter what the problem is. He makes up a name for it, gives them some phoney analysis, walks away with a hundred bucks.'

I made weaker and weaker tea from the tasteless grey sachets and we talked on, forgetting our idea about going for a drink in the bar. Her mother was in Cornwall and, again, they had almost no contact. All this was more exotic than my own background, and more excitingly fractured too: a broken home, estrangement, all the things people never admitted were possible.

I said I was a photographer. She told me her dream was to be a writer and illustrator of children's books.

'I have a few written already.'

'What kind of thing?'

'I have this character called – it sounds kind of dumb – Cautious Rabbit,' she said.

I wanted to pick her up and take her to bed straight away. 'Cautious Rabbit?'

'He's ... so, obviously, he's a rabbit. And he always wants to go to the big city or talk to a girl rabbit or drive a fast car, but he doesn't have the courage, and his friend always gets there first. His friend is called Confident Hare. But then Confident Hare usually gets some kind of comeuppance.'

'I'd love to see one.'

'The idea is to teach kids that loud brash people don't always win, and to follow their own ... sorry. It sounds so stupid.'

I watched the earnest way her green eyes scoured my face as she spoke, her arms whizzing out at right angles, and thought about what it would be like to remove her clothing one item at a time. Out in the corridors trolleys were being wheeled creakily along and porters were knocking on doors; the lift which had arranged our meeting was continuing its endless ups and downs.

When the light had gone outside, I drew the curtain across and thought briefly of the bride mourning her father, the helpless groom sitting by, the silence. The day felt as if it had lasted a week and my muscles ached. By about ten, Lauren and I had progressed to sitting cross-legged and side by side on the bed like a couple of children, our thighs just touching, and I'd just started to feel that something must happen soon when something of the wrong kind did: there was a sharp knock at the door. The visitor was a beady-eyed older lady in gloves and horn-rimmed glasses. She flashed me a glance as if I were an ogre which had narrowly failed to capture its prey.

'I've found someone to give us a lift,' said the newcomer.

'Unless,' she added with another look at me, 'you have business here.'

'I guess I should . . . I should go back,' said Lauren.

'You'd be welcome to stay with me,' I said.

'I'll bet she would,' remarked the friend tartly. Lauren coloured.

'I mean, on the floor.'

'We'll be off in ten minutes,' said the friend briskly. 'Car's outside.'

I made attempts to change Lauren's mind, but the atmosphere had been made awkward, and she was already checking herself in the mirror and gathering up her cardigan and coat. Even as she opened the door – pulling a sleeve over her hand, I noticed, so as not to touch the handle itself – I had some idea that she might be persuaded.

'I hope you're not just going because of your . . . bossy friend.'

She sniggered. 'Marjorie? No. I'm going because I think we both know what would happen if I stayed.'

And what would be wrong with that? I wanted to ask, but sensed it would be a mistake. We rode down together in the lift. As it made its rocky descent we finally kissed. The taste of her was like a hit of some drug; I wanted to swallow her whole. I clutched her arms and moved in for another kiss, but the lift jerked suddenly to a stop, the grille was yanked across, and two sweaty Irishmen got in and started talking about horse-racing. I grabbed Lauren's hand as she stepped into the lobby.

'See you very soon.'

'Yes,' she said, and that was that.

At midnight I met Daley in the hotel bar. He had been going back and forth from the hospital, sitting with stunned relatives, making emergency arrangements.

'I could do with a drink,' he admitted.

'I'll get you one.'

'I'll have a whisky, please. And I'd better look into getting a brown bowler from somewhere.'

The bar, with its maroon carpet and dutiful watercolours, was very quiet. Lauren would be in bed by now, I supposed. It was perplexing to think how often we'd been within a few miles of each other, doing similar things, yet never to meet unless destiny suddenly took a hand as it just had.

'Strange day,' said Daley, nodding to the barman to refill his shot glass almost immediately. 'What did you get up to all evening?'

'Well, actually, I was falling in love.'

'Ah. Anyone I'd know?'

'Lauren.'

Daley smiled and gave a slow nod. 'Makes sense.'

It wasn't how I would have put it at the time, as I lay awake thinking about her, but it was the right description. I'd always said I would know the right moment, and here it was. It just made sense to be with Lauren, and very soon, it would make no sense to try and recall what things were like before her.

VII

Six weeks earlier I had never met her. Now I was trying on a top hat and glasses and doing my best to look like Oliver Hardy for her. This is what I remember most about the start of love: the sense that everything was possible all of a sudden. Here we were in a fancy-dress shop in Kentish Town, trying to find a pair of costumes for her friend's engagement party on the theme 'famous duos'. Lauren surveyed me critically.

'Even if we push a cushion up there, I don't know, you just don't have the body type for it.'

'Well, I'm sorry for not being a fat man with a moustache.'

'What do you suggest, then?' Lauren shook her head in mock outrage. 'Am *I* meant to be Hardy?'

'Could we have chosen a man-and-woman duo,' I asked, 'or would that just be making things too easy?'

She folded her pale arms across her chest and grinned. Her hair shimmered gold beneath her top hat and her eyes darted over the dusty racks of Navy uniforms, gorilla outfits, tutus, all hung so closely that we had to peel them apart to try them on. Everything was funny at the moment. Lauren's laugh was as dramatic as her tears; it started light and nimble like a flute, but often built up steam until it resulted in a choking fit.

The girl behind the counter fanned herself with a leaflet and glared at us. It was a muggy, white-sky Saturday afternoon; our laughter lingered like a stench in the airless room.

'Do you have any better moustaches?' asked Lauren.

'Any what?' The girl turned down the Velvet Underground with an audible sigh.

'Moustaches.'

'Mous-*taches*,' I corrected Lauren. 'You're saying it wrong.' She put the emphasis on the first syllable, *moust*-aches. Pantomime bickering over this sort of thing was a feature of our early relationship.

'Whatever's there is what we've got,' said the girl. After a stony pause, she added, 'I could look in the back for you.'

'It's OK,' said Lauren, 'I'm thinking maybe cat and mouse anyhow.'

'Which one am I?'

'A lady,' said Lauren, 'does not dress up as a mouse.'

The party was in Highgate, minutes from the little studio flat I'd recently bought, but in much more opulent surroundings. The host, Kerry, had done the place up to look like it was in Manhattan, though Lauren – with her inside knowledge – was scornful of the results.

'This is what they call a loft apartment, here? We're barely above ground level. Why are your buildings so small?'

'Because our people aren't as fat. And because we don't have delusions of running the world.'

'*Kerry* sure does.'

Any unease I might have felt at the idea of joining Lauren's social circle – composed of people further on in life than me, since she herself was five years older – dissipated in the face of Lauren's arch remarks about her friends. Though she had plenty of them, she was always cutting them down to size for me in private, implying that I had gone straight in ahead of them in the queue for her attention. Perhaps there was an echo of Victoria in all this, but Victoria was far from my mind as we ascended the stairs towards the leaking stream of party noise.

'Are you looking at my ass?'

'Well, where else am I meant to look?'

Lauren's cat costume consisted of a black all-in-one, with accompanying ears and tail handmade from crêpe paper. Her thighs and buttocks swayed lithely inside their polyester wrapping. It was hard not to reach out and grab her at every step; except that my hands were sheathed in little mittens she had picked apart and re-knitted to look like a mouse's paws. I had on a pair of large cardboard ears, too, but had been allowed to get away with a T-shirt and dark jeans. As we reached the door, she stood back to let me grasp the handle. Over the past few weeks she had entranced me with quirks like this: the way she bent to sniff a plate of food before eating it, the way she avoided walking on drains, and in particular her fear of electric shocks, which had come up straight away in the hotel on that long first evening.

'I saw someone get killed this way.'

'Get killed by opening a door? Are you serious?'

'Kind of. Well, not opening a door. Being struck by lightning. But, hey, why take a risk?'

Now as she followed me through the doorway, a large figure in a black gown loomed in front of us. It was Daley, dressed in the regalia of a priest. He waved his hands ecclesiastically above our heads. 'Peace be with you.'

We burst out laughing. 'What the hell, Daley?'

'I thought it would be nice to have a man of the cloth present,' said Daley, 'in case anyone decides to pop the question tonight.'

With a sidelong glance I registered the trickle of pink stealing up Lauren's cheeks and longingly pictured the reddening flesh beneath her costume.

'It's meant to be famous duos.'

'I have come as a priest and his God,' Daley clarified. 'Teresa is God.'

'Where is she?'

'She's at home. She rules me from a distance. Just like God, you see.'

The heat of the party propelled me from one conversation to another, goaded me into making ever gutsier statements. I am a wedding photographer. I am a freelance photographer, weddings and other stuff. I'm a photographer – all sorts of things, really. Now and again I would dig out my little Kodak and snap Lauren across the room. She would be gesturing expansively with her cat-arms, smiling her two-stage smile, laughing in that way that made her face flush in delight. She swigged from a bottle of Harp and wiped her mouth with one paw. She talked about Andy Warhol, used words like *subway* and *semester*, mentioned the Lower East Side in a manner which shone a harsh light on the wannabe-Americanisms of everyone else present. Around midnight a boy who had been in my brother's year at school, but whose name I had never known, caught me gazing across the low-lit room at her.

'She's worth staring at, isn't she.'

I checked myself and looked at him. He had dirty hair and a cheesecloth shirt and was looking at Lauren as if halfway into her bed already.

'She is.'

'Do you know if she's here with someone?' he asked.

'I do know,' I said. 'She's with me.'

'You're having me on!' His ratty face twisted into the purest expression of envy I had ever seen.

'No. Her name's Lauren.'

'How . . .?' He looked me up and down. 'I mean, no offence, but how did you . . .?'

I saw myself as he must have seen me, a skinny fellow with a mop of hair and cardboard mouse-ears.

'I'm a photographer,' I said, as if that answered everything.

Shortly before we left I pursued Lauren drunkenly up a flight of stairs to a bedroom painted all white with a huge red-brown Rothko print above the bed. She turned, her eyes – extraordinary wine-bottle green – flicking rapidly and amusedly over me.

'You're drunk.'

'What are you doing?'

'I've come up here to change.' She patted her shoulder bag. 'I've been a cat long enough.'

We looked at each other. She pulled down one corner of the all-in-one, revealing a pink-white shoulder.

'Are you just going to stand there watching me?'

'I could help,' I said, and advanced towards her. Lauren stepped back teasingly.

'I'm not sure how much help you'll be. You're still dressed as a mouse, for one thing.'

I took hold of the other shoulder and she put a hand on my arm to restrain me. 'Someone will come in.'

'And . . .?'

She sighed, as if at a troublesome child. My fingers, captive in the mittens, fumbled vainly with the skintight costume. She shook her head and began to ease the material over her shoulders. Her bare breasts hung in front of me. I leaned in and kissed them in turn.

'I don't think this is the place, Dom.'

'I can't help it. You're so beautiful.'

I took her by the thighs and buried my face in her cleavage. She kissed the top of my head. I grasped for her, desperate to peel off the costume. She shuffled backwards against the wall.

'At least take off the damn mouse-ears.'

'If we'd been Laurel and Hardy this would have been easy,' I muttered. She laughed. My breath was heavy. Then suddenly Lauren stiffened and rolled the material back over her shoulders. A couple had blundered into the room, a stocky man leading an Indian girl by the wrist.

'Sorry, are we disturbing you?'

'I was just going to change in the . . . in the bathroom there,' said Lauren.

'Ah,' said the newcomer. 'I was just going to make love to this lady on the bed.'

The moment had gone; I was a pulsing ball of lust, but this had more or less been a normal state since I met her. Finally home at 3 a.m., I lay on the bed in my new studio flat, unable to stop smiling. Lauren had resisted my slurred attempts to make her stay, as she had done every time so far, no matter how euphoric the activities of the day. I looked around the room, grainily illuminated by the streetlights outside and dominated by the stereo system with its giant speakers, the shelf with cameras arranged in ascending order of size like Russian dolls. I willed the night to disappear, my brain to fall asleep and wake refreshed, so I could see Lauren again.

I was always grateful to have met her in spring; summer was a great time to be hurtling ever deeper into love. There were barbecues, and open-air concerts at Alexandra Palace like the ones Victoria used to go to. They set up a drive-in cinema in Regent's Park and Lauren, thrillingly prone to blasts of emotion, wept a barrel of tears into my shoulder when two forgettable sweethearts were parted by war. Afterwards I took her to a Japanese restaurant whose expensiveness, in my unsinkable mood, only added to its appeal.

'Are you sure we can afford this?'

'No. You're right. I'll have to offer them my coat.'

'Don't joke about it. What happens if you overspend and we end up in a . . . in a debtors' prison?'

'A debtors' prison? Well, why stop there? What if we get consumption?'

'I guess I do still rely on Dickens for my understanding of the legal system.'

'That'll be why you keep trying to adopt orphans, then.'

'You shouldn't mock.' She waved a fork at me. 'I've told you, this country is very old-fashioned.'

'That's exactly what Victoria says.'

'I think you'll find Victoria died a while ago.'

'Not the Queen. My sister.'

'Oh, sure, your beloved sister. Who you have a picture of in your bedroom *instead of me*.' She shook her head accusingly.

'Let's put that right.'

I snapped her across the table sucking at her cocktail through a straw. The blast of light from the flash drew tuts from the stroppy couple at the next table. Daley took the film into his darkroom the next week and emerged with a portrait which displaced the one of Victoria from my bedside table.

*   *   *

In high summer Daley and I drove down to Brighton for a wedding. We were staying the night in a b. & b. and Lauren was going to join me on the Sunday for a day trip. She loved the Englishness of seaside resorts, the fish and chips, the low-grade hubbub of the pier. These days I normally drove the Capri to jobs, but today Daley was at the wheel and I sat in the front seat with a four-pack.

'Easy with those. Best not to be drunk when we introduce ourselves. Afterwards, no problem.'

It felt as if everything was on our side. We had weddings every weekend up to Christmas, and the weeks were full too. Lauren's commemorative albums and artful framing gave us an edge over the more workmanlike Boots the Chemist, and there was no other photo studio for miles around. I was absolutely at home in my job.

A few miles out of Brighton I felt the liquor begin to take hold of my brain in a pleasant way. I glanced across at Daley, his hands shuffling clumsily across the wheel, a couple of beads of sweat collecting in his close-cropped hair.

'Daley, can I ask you something?'

'You can ask. I won't make any promises beyond that.'

'Lauren and I have been together for, you know, a few months now.'

'You don't say.'

'But the thing is, we've never . . . she still hasn't . . .'

'You've not slept together.'

'I just wonder if . . . what's normal. I've never really been with someone for long enough to know.'

He turned his big head and peered at me with a grin. The driver behind, who had been planning to overtake, honked indignantly as we drifted across the lanes.

'It's not *that* serious. I'd rather you concentrated on driving.'

He scratched his nose – again leaving the wheel in perilous limbo for a few seconds – and gave me a quick, calculating look. 'As I'm sure you know, the idea is to wait till you're hitched. People tend to get married if they love each other. Not sure if you've noticed, but that's how we make a living.'

'But do people really wait? Isn't that just . . .?'

'Just religion?' Daley shrugged. 'Maybe. A lot of things are, though, if you trace it back. People still do them.'

'So you don't think . . . I mean, she doesn't actually believe in God or anything, does she?'

'She believes in doing things pretty much by the book,' said Daley, 'whatever she might say.'

In the balmy dusk next day I resolved to bring it up with her. We sat on the beach watching the sun set, as if unwillingly, a dazzle of orange-pink above the sea. At last, I had stopped associating beach scenes with some past Eden of my childhood: new rules were being written.

The seafront was almost empty, only scattered pairs of sweethearts still out on their blankets. There was a smell of seaweed and of the summer night. 'This has been the most wonderful day,' said Lauren. 'I wish it didn't have to end.'

'It doesn't have to end. We can do anything we like.' I gestured behind us to the line of Victorian beach hotels, their façades white like wedding cakes. 'We could check into one of those and spend the whole night together, and wake up late tomorrow morning and have breakfast in bed.'

I felt her shiver under the drape of my arm. She picked up a handful of pebbles and let them run slowly between her fingers to rejoin the millions more around us.

'I wish we could.'

'We *can*. I can afford it.'

'It's not that.'

As if part of an advertisement, a couple came crunching through the pebbles towards us and swung away towards the line of hotels. A laugh ghosted away from them and reached us on the light breeze.

I cleared my throat. 'Will there be a time when we . . . when are we going to take the next step with this, Lauren?'

'The next step being . . .?'

'You know.'

Lauren looked down at the carpet of pebbles under our feet. 'What kind of question is that?'

'I mean – would we have to get married before you'd be . . . comfortable with it?'

She swallowed hard. 'You don't ever *have* to marry me, if you put it like that.'

'You know what I mean. Do you think it would actually make a difference, if we signed a piece of paper? Do you think that would suddenly make it all right to have sex?'

'Is that how you see marriage? Just a piece of paper?'

'No, of course not.' It was an unexpectedly difficult question, how I saw marriage: all the *till death us do part* rigmarole was so familiar that the words hardly struck me with any more force than a shopping list. And yet nobody was better placed to appreciate the magic that these occasions worked on people. 'No, getting married is a huge thing, of course. Just . . . it doesn't actually change anything, as far as I can see.'

She considered. 'Well, then, would it really matter if we did it?'

I grinned, wrongfooted. 'I'm twenty-five!'

'*I'm* nearly thirty. I want to have babies before I seize up.' She glanced across at me in the failing light. 'Sorry. I don't want to scare you off. I would like children some day, that's all.'

'So would I.' I was surprised to hear myself say it. I squeezed her shoulder and checked my watch. 'We'll have to get the train soon.'

Lauren's eyes dipped sheepishly. 'I'm sorry I killed the romance.'

'You're just making me want you more. You know that.'

I helped her to her feet. She bent to pick up one of her shoes. 'Can I ask you something quite intimidating?'

'I'm not going to be intimidated by you.'

She grabbed my hand and we picked our way up the beach, towards the empty chip vans and stilled amusement arcades. 'Do you think you'll fall out of love with me? Get bored? Because I'm older than you?'

'What a question. We've only been together five months.'

'Well, exactly. Is this, you know, is this a fling for you, or . . .?'

Lauren's fingers were creeping over mine. She had a way not just of asking you to make a big statement – any girl could do that – but of making you want to go along with it, making you desperate to say what she was hoping.

'This is a lot more than a fling, Lauren.'

Her eyes sparkled. 'It's just, you know. I know it's early to talk about getting married and all. But if you think I'm the right person, well, I'm still going to be the right person in a few years.'

This kind of talk was unnerving, but in her smoky accent, and spoken as her hips moved with such unwitting lusciousness against the tight folds of her dress, it was also captivating.

'Well, am *I* the right person – the definite right person – for you?' I parried. 'After five months? Can you honestly say—'

She put a finger suddenly to my lips, sending a bolt through me. 'Hush. Yes. I can say that. I've met a lot of men. I've never met anyone I felt this way about.'

We kissed almost violently on the pavement. A hundred yards up the road, the hands of the Clock Tower clock had moved along and I wriggled away from a follow-up kiss.

'Come on! We're going to miss the bloody train!'

I grabbed her hand and we ran the rest of the way, blood throbbing at my temples. I had no idea whether I wanted us to catch the train or see it pulling away and deal with the consequences. We hurtled through the station foyer and leapt on board, laughing wildly, as the guard gave a blast on his whistle. Other passengers gave us looks of distaste or grudging acknowledgement. Lauren's cheeks were flaming from the run.

We drank all the way home from a half-bottle of vodka she had in her bag. My hand was on her thigh and we gazed out through the mist of cigarette smoke at the dark grubby suburbs. My heart was beating a furious time in and out of the chugging rhythms of the train on the track. At Victoria Station we slid out of the tide of sleepy drunks on the platform and into a dark corner where a florist's stall stood. Her fingers dug into my shoulders and I eased my hands inside her dress and began to kiss her. Our lips were glued together as my hands stole their way down her body, between her legs. My eye caught the words *LONDON VICTORIA* on a big iron sign above our heads, and then she was leading me deeper into the station's shadows.

Younger generations always look back on their elders' romances as if they must have been cute, homely affairs: bunches of roses and helping a lady down from a steam train. In my childhood this was because the old pictures were black-and-white. Colour film seemed a big progression, but time has not got any kinder to its victims. The photos I took that summer of Lauren look as old now as those wedding photos of my parents did to me. Red lipstick and a pink cocktail in a purple-brown restaurant, sun-yellow hair against blue Brighton sky: no matter how lurid they seemed at the time, the prints are so washed-out, the inks so jaded, that anyone who wasn't there would conclude that the world was simply less bright in those days.

Today's kids will have to go through it all too of course, their most treasured photos looking more and more absurd: fashions crushed mercilessly by time, key people dying or slipping slowly out of the address book. But at least the pictures themselves won't look as outdated as mine do. Computers will keep them safe from fading and scratching, from being lost or spoiled or neglected in an attic. Mine is probably the last generation literal-minded enough to put its trust in something as vulnerable as a little photo in an album, or a dusty yellow packet. Ours will be the last non-digitized set of memories, the last ones to fade year on year and disappear bit by bit from the world, the way we ourselves do.

She expertly cut a jagged mouth into a pumpkin, I took her to a damp firework display in Alexandra Park, and before long she was glancing nervously at the Christmas lights on Regent Street.

'Don't you like Christmas?'

'Sure, I like it. I like any opportunity to explain to my mother why I don't have babies yet and why my books aren't published and why I don't become a doctor.'

'Well, why don't you come to mine?'

'Because if there's one thing Mom would find more disappointing than my presence, it's my absence.'

'Come to my folks' on Christmas Day, then, and you can see her on Boxing Day.'

As boys hawked the last of their felled trees outside the garage and Daley's butcher friends took the final turkey orders, I wondered what I was getting her into. The Cricketer and his little gang – Max, Victoria, Max's latest powdered girlfriend – were out in Australia for some match or other, so it would only be us and my parents. But when we arrived on Christmas Eve, Mum and Dad appeared to have raised their game. A tall wide tree confronted us in the hall. Baubles and party lights had been hung in my room, where there was a camp-bed for Lauren. Dad, his glasses misting, served punch and mince pies to neigh-bours as festive dusk fell over Park Street. Daley dropped in wearing a pair of reindeer antlers. He was well-oiled already, and proposed four or five toasts.

'To Kitchen and the future Mrs Kitchen!'

'Shut up, Daley.'

'He's only saying what we're all thinking,' said Dad, a glass of punch in his hand. 'You could hardly have met a lovelier lady, Dominic.'

Lauren's pale arms and neck were spotted with pink; the present Mrs Kitchen beamed maternally at her. I downed a couple of glasses and felt my heart flush with pleasure. I was the one making my parents proud these days, not the other two with their far-off capering and their cheque-books. Tomorrow we would all go for a walk and Lauren and Mum could chat, and I would take Dad for a pint on Boxing Day.

The doorbell rang several times.

'Carol singers!'

Lauren, who was closest, slipped her hand inside her sleeve to open the door. A group of singers immediately launched into 'God Rest Ye Merry, Gentlemen' and Lauren squealed with glee. Muttering good-naturedly, Dad went back down the hall for some change, but Daley was ahead of him.

'I'll cover this.'

'You're too kind, Mr Daley.'

'Ah, well. I'd only spend it on the hedgehogs.'

Mrs Linus, her face holly-red and creased in the search for breath, led the singing in a voice that overwhelmed all but one of her team, screeching her *'tidings of comfort and joy'* so loudly that Lauren took an involuntary step back. A solitary singer at the back of the group matched her for volume until the carol came squealing to an unholy climax. Lauren whooped and applauded as Daley tossed the cash into a cloth cap. Mrs Linus nodded at me.

'Looking very well, young Dominic! This your missus, is it?'

'Girlfriend. Lauren.'

'Much appreciated,' said Mrs Linus, who meant something like 'Pleased to meet you'. She stuck out a tubby hand for Lauren to shake. 'And how's Max? Out in Australia, is 'e?'

'He is.'

'Clever one, that one is. 'Ow about Victoria?'

'She's in Australia too.'

'I don't think she is!' said Mrs Linus with a breathy chortle. The group of singers scattered in laughter and I saw at the back of the crowd a figure utterly familiar to me, yet so unexpected these days that I had to catch my breath.

'Victoria!'

She laughed. 'Old boy! Thought you'd never spot me!'

I fought my way through to meet her. The carol singers shuffled out of the way and Victoria kissed me on the cheek in the doorway. 'What the hell are you doing here?'

'I decided to pop back for Christmas. Awfully dull out there. Too much cricket. Compliments of the season!'

'Were you really carol singing?'

'Of course not. They were on the doorstep when I got here. Thought it might be a laugh to surprise you.'

Dad had called excitedly for Mum. Daley gave a cheer and waggled his antlers in welcome. Victoria's arm was still around my shoulders when I glanced back to see Lauren watching nonplussed.

'Victoria,' I said, 'this is my . . . this is Lauren.'

The two of them greeted each other and stood in an awkward embrace, and a look passed between them which I had seen countless women exchange at weddings: a look of instant appraisal.

Lauren stepped aside to let Victoria come crashing through. She was wearing leather boots with thick heels, and looked taller than I remembered her. She pulled off her hat and flung her coat casually to the floor.

'How did you get home?' asked Dad. 'We would have picked you up from the station, if you'd . . .'

'I cabbed it from Heathrow. Easier all round.'

'A taxi from Heathrow?' Mum could hardly contain her delight or her horror. 'That must have cost an arm and a leg.'

'Don't worry, I'm rich!' cried Victoria. 'Someone put the kettle on!' She went galloping up the stairs and I heard a thud and creak of springs as she heaved her suitcase onto the bed. Lauren and I stood in the pocket of cold by the door.

'Why did she call you old boy?' Lauren murmured.

'It's just a sort of tradition,' I said.

'Everyone seems pretty excited to see her.'

'Oh, she's just . . . larger than life.'

'She's very attractive.'

I thought briefly and involuntarily of the tortoise tattoo, and tore my thoughts away from it.

'No one's more attractive than you, Lauren.'

'You don't have to say things like that.'

'I'm saying it because it's true. And I'm proud you're here. I want to show you off.'

I folded her up in my arms and considered what I'd just said. It was true enough, and yet I felt quite strongly that it was going to be a long Christmas Day.

Victoria glowed with thickly applied make-up; she was wearing a pair of large hooped earrings of the kind she would once have made fun of. Looking at her was like walking into a favourite pub that has undergone an impressive but rather clinical refurbishment.

Throughout lunch she talked about the Cricketer's introduction to the Pope, about the children at an Indian orphanage, about New York, Sydney, parties, cars. Dad sat nodding eagerly at everything; Mum bustled to and fro with heaped trays and plates. Lauren bent instinctively to smell the slice of Christmas pudding that was doled out like a slab of concrete in front of her, and Victoria gave her a wary look as if suspecting her of rudeness.

'She always does that with food,' I explained.

'It's kind of a habit,' said Lauren, staring at her plate.

'Well, Dom has a few habits as well, as I'm sure you've noticed,' said Victoria. I felt my face darken and scraped my chair a little closer to Lauren's.

Victoria had bought extravagant presents for everyone – two designer shirts for me, some French perfume for Mum – and these store-wrapped silver-paper packages sat conspicuously alongside our homelier efforts. Of course, there was nothing for Lauren.

'I didn't know you were coming,' said Victoria apologetically.

'Hey, I didn't know *you* were coming either!' Lauren replied, trying to make a joke of it. They blinked awkwardly at each other.

'I mean, I do live here,' said Victoria.

'Of course, of course you do,' Lauren backtracked. 'I didn't mean any . . .'

'Oh, nor did I, nor did I,' said Victoria, and the moment died rather heavily in the room.

Later on, after a few more drinks, she got some discarded wrapping paper, wrapped her hat in it and gave it to Lauren, saying, 'Better late than never,' and everyone laughed; but even this felt somehow condescending. At nine o'clock, with Dad asleep in a chair, Lauren went upstairs for a bath, and about an hour later I realized she was already in bed. It would be the first time we'd shared a room, but it was going to be a lot less of an occasion than I had imagined. Even as I was framing this thought, Victoria tried to interest me in a nightcap.

'I'm done in, Victoria.'

'Good heavens. One more drink. It's Christmas bloody Day.'

'I'll see you in the morning.'

I saw her bite back some possible rebuke. 'Goodnight, then.'

Lauren was practically asleep in my bed when I went up. I lay awake on the camp-bed for a long time, until I heard the decades-old, familiar sound of Victoria clumping up the stairs and closing the door of her room behind her.

Lauren caught the train to Cornwall the next morning. I went home intending to get some lunch and then go out somewhere with my camera. A dusting of frost lingered on lawns and the trees were stark against the white sky. When I came in, Victoria was gouging chunks out of a huge Camembert.

'Glad you're back, Dom. Mum wants to talk to us.'

There was an edge to her voice, even filtered through a layer of cheese.

'When has Mum ever wanted to talk to us? I mean, about a specific thing?'

'Exactly.'

Our mother came in from a walk and ushered us out into the garden. The Linuses' house was full of people; through one window I could see a huge Christmas tree shedding a rain of pine needles as Mrs Linus waddled past it.

'It's ever so nice to have two of my three children back for Christmas,' said Mum.

'You know I always . . .' I began.

'What did you want to talk to us about?' asked Victoria.

Mum brought out a handkerchief and dabbed at her nose. 'I just wanted . . . well, it's to do with Dad,' she said. 'He's not reporting on the football today, or . . . or very much, recently.'

'What do you mean, "very much"?' asked Victoria.

Mum sighed. 'He's . . . they've sort of taken some of his reporting duties away.'

'What's he doing now, then?'

'Well, he does more . . . more administrative things, less of the actual writing.'

Victoria was staring hard at our mother. I shivered.

'Why?'

'There's nothing wrong with him, Victoria. He's just a bit . . . he gets a bit vague.'

Victoria tossed her head impatiently. 'My God. This comes up every time and nobody does a damn thing about it.'

'How are you managing?' I asked. 'I mean, are you all right for . . .?'

'*We are absolutely fine*,' said our mother, in a tone so pained that it made us both flinch in shock. Victoria looked towards the Linuses' house, and I at the overgrown fringes of the garden where she sometimes used to feed the tortoise.

'All I was going to ask,' said Mum in a more measured tone, 'is whether you might think about taking him to the football today. I know neither of you likes football particularly.'

'Of course we will,' we said, almost at the same time.

'It would mean a lot to him,' said our mother.

She turned suddenly to go, brushing at her eyes with one hand. I searched for something to say and then, as in days gone by, followed Victoria mutely into the house.

Later that day we went with studied merriment towards the Arsenal ground, past the squat terraces hung with decorations which seemed to sense that their time was nearly up already. Dad, walking between his children, had on the old red-and-white scarf under his big mac.

'It's been a few years since you came down here, Dominic!'

'Better late than never,' I said gamely.

'Dommo only ever came the once,' said Victoria. 'He needed to pee and then he fell over and whacked his knee and cried, by all accounts.'

'I'll try and do better this time.'

'We'll look after you,' said Victoria, grabbing my hand in one glove. 'If you need any help, just ask a grown-up.'

I felt myself shudder at the contact; forced back the feeling again, told myself it was imaginary.

We walked past the programme stalls, the police horses surrounded by mounds of ripe-smelling dung, and took our place in the stands. As Victoria settled in her seat, a few people nudged each other and pointed at her; she smiled cheerfully back at them. Dad went up to the press box to see his colleagues, but returned looking rather disconcerted.

'Getting younger all the time, those chaps.'

'Look,' said Victoria, 'are you sure you're all right, not reporting on the games?'

Dad gave one of his jaunty smiles. 'Probably all for the best.'

The teams had come out onto the field and a huge belching roar from the crowd put an end to the conversation.

The game played itself out. There were several goals and we joined in dutifully with the cheering and booing. A man in front of us, blowing huge clouds of smoke from a fragrant pipe, shouted furiously throughout, 'Bunch of fucking clowns! What a disgrace!' Each time he yelled, Victoria would snigger and I would grab her sleeve to shut her up. The man got more and more vocal and I was worried Victoria might get us into trouble as Daley was always threatening to.

'Shut up, for God's sake!'

'*Bunch of fucking clowns!*' she mimicked, and we giggled silently.

The sky went black above the grandstand with its solemn clock; the winter air grew colder. Victoria wrapped a cashmere scarf around her shoulders: she stood out even more now. Finally it was all over, and we applauded the muddied men off the pitch and turned to go. Victoria took Dad's arm and guided him slowly down the old concrete steps. The crowd poured out of the ground, watched by policemen shivering on the backs of their patient horses.

At the bus stop, Dad said suddenly, 'You owe me money for that, I think.'

There was a pause. 'No, Dad,' said Victoria. 'I bought *your* ticket. It's fine.'

'Are you trying to get out of paying?' Dad asked. I waited to hear that this was some joke, but there was suspicion on his face. My heart began to drop; I thought I could feel it, like some foreign body edging through my guts.

'Now, Dad,' said Victoria, still gently, 'I actually bought three tickets, do you remember, and . . .'

'Trying to con me out of what's mine!' he said loudly, and several people turned to look. 'Where's my money? I'm just trying to . . . where's my money?'

Victoria and I exchanged a helpless, appalled look. 'Dad,' I began, 'it's all a misunderstanding . . .'

'This is what I get!' said Dad, gesturing vaguely. 'Everyone taking advantage! It's only Max who chips anything in!'

Victoria tugged anxiously at her hat. 'Come on, Dad. We can sort this out when we get home.'

'Isn't it enough,' said Dad, 'having to . . . not being able to . . .'

A bus came creaking to a stop at the side of the road, and the throng pushed impatiently towards it. Victoria steered Dad by the arm. 'Let's not get on the bus.'

We walked through Finsbury Park, the chilly quiet broken up by Dad's occasional mumbles. 'Bring some money next time. Any money you can. Just all helps, you know.'

'Dad,' said Victoria, 'Max and I are both doing very well . . .'

'So am I,' I put in petulantly.

'. . . and we can easily lend you . . . or, I mean, give you money, whatever you need . . .'

'People don't understand,' said Dad. 'They don't know at all. That's the long and short of it. That's the long and short of it.'

The wind moaned in the trees. The silence between us seemed not just prolonged but unbreakable, permanent, like the silence in space. We passed one of Mrs Linus's plump daughters, home for Christmas, out walking her Labrador. She began a cheery hello, but Victoria rushed past her, practically dragging the other two of us along. Victoria's face was almost stone-like in its composure; her eyes glinted coldly in the dark. I felt myself, by force of habit, looking to her for leadership, waiting for her to say it would be all right.

Our mother, in her blue oven gloves, was just taking a cake out of the oven when we got home; Victoria's face stopped her dead.

'What's the matter?'

'What's the matter? Dad has a mental problem, that's the matter,' said Victoria, 'as well you know, and . . .'

'Victoria . . .'

'I've been saying this for *years*.'

'What did he do?' asked Mum, with a raw fear in her eyes. She turned her face away and pretended to rifle through the cutlery drawer.

'He was talking about money and just rambling on and he doesn't seem to know what he's on about. He needs to see a doctor, Mum. I'll take him tomorrow or whenever they open.'

'You don't have to do that,' said Mum so quietly I barely heard it.

'I *do* have to do it, because he won't do it himself, and you won't do it, and no one talks about a fucking thing in this house.'

'Please.' Mum winced at the swearword. 'I'll take him.' Her voice was shaking. 'I'll take him to the doctor.'

'Will you?' Victoria's eyes were round and heavy as marbles. She was circling the kitchen as if about to finish off prey. 'Or will you just keep pretending everything's fine as long as we keep a stiff upper lip and—'

'*I'll take him.*' It was a cracked shout, falling off at the end as if the words were disappearing down a hole. 'Please,' she said, sitting down at the table and resting her head on her hands. 'Don't humiliate me, Victoria. I'll take him. I promise. He's so hard to talk to, he . . .'

She sat there staring at her hands, the old beaten silver of the wedding and engagement rings on her pale finger. I would rather have been anywhere else.

'He said . . .' began Mum, and stopped. Victoria stole around beside her and took her hand, squeezing it gently.

'It's all right, Mum.'

'The other day,' she continued, 'I was just in here singing along to the wireless, you know, not really concentrating, and he came in suddenly and said, "Why do you never know the words, you silly—!"' She mouthed the word 'bitch'. ' "Why do you always sing something-something this-and-that, you silly—!"'

I met Victoria's eyes. She was chewing on her lip. 'Dom,' she said softly, 'put the kettle on.'

'I'll do it, let me do it,' said Mum, but Victoria had hold of her shoulders.

I filled the ageing kettle, feeling it get heavier and heavier in my hands. I wanted this simple task to go on until everything else had disappeared. Beneath the rush of water through the taps, I could just hear Mum continue, in a voice which sounded as if it had been squeezed out like a dishcloth.

'And then five minutes later he couldn't even remember it. Just seemed confused, and . . . and it was impossible to believe that he *had* said it. And he went right back to normal, and, you know, once again I just sort of thought everything was all right.

'Well, I don't know if I really did think that, or not.' She waved her hands in a small, hopeless gesture. 'He . . . well, he's my best friend, you know.'

However passive my relationship with Mum might sometimes have been, I felt at that moment the ferocious protective love of a son. I would have done anything to show it. But she had grown up in a family where demonstrations of affection rarely took place, and now somehow we were that family. All we could do was creep around one another and hope that our true feelings would somehow materialize in each other's minds.

Even Victoria was not above this rule. Still, as she sat with her arm around Mum's shoulders, a part of me that I could never acknowledge was grateful for the day's drama. It had brought back a version of my sister I recognized.

VIII

On the day before New Year's Eve we went to the doctor's in Muswell Hill. Dr Etherington looked exactly as doctors do in old films: hair slicked back into a shiny helmet, thick brown-rimmed glasses, grey suit. In his waiting room there were pea-green armchairs and cheerless magazines about the British countryside. Our parents followed him meekly into his room and we trooped down the corridor to the smoking room. I lit up a cigarette and passed one to Victoria. She shook her head. I thought for a moment that the tension had made me delirious.

'Forgotten how to smoke, old girl?'

It felt good to be talking; like a small resistance against the horrible flat atmosphere of the place, the pervading sense that nobody ever went there willingly.

'I've actually not had one for months. Didn't you notice?'

I hadn't, somehow, perhaps because so much else about her seemed to have changed.

'I think I've succeeded in giving up,' she said.

'You, giving up! But you're a champion smoker. You got *me* into it.'

'Tom's constantly trying to convince me I should be looking after myself, and . . .'

'To hell with Tom!' I snapped. 'I mean, sorry. I don't mean anything.'

Victoria smiled. 'You've made your point. But you won't get me smoking again.'

I shook my head, taken aback.

She put her hand to her stomach. 'I don't suppose you've got any cheese?'

They were in there for a long time. Victoria kept taking off her tweed cap and twirling it distractedly around her finger.

'Your girlfriend's very pretty,' she observed, looking out of the window.

'Thank you.'

'I wasn't complimenting *you*.' She grinned. 'I was implying you'd got lucky.'

'She's not just pretty,' I said, feeling that Lauren had in some way been damned by faint praise. 'She's really . . . she's amazing, actually.'

Victoria nodded and looked out of the window again. The clock ticked on and the deliberations continued behind the closed door. We went back to the main waiting room and sat there together, making uneasy wisecracks, drawing strength from our shared wish for all this to be over.

Eventually Dad came out, smiling blithely as though he had been visiting an old friend. Mum's smile was a pained one, and I felt my heart slide into my stomach exactly as it had on Boxing Day. In the car, she summarized the situation. Dr Etherington suspected that Dad was in the early stages of dementia.

'The doctor said there was no need to panic, and that he can stay at home, and we should see how it develops over the next few months.'

Victoria and I glanced at each other, thinking the same thing: illnesses can only 'develop' in one direction.

'Is he . . .?'

'*He* does have ears, you know,' Dad chipped in merrily from the passenger seat.

'Is there some medication you can go on for it?' Victoria persisted. 'Did he prescribe something?'

There was hesitation in the front seats. 'It's not really the sort of thing they can . . . treat with anything much,' said Mum.

'So, so what do you do about it? Can it just . . . go away or get better?'

'It can,' said Mum, in a tone designed to end the conversation. She flicked the indicator switch, and its clicking counted the seconds of silence in the car.

'Or it can take a very long time to become serious,' said Dad, turning around to peer jovially at us, 'so by the time I've gone bonkers, something else will have carried me off instead.'

'Well, fingers crossed for something else to carry you

off, then!' said Victoria. It was a bold joke even for her, and everyone – Mum included – burst out laughing.

We went home, ate a reassuringly weighty late lunch, drank tea in the living room. I perched on the Chesterfield next to Dad, who talked ten to the dozen about an idea he had for a book about Arsenal, and the excellent Christmas it had been. Everyone was studiedly positive, agreeing with everything that was said.

The short afternoon was ebbing away, and I was about to walk to the phone box so I could call Lauren in private. It had been a long four days apart, and I was planning to take her for an extravagant dinner that night. She'd sounded miserable when I called the night before, speaking in a hushed, uncomfortable voice on her mother's phone. 'I can't be here much longer. Mom is worse than ever. I miss you so much.'

'You, too.'

'Let's not have another Christmas apart, ever.'

'Yeah. Let's not.'

'You know, we don't *have* to have dinner tomorrow. I know Christmas is expensive.'

'Not for me. I give everyone photos.'

That made her laugh. 'But seriously. I'd just like to see you. I don't care what we do.'

'Nor do I. All I care about is seeing you and eating Oriental food.'

Her trickling laughter on the other end of the phone had made me seethe with wanting her. It was still a thrill to feel this way about someone, to be on the right side of the line which divided the single and the in-love. I did not trouble myself at this point with the idea that there was at least one more possible category.

As I was on my way out, Victoria cornered me in the hall.

'Dom, let's go somewhere.'

'What?'

'Just for the evening. I can't stand it here with all this trying-to-be-cool-about-Dad. It's exhausting.'

'I thought you'd be seeing your friends tonight, or something.'

'They're all ... there's no one around,' said Victoria. She swallowed. 'You know, I never was as popular as you probably thought at the time.'

For a moment, and for the first time in my life, I felt a little sorry for her. I hesitated. 'I was meant to be seeing Lauren tonight.'

She had taken her hat off and was playing with a strand of her hair. She stared at the banisters curving up towards our former bedrooms. 'I don't want to get in the way of that. I just ... I would just love to spend a bit of time with you.'

'Where would we go?'

Victoria's eyes sparked for a second. 'We could go to Southwold.'

'Southwold! Why stop there? Why not get the ferry to Holland and then on to Africa?'

'Ah, come on. Southwold's not that far. We could jump in your Capri. There'll be no traffic today.'

'No, because nobody apart from you is mad.'

'We could just go up for the evening and stay somewhere, and come back in the morning. Just for the sheer stupidity of it.'

'It would certainly be stupid,' I agreed, but her eyes were peeling away my resistance as if it were cling film.

'Please,' Victoria wheedled. She took hold of my elbow. 'I'll be out of your way in two days and you won't see me again for months.'

She saw my face change and wrinkled her nose in disgust. 'I'm sorry. I didn't mean to make a big emotional deal of it. God, I must seem really spoilt.'

In a way she did, yet the idea had taken hold of me. I imagined visiting the old beach hut, listening to the sea in the dark.

'Go on then.'

Victoria whooped in excitement. 'Hurray!'

'We should leave straight away, or it will be the most pointless trip of all time.'

She was already sprinting up the stairs. 'Five minutes. I'll pack an overnight bag. Meet me out at the front of the house.'

'I'll be the one in the Capri,' I called back, my heart jumping. But it landed awkwardly as I remembered I would have to let Lauren know. The giddiness in her voice when I called was painful to hear.

'Hey, so I was thinking, have you had Vietnamese food? I met this guy at a Vietnam protest and he was telling me about this amazing restaurant.'

'Listen, Lauren, I can't do tonight.'

The silence on the end of the modern mobile phone will never compare to the silence a slighted person could achieve on an old-style telephone. I could almost hear Lauren's brow furrow.

'Why?'

'There's kind of an emergency,' I heard myself say.

'What?'

I swallowed. 'My father is . . . he's seriously ill.'

'Oh God. I'm sorry.'

'He's . . . it's a mental thing.'

'Is he going to be all right?'

'Well, hopefully. I'm going to be away just for the night.'

'Hey, don't worry about it. We can still do New Year tomorrow, right?'

'Of course. Sorry, Lauren.'

'Don't be silly. Your dad has to come first.'

As I swung open the door and walked up the road to where the Capri was parked, fumbling in my pockets for the keys, I felt as if the freezing air had taken on the unease of my conscience. It was true, I tried to tell myself: Dad *was* ill, and I deserved sympathy, and so did Victoria. All we were doing was going for a little trip, for a single night, two siblings who barely saw each other these days. Nothing could have been more innocuous, but as Victoria came bounding out of the front door in one of her old winter coats, and ran down the street clutching her hat to her head, that was not quite how it felt.

*　　*　　*

'*Plumpness*. Nine letters. I'm out of practice.'

'*Palimpsest*. Ten.'

'What?'

'*Palimpsest*. It means, um, it's a piece of paper you can scrape the words off so it can be used again.'

'It sounds made-up to me.'

I waved at the glove compartment. 'Dictionary's in there.'

She reached to open it and burst out cackling. 'What's that doing in there!'

'I play this game with Daley. Disputes come up quite a bit.'

'How *dare* you become good at the number-plate game while I'm indisposed.'

'By "indisposed" you mean "living like a princess"? Get the *A to Z*.'

'This grubby old thing? Half the pages are missing.'

'Well, as long as the S is there, we should get to Southwold.'

She began to flick through the book. 'Anyway, I don't live like a princess. I'm a cricketer's wife.'

'A rich, famous cricketer.'

'Yes, I've certainly got a lot of nice dresses and I get to go to India a lot.'

'But he doesn't play the number-plate game with you?'

'He only likes games he can win.'

The sky was slate and the road, as she'd predicted, empty. I lit a fag; Victoria declined. Her abstinence was going to take some getting used to, I thought to myself. I stepped on the pedal and we rattled our way east. It was pitch-black outside by the time we started to pass the familiar landmarks: the monkey-puzzle tree, the *FRESHLY PICKED VEGETABLES* sign, which made Victoria exclaim with delight. The town did, after all, exist outside summer, and outside the idyll of our past. All the same, it was odd to come out of season. The streets were deserted when we arrived; the sea prowled silently like a big cat at night. We browsed a couple of unpromising b. & b.s before coming to the Swan.

The half-asleep old man behind the desk confirmed that there was plenty of space. 'Twin room?'

'Yes please,' said Victoria. 'Two beds. The name's Shillingworth.'

The old duffer narrowed his eyes as if to make us out in the distance, though we were close enough to touch. 'Shillingworth. Victoria Shillingworth?'

'Yes.'

The receptionist glanced wryly at me. 'I see. Well, we don't ask too many questions, round here. We had Winston Churchill himself, you know.' He waved a hand towards a stern photograph.

'This is my brother,' said Victoria sharply.

The man looked embarrassed. 'I see. No offence meant, of course, madam.'

'I quite understand.' Victoria's tone was now rather regal. *THREE HUNDRED YEARS OF HISTORY!* boasted a certificate under the Churchill picture.

'I think you'll like this room, madam,' said the old man, suddenly deferential, handing over a chunky key.

* * *

The chip shop was still there, its rust-worn adverts for pies and CRAVEN 'A' all exactly as they used to be. The 'ding' of the bell as Victoria opened the door was a peculiar sound, familiar and nostalgic all at once. At first it looked as if there was no one behind the counter. Then from the corner emerged the fat proprietor with his monocle, and his perspiring wife. Neither looked any older than when we were children. They were holding hands and I spied with surprise a bottle of whisky next to the till.

'Sorry about that,' he said, 'we were just enjoying a moment to ourselves.'

'It's our forty-fifth anniversary,' the wife added.

'Now, old girl, what will it be?'

I had almost forgotten that he was the original source of the old boy/old girl joke, it was so long ago. As always, he stood in a leisurely manner, arms folded, while his wife sweated over the chip trays and the newspaper.

'Forty-six years ago, we met. Asked her to marry me straight away. Married Christmas of '30. Lots of our friends turned up late, because it was out in the countryside, you see, and there was a business with a cow, which—'

'I shouldn't think they want to hear about the cow, love.'

'Opened the shop New Year's Day '31, been here ever since, fifty-one weeks a year,' the owner continued. 'And we've never had a moment of unhappiness, have we, Hettie?'

'Too few to mention,' said the wife, shoving the greasy packages into a bag and handing it to Victoria. The bell dinged again as we went out into the night.

We walked down towards the sea. 'Forty-five bloody years!' said Victoria, throwing a chip to a seagull that screeched hopefully at her.

'Well, you've done a few years yourself and you seem pretty happy.'

'Yes, I seem it all right. Do you reckon you'll marry Lauren?'

'We have talked about it.'

'I can imagine. She looks like she can't get you into the church quickly enough. I bet she wants kids, too.'

'She does. She's a bit older, though, so . . .'

'By *a bit older* you mean a bit *younger* than *me*,' said Victoria stiffly. 'I don't see me having kids left right and centre.'

We came down the slope past the long line of beach huts. The water was black as the sky, and above us the moon looked as if it were hemmed in by clouds, trying to escape them like a suspect surrounded by police.

'I'm sorry,' I said.

She reached into her coat, brought out a hip-flask, and took a long gulp.

'Not your fault,' she muttered, passing it to me.

I was reminded inescapably of the night that I glimpsed her naked: we must be pretty near the original spot. 'How's Maudie getting on now?' I asked. It was a deliberate subject-change, but a bad one, I saw too late. Victoria grabbed the flask and swigged from it again.

'She's in a place in Hertfordshire. She's allowed out fifteen minutes a day; the rest of the time she stares out of the window. When I went to see her, I talked on and on about India and Lord's and whatever else, and she smiled and nodded as if I was in some fantasy world. I felt sick. It was like we'd never met.

'And now Dad's going that way,' she concluded.

'He's not. He'll be OK. He's getting on a bit, that's all.'

'People said the same about Maudie. She's OK. She's just a bit down. Now she's basically a shop dummy.'

I felt out of my depth, as I had so often in the past with Victoria. She stared at the sand, looking as if she might weep. Stripped of her new gloss by the moonlight, she looked spectacular and a little ghostly.

'Funny how things work out,' said Victoria quietly.

'Are you going to tell me about you and Tom?' I asked. Surprised by my own boldness, I held a cigarette out in front of me and began to click with numb fingers at my lighter.

Victoria was avoiding my eye; she looked out to sea.

'It's fine. It's really fine. It's what happens to a lot of people, I think. He wanted kids and I couldn't seem to get pregnant, and sex became . . . it was wrapped up in all this guilt. He's been quite aggressive about it at times. Not cruel, just . . . he talks about it as if I have something wrong with me. Which puts me off more, of course, and it just, it's just died away a bit. Sorry. You don't need to hear this.'

'I do need to hear it,' I persevered, 'because it's you.'

Victoria took the lighter and prodded it into life with an expert thumb.

'You smoke that one,' I goaded, 'and give one to me.'

She shook her head. 'Seriously, I need to give it up. Tom's forever lecturing me.'

'It sounds like you have more respect for Tom's opinions than your own,' I said.

Victoria raised her eyebrows. 'God. You really do hate him, don't you!'

'I don't hate him,' I said, my face suddenly warm. 'I just feel like you shouldn't be trying to keep anyone else happy.'

'Dom, pretty much everyone in the world does everything to keep someone else happy.'

'That,' I said, 'is the least Victoria Kitchen thing I have ever heard.'

'I'm not Victoria Kitchen any more, am I?'

'Obviously not.'

She stared at me, then turned and walked rapidly back up the beach. I struggled to keep pace with her, my feet sinking into the softer sand as we reached the top.

'Victoria. Hey. I'm sorry.'

We had stopped next to the old beach hut. On a whim she tried the door, but it was locked. Both slightly out of breath, we turned and surveyed the scene. There was nobody anywhere. Down the path, the caravan park where we used to stay would be deserted too, on this strange night of the year.

'I'm sorry.'

'Give me the fag,' she said, her eyes hard.

'You don't have to smoke it, just to prove a—'

'Give it to me.'

She snatched the cigarette and smoked the remainder with aplomb, taking an in-breath which seemed to last a whole minute, and then sending a spiral of smoke up into the cold air.

'You didn't have to do that.'

'I'm prepared to smoke just one fag,' she said, 'to prove my worth to you.'

This made me cough; it felt as if our natural hierarchy had been inverted. 'I just think,' I said, 'well, you said it yourself. You only live once. Some people, not even that.'

She smiled and then shivered as the wind surged up and rattled the doors of the huts. Instinctively I grabbed her and held her close. She smelled of gin and chips, peaches and cigarettes.

'Come on. Let's get back.'

The man behind the desk was asleep; the clock above him showed midnight, and Churchill stared at us in disapproval. Victoria went into the bathroom. There was a double bed and a single. I lay on the bigger one, looking up at the ceiling's gnarled beams. I reached for the hip-flask and downed what was left, grasping for a hold on my out-of-focus thoughts. The doctor's appointment seemed days ago now; with the fatigue and the drink and the mixed emotions, I felt as if I had been flattened against the bed, was being pinned there.

I stared at the ceiling again, the patterns of swirls and knots in the wood, and thought about all the things that must have taken place in this room: all the deeds that had been done, all the desires that had been frustrated. In the end, did it really matter which was which? One hundred years later, who cared if two people once committed adultery in this room, or conscientiously decided not to, if both of them and all the other people concerned were now rotting in the ground? Without a God to keep track of it all, who would ever know and how could it matter? These thoughts were impostors and I manhandled them out of my brain. You are normal, I told myself fuzzily; you have a girlfriend.

The bathroom door was pushed open. Victoria was in her nightie, a towel tucked under her arm. I rolled onto my side to avoid seeing her.

'Excuse my semi-nakedness. I see you've commandeered the double bed.' She sat on the edge of the bed and rummaged in her case.

'Budge up.'

I glimpsed, through the fluttering folds of her nightie, the tortoise tattoo, the green and brown somewhat dulled by the years. Her eye followed mine and for a moment, we both stared at the small motif on her thigh.

'*Stupid little thing, i'n' 'e!*' said Victoria in Mrs Linus's voice.

'He's a bit smaller than I remember.'

'I think you'll find it's that my thighs are a bit fatter than you remember,' said Victoria. 'Unless someone has sneaked in and redrawn him in my sleep.'

'Your thighs aren't fat.'

She settled back against the pillows and pulled the cover over us. 'It's fucking freezing. You're not going to banish me to the other bed, are you?'

I grunted and moved as far away from her as I could. We lay there, side by side like an old couple, not touching. I was conscious of nothing but that familiar knot and the attempt to deny that it was there, which felt as if it were consuming every ounce of effort in my body.

'Are you all right, Domino?'

'I'm fine.'

'Do you not want me in here with you?'

You don't understand, I thought, and maybe it's just as well.

'It's fine.'

Her foot brushed comfortingly against mine. Had she somehow forgotten what happened in the Shillingworths' library that night, or did she remember it as something quite different, something much more innocent? Perhaps it *had* been, for her, something much more innocent. A feeling of loneliness clamped my heart like a cold hand. It was only me that felt this illegitimate passion, only me out of the two of us, only me in the whole world, surely.

'Sure you're all right?'

'I'm just tired,' I muttered, 'and I was thinking about Dad, and I've had too much to drink.'

Her arm settled around my back and we lay there in the dark. The only sound was the occasional creaking of the old wood around us. I thought about Lauren, trying desperately to focus on every aspect of her beauty: the violent green of her eyes, the way her hair fell around her shoulders, her voice, her hands.

Victoria fell asleep. Her shallow breaths tickled like a light wind at my back and her arm still lay round me. The minutes collected themselves grudgingly into quarter-hours, half-hours. I wriggled gently out of her grasp and went to the window. A shaft of light fell over the bed; my sister shuffled in her sleep. It was a quarter past four. Eventually, though it felt impossibly far away, the last morning of 1975 would settle over the still streets outside; the two of us would wake and drive back to London. Then Victoria would disappear once more, perhaps for months or the whole year, and I would try even harder than ever to forget what I feared I felt for her.

Divorce was meant to be at a higher rate than ever and there were articles in the papers about a new age of sexual liberation. But people were certainly still getting married, and holding receptions in ever more ingenious places. We did photos at an underwater ceremony: I had to have scuba lessons, and hire special cameras, and endure Daley's endless remarks about the bends, all of which meant we could name an astronomical price. We took photos in the Arsenal stadium ('Perfect place to tie the knot,' said Dad), and in a revolving restaurant ('I don't know why the hell people can't just eat and then go round and round afterwards,' Daley complained). One couple, who had met in Morocco and were tediously obsessed with the country, insisted on posing on the back of a camel in a wildlife sanctuary.

'Now then, smile!' yelled Daley at the groom's parents, perched miserably on the animal whose own face betrayed a similar distaste. 'That's it, smile – all those who have the necessary muscles! What a wonderful time we're having!'

'What a complete bollocks of a wedding,' he breathed to me as the shutter went down.

We spent one hot July afternoon at a three-part wedding: a civil ceremony in the Old Marylebone Town Hall, followed by an extravagant Greek Orthodox service where the couple effectively got married all over again to placate the godlier side of the family; and then finally a reception in yet another part of London. In the Town Hall they were ploughing efficiently through wedding after wedding. I saw two couples chat for some while before they realized they were not there for the same ceremony. We hared down the stairs into Baker Street Tube to get to the next stage before the guests did.

'When are weddings going to go out of fashion, Daley?' I panted as we wedged ourselves onto a train. My back was gummy with sweat, rolls of precious pictures weighing heavily in my rucksack.

'Not in this lifetime, I think,' said Daley. 'There are certain rules which bind the world together. Will I help you with that?'

Daley, who already had the huge tripod bag over his shoulder, took my camera and held it like a toy in his hand.

'So, you think it's – what, a law of nature that people get married?'

'Well, it's been happening since the beginning of time.'

'But that just means it's a habit. You've had that jumper on since the beginning of time. Is *that* a law of nature?'

'It is indeed,' said Daley, 'until such time as the Authorities give me another pullover.'

'Marriage sounds pretty exciting.'

'I don't see what *you* have to worry about,' Daley laughed, 'with a beautiful girl like that.'

Lauren sometimes brought the commemorative albums to my flat and worked at my tiny dining table. I would watch her snip-snip with her nail scissors, shaving the edges off photos to smooth them into the sentimental shapes that were in vogue. Now and again she would pass comment under her breath – 'Wow, what a dress', or 'I would *never* have my hair like that' – and then glance up. 'Oh, I didn't mean . . .'

'I know, darling.'

The subject kept getting stuck under our feet, tripping us up, and the more aware of it we were, the less we discussed it. It felt as if things had to tip one way or another.

For the anniversary of our first meeting I took her on the plane to Paris. We stayed in a hotel with crystal chandeliers and a string group playing perpetually, it seemed, in the bar. On the second night we went to a restaurant on the Seine. An excitable maître d' all but bowed down to us as we entered. The weather was warm and the river with its low bridges melted artfully into the dusk, like a butler withdrawing from a room. Lauren and I held hands across the table.

'It's been the most unbelievable year. Thank you.'

'Thank *you*. Thanks for being in that lift.'

'Thanks for not running away when I came out looking like a mad witch.'

There was a disturbance at the table to our right; a man was on the floor. I had a stark memory of the doomed father of the bride who had inadvertently brought us together. Then applause broke out and we saw that the man was on one knee, the woman was in tears: it was a successful proposal. The man sprang to his feet and the two of them shared a long kiss. More and more people were applauding and whistling; the maître d' came bounding over, punching the air as if this were a personal victory. A string quartet materialized out of nowhere – Paris seemed to be full of them – and began to play. A bottle of champagne was uncorked. Strangers approached with congratulations.

'Lucky girl!' murmured Lauren. At the next table a baby was gurgling and kicking happily on its mother's lap. The baby reached out to swipe at a wine glass which was hastily moved away.

I took a gulp of velvety red, looked at Lauren's face, saw the past year of bliss as if it had all occurred on a single day, and felt caught up in an unstoppable tide. I dropped onto one knee, so hard it cracked painfully against the floor as it had at the football years ago.

'I'm not being outdone,' I said. 'Lauren, will you marry me?'

She gaped at me. 'Are you serious?'

'Marry me.'

Her hand flew over her mouth. Then it was all some-thing of a blur: nudges and turned heads at the other tables, applause starting up all over again, the string quar-tet laughing as they reorganized themselves around us. Champagne, whistling, Lauren's eyes brimming. In the middle of it all, I saw for a second the irritated expression of the original proposer. The waiters in their jackets brought over more champagne, I shook hands with strangers, was kissed on both cheeks by a middle-aged American tourist.

'Greatest night ever!' she warbled. '*Two* proposals! So much happiness!'

'In the city of love,' drooled the maître d', 'we are now the restaurant of love.'

He made us pose for photos with the other couple, a pair of estate agents from Liverpool. I helped him adjust his flash – 'Dominic is a top photographer in England,' Lauren explained proudly – and then with my own camera I shot a series of pictures of my bride-to-be, pink-nosed, grinning.

'Is it a horrible cliché if I say I'm the happiest girl in the world?' she whispered into my ear as we slunk back to the hotel along the river, my hand on her backside.

'Probably. But clichés are mostly true, aren't they? I tell you who *wasn't* the happiest girl in the world – the other woman! They lasted about ten minutes before we took their place.'

She giggled. 'I feel bad.'

'You shouldn't. He timed it wrong. Proposed too early.'

'Were you planning it all along?' she asked.

'I think I was planning it from the second you stepped out of the lift.'

In the weightlessness of this moment, in the still warm spring air, it seemed true: I really could believe that everything had been leading to this proposal.

We toppled up to our room and I flung her onto the antique bed and ripped at her dress.

'I love you,' I whispered.

'Do you mean let's have sex?'

'No. Yes. I mean I love you *and* let's have sex.' She flushed and grinned. 'Does this count, now?' I was half joking. 'Does this count as being married?'

She screwed shut her eyes and threw her head back. 'Go on,' she whispered, 'go on.'

Afterwards, as we lay exhausted in each other's clutches, I felt fully purged for the first time of everything I had ever been uneasy about feeling. I could see a future which consisted of nothing but this blissful normality. I kissed her eyelids as she slept.

We made love all that stifling summer, the hottest on record. We did it on airless afternoons in my flat with Wimbledon commentary on the radio – the chatter of sport was suddenly inoffensive – and in seedy bed and breakfasts after day trips; in hotels after other people's weddings, and in the Daleys' house where we were looking after their cat. For a while we couldn't be in a room together without undressing each other. It was as if, having waited so long, we had to compensate for every single time we had passed up the chance.

'Why *did* we wait so long, if we were going to end up doing this before marriage after all?' I asked Lauren.

'This isn't really before marriage. We're as good as married now. We've made the commitment.'

'And they definitely know that, do they – God or whoever made these rules? We're not going to get damned on a technicality? I'd hate that.'

'Just kiss me, will you.'

Cautious Rabbit appeared in special editions, for my eyes only: *Cautious Rabbit Is Caught with His Pants Down, Confident Hare Teaches Cautious Rabbit a Game*. With the Instamatic I photographed her naked, stepping out of the shower. The photo was a classic: her mouth frozen open in indignation, her hair matted over her forehead, one hand ineffectually shielding her breasts. I kept this picture until only a couple of years ago, when it was among the last batch from the seventies I destroyed.

We were married in October, in my parents' church with a beaming Daley by my side as best man. Autumn weddings had always been my favourites: none of the festivity-fatigue of midsummer, with all the hot men in their tuxedos silently lamenting the loss of another week-end. There was spirited sun all day, and then a cool crunch in the air as darkness came down. Having witnessed so many weddings that I could have recited the vows easily, it was odd to be saying them myself; the whole thing felt not quite real. Victoria whooped as we walked down the aisle with Mendelssohn barking victoriously into the rafters. Mum and Dad applauded, and Lauren's estranged parents beamed at one another. There was a dinner, Daley rolled out a sparkling compendium of best man gags hoarded over the years, and a ceilidh band – friends of Lauren's mother – whirled everyone into a dance.

I thudded between dancing groups, whisky in hand, being slapped on the back and having witticisms yelled in my ear. My hand was squeezed by people I hardly recognized. Someone yelled that I had done well for myself. The musicians – every one of them bald – bashed away relentlessly on their fiddles and pipes, the band leader yelping arcane instructions to the dancers below: 'One, two, and a do-se-do!' The dances seemed endless, the melodies doubling back on themselves, like records that kept jumping back to the start. I felt arms around my neck and spun to face Victoria.

'What a day, Dommo!'

Her forehead was damp, and disarranged strands of hair poked from the brim of her hat. Her dress was green and gold and brown.

'Yes. What a day.'

She leaned in and kissed me on the lips. It must have seemed, to everyone else, a tipsy, innocent gesture between siblings. Victoria took a step back and her eyes scorched mine with a look so full of emotion that I experienced it almost as a slap in the face.

Now, at last, we were both married; perhaps now this dizzying thing we shared would finally evaporate, even as I became vividly aware of it once more. Victoria turned and made her way through a crowd, which parted, as ever, in front of her. I watched her go with a sudden gasp of the heart as if she were leaving for ever. Then Daley took hold of my arm and dragged me back into a circle of jostling, perspiring dancers, the music began its gallop again, Lauren was by my side and the preceding few moments – like all such moments with Victoria – might never have happened.

On a balcony in Rome during the honeymoon, with traffic horns blaring below and an evening sky of blood orange, Lauren told me she was pregnant. Perhaps we had already guessed it, perhaps even the wedding guests had. I held her tightly and we stood in silence. What the news stirred in me initially seemed like joy, but when its first flurry had eased off I realized it was closer to relief. I had gone from nothing to the full set: steady girlfriend, wife, wife with child. After growing up feeling that I was always last to catch up with the ball, now I had planted both my feet solidly in the world. Whatever I might have felt that was not right, there would simply be no space for it any more.

Part Three

IX

Life has to be lived forwards, but you can only understand it backwards – that's what some Victorian philoso-
pher said. Even trying to understand it backwards is hard
enough. The more I write down these far-off events, the
more it feels like I am describing someone else's life: someone I knew, but never quite came to grips with.

Lauren spent the long hours of labour under a strip-
light which flickered on and off. Her face was shiny with
sweat, and yellowish like the hospital nightgown.

'Not long now,' I kept saying. 'Not long now.'

'How the hell do you know?' she snapped. She was
right; I hadn't a clue what was happening. The hospital
staff were surprised even to see me there.

'Planning to stay here for the birth itself?' asked a grey-
haired orderly, eyeing me as if I were a tradesman whose
work was taking longer than expected.

'Depends if it comes before Christmas!' I said.

'It's only June,' said the woman, not blinking.

'I was joking. Sorry.'

She glanced at her clipboard. 'Do you not work, then?'

'I'm a photographer. Wedding photography, and I'm starting to take on other . . .'

But she had stopped listening. 'Nice job,' she said, with a tone of bright accusation, 'if it allows you this much time off. Has your wife had her blood pressure taken?'

Day and night cancelled out into a formless yellow-grey haze. Daley dropped in with a thermos of tea and some magazines for Lauren. One of them had a story about Victoria and the Cricketer in India. I flicked through it trying to believe that the bronzed lady in the picture was the same woman I had shared a bed with in Southwold; then trying to believe it wasn't.

Eventually baby Elizabeth was handed to me. Lauren's face was a mask of sweat and tears as she squinted at our daughter.

'Isn't she beautiful! Isn't she the most beautiful thing!'

She was smaller, messier, more rumpled than I ever imagined babies were.

'She is. She certainly is.'

The worst is over now, I thought, the hard part is over. As I look back, it is safe to say this is one of the least accurate thoughts ever to have entered my head.

I still can't quite account for the two or three years that saw Elizabeth struggle from birth to infancy to recognizable personhood. How can all those nights of broken sleep, the anguished conversations, the mess, add up to two or three years of my life? I only know that one summer afternoon in 1979, in the overheated Capri which now boasted a baby-seat in the back, I almost fell asleep at the wheel.

On the car radio two professorial types were discussing whether the sixties had seen a sexual revolution after all, or merely a lot of posturing. I was thinking how odd it was to hear 'the sixties', once the place where we all lived, now taking on a quaintly archaic ring, like 'the Blitz'. When Elizabeth grew up, she would talk about 'the sixties' and for that matter 'the seventies' the way imperialists used to mention foreign outposts. The thought of Elizabeth reminded me, like a gnawing at the guts, of everything that was waiting for me when I finally got home after what would be a long day's work.

Lauren and I had had a row as I was leaving. Elizabeth was waking up from the lunchtime sleep and beginning her lamentations. She could hold the same crying note for an astonishingly long time, like a tenor showing off. She had done this almost since birth, and there were signs that she was only beginning to hit her true form.

'So, as well as today, suddenly you're working tomorrow now? You couldn't have told me this?'

'It's just come up. I couldn't have told you before it happened, could I?'

'So, on a Sunday, when we were meant to have time together . . .'

'I know. I'm sorry. But it could be a good client.'

'You can't just do everything. You have to make time for your family.'

'I'm trying to feed my family, in case you hadn't noticed.'

'Maybe I didn't notice because I'm trying to keep our daughter alive single-handed?'

When we weren't arguing with each other, we were arguing with the neighbours, who seemed to think Elizabeth's crying was specially laid on to antagonize them. From time to time, a beaky man would ring our bell and ask if we could keep the noise down.

'Believe me,' I'd say, 'we would really like her to stop crying, as well.'

'Well, have you fed her?' He looked a bit like a malevolent bird, I always thought, with narrow cynical eyes. 'Have you changed her? It can't be normal for a baby to cry *this* much.'

'I can assure you' – through gritted teeth – 'it is.'

'In that case, do you think you could at least be a little quieter when you're arguing? Or are you going to tell me that's normal as well?'

'At the moment, it is, yes.'

On her good days Elizabeth was mesmerizing. She guided a toy kangaroo around the house in careful hops, bandaging its paw with tissue when it got hurt; sometimes she picked up a leaf in the park for me, and handed it over solemnly for safe-keeping. She had strawberry-blonde hair and green eyes, and wore tiny polka-dot dresses.

But when I got home that night Lauren would hardly have the energy to greet me at the door: she would be mashing vegetables, or shoving a pile of washing into the knackered machine. There were bills to pay on the table, and things needed doing around the house, and the men on the radio said that the sixties had reinforced as many old prejudices as they had broken down. I thought for a second I was back in the garden at home watching Victoria feed the tortoise, and that was when I nearly steered us straight off the motorway into a ditch.

'Dom, for the love of . . .! Watch out! Hey!'

Daley seized me by the shoulders and on instinct alone I wrenched the wheel back the other way in a rain of furious horns.

'Holy Jesus and Mary!'

'Sorry. I'm sorry.'

'Is it because of me winding up football fans, is that it? Have you been planning all along to kill me?'

'I'm just so tired.'

'We'll have a coffee. Are you wanting me to take over driving?'

'You haven't driven for years.'

'You've not *slept* for years, by the looks of you.'

He shook his big square head. His appearance hadn't altered at all in what was now well over a decade since we began working together. His cropped hairstyle had almost ridden out the seventies and was now starting to seem less incongruous. The grey jumper hadn't changed either, although he claimed it was a different one.

'Come on. Services.'

'We'll be late if we do that.'

'We'll be late, in the sense of "the late Roger Daley", if you drive like that any more.'

This job was a big drinks reception in Manchester to celebrate the anniversary of a tennis association. Max was going to be there with Old Man Shillingworth and some other cronies, and that thought alone made me feel hot and twitchy in addition to the fatigue. By the time we had stopped at a garage and I'd forced myself to drink a tar-like cup of coffee, we were dangerously short of time. No sooner had we got under way again than we got caught in traffic and by the time we arrived at the exhibition hall we were already late. Inevitably, Max was the first person I saw as I arrived, lugging the bag over my shoulder, sweat building in my too-long hair.

'Ah, here he is,' said Max. 'Every inch the professional.'

This was aimed at a little clique of blazered individuals who chortled unctuously at it. One of them was Old Man Shillingworth, cigar in hand. Another was a boy barely out of school, by the look of him, unnervingly clean-shaven – his face shone as if scrubbed every hour – and wearing an awed expression which he turned on my brother at every opportunity.

'This is Roly, my assistant,' said Max.

'Pleased to meet you,' I said. 'We'd better get set up.'

'I had no idea photography was so complicated,' smirked the Old Man. 'Just a question of pressing a button, isn't it?'

'No, no, they have to *set up*,' said Max, while the assistant ha-ha-ed dutifully. 'They need to *set up* the *shots*.'

In the room there were fifty or so old fellows in blazers, all with the comfortable flab of long-time administrators. A separate pack of wives and assorted other women stood chattering in one corner. As I sweatily set up the Rolleiflex, Daley tried to organize the men into a neat group. 'OK, gents, tall ones at the back, please.' The subjects muttered among themselves; no one moved.

Daley used his old joke. 'You can tell you're one of the tall ones, if your face is higher than other people's.'

'Planted a bomb anywhere round here, Paddy?' shouted one of the men.

Daley's face set in a grim smile. 'Not yet, but I shall certainly consider it.'

There was catcalling from some of the better-oiled men. We squeezed them slowly into formation and I stepped back and looked through the viewfinder on top. 'All right. Everyone smile.'

I pressed the button; nothing happened.

'Sorry. We'll try that again. Three-two-one . . .'

Again, the button seemed to jam halfway down. I felt myself fill with misgivings. My brain was like wet cotton wool.

'Daley? It's not working.'

He tried the button. 'Have you got the spare?'

We had another Rolleiflex, but it was in the boot of the Capri. Daley went striding out to the car park and I was left standing next to the suddenly useless equipment, while the group offered their witticisms.

'There you are,' said Old Man Shillingworth, 'obviously there *is* an art to taking photographs after all. Not only do you have to set up the camera, you have to be competent enough to have one that works.'

The smooth-faced assistant laughed so hard at this that he looked in danger of falling over. He had girlish lips and big white teeth; I fantasized for a second about planting an elbow right in his mouth. Max was moving away towards a drinks-laden table. The group we had assembled began to unravel.

'Gentlemen, if you could all stay in your positions for just a second longer . . .'

'How long's that bloody Mick going to be with the camera?' exclaimed Shillingworth, lighting another cigar. 'Are we going to stand there all bloody day?'

One woman, considerably younger than his wife, stretched out an arm and pawed him in mock-reproach. 'Georgie! Are you making mischief again?'

I looked at my brother. His hair was neatly cut these days; he had a pricey blue suit on, and heavy shoes. Fine living had filled him out a bit from the wiry scholar he had once been.

'Max. Do you think you could possibly get your friends to come back into a group?'

He looked at me with the old fox-like scorn. 'I sort of assumed, with you being the photographer, you might take charge of the photos.'

'I am. We are. We've just had a slight technical hitch.'

Daley was barging his way back into the room with the replacement camera. In his haste he misjudged the door, which swung quickly back and hit him in the face. A huge, malicious guffaw filled the air. I felt myself turning purple.

'You two are quite the Laurel and Hardy,' Max observed, unconsciously inflicting a flashback to a happier moment, in the fancy-dress place in Kentish Town.

'It's normally a bit smoother than this,' I said. 'As I said, I just want to make sure we've got the pictures they ordered, because—.'

'Whatever you say,' said Max, but he was already into another conversation, introducing Smooth Face to some bejewelled lady. Daley bent over and began unpacking the reserve camera. More people had come barrelling into the room, and seemed not to see us at all; one of them almost tripped over Daley and upset the camera.

'Can I just . . . excuse me, gentlemen. Can I just ask you . . .' I shouted, into the building din. I caught Max's eye desperately once more, and he shot back a dry, unapologetic smile. I can't stop you being here, it seemed to say, but don't expect me to *help*. I had seen the look before, but this time there was no Victoria waiting at the school gates.

That was probably the last moment that I thought of Max as my brother.

Even with the substitute camera set up, the group shots were a mess, and the individual ones with the handheld were no better. Fatigue had gummed up my reactions and I knew straight away that the pictures were going to be awful. The organizer was an important client – he put on these receptions all over the place – but it was Max's judgement I really feared. He would now have the perfect opportunity to sneer at my work. I was all fingers and thumbs changing films. I backed away from a table to frame a shot and walked straight into a waiter. I was pinballing between exhaustion and a crazed desire to prove myself competent by doing everything faster, faster, faster.

When our job was finally over, I found an empty function room and sat with my head in my hands, wishing everything and everyone would vanish.

I don't know how long it was before I felt Daley's giant hand on my shoulder. 'We've to be going, if we want to miss the traffic.'

I nodded, but didn't move. Daley lowered himself slowly down to meet me, grunting as his long backbone crunched into its new position.

'You don't look so good, Dominic.'

I found I couldn't speak, and began to shed tears into my locked hands. Daley patted me on the back. Then he got up and locked the door, and when I opened my dewy eyes, he was holding out a shot glass.

'I've got to drive.'

'You can have one. That's the rules of the road. If you're down, have one to help you drive better.'

I took it and downed it. 'I'm just so tired.'

'I know. Babies, kids. Toughest game in the world.'

'Did you ever want to . . .?'

Daley frowned, as if it was an effort to remember. 'A good while ago, now. But Teresa couldn't.'

'I'm sorry.'

He gave a shrug of his broad shoulders. 'The will of God, or what-have-you.'

We sat in silence.

'She's just so exhausted all the time,' I said. 'It's as if she never quite recovered from having Elizabeth. Well, recovered isn't right, but you know. Never quite went back to the way she was.'

'She's happier, deep down, in some ways,' said Daley, 'kids do that. But she's unhappier in other ways too, and those are the ways you hear more about. Lauren's a . . . I suppose a volatile person, is the word. You know that.'

The fact was that I'd been with this new, changed Lauren longer already than the one I had met and fallen in love with. Having known her only in the peaks of romance and now in the impossible terrain of young parenthood, I had no real measure of what her normal self was. Already there were moments when it was difficult to remember how much fun we used to find one another.

'This can't be *it*. This can't be the rest of our lives.'

'It'll get better,' said Daley, ruffling my hair. 'Then it'll get worse again.' We laughed. 'Then, better. That's life.

'You should always remember you can talk to me,' he said, getting up with another little sigh as his limbs straightened out. 'And to others. How's that sister of yours?'

Victoria and I had reverted to irregular contact. She'd sent me postcards from this and that unlikely outpost, including quite a few with *Beautiful Victoria* or *Scenes from Victoria* on the front. It was amazing how many places called Victoria there were. I'd bought a job lot of miserable-looking cards published by the Royal Institute of British Architects, showing off the new concrete monstrosities of Milton Keynes and Letchworth. The more exotic the pictures she sent me, the grimmer the card I would send back.

Hope this finds you all well, OB. I am back out in Zimbabwe, as you can see. Very drunk last night. I'm afraid Victoria Falls ended up being a pretty good description of events. Will be back in London soon to keep eye on Dad.

Dom – thank you for the appalling vista of Bletchley. Don't know if you're trying to put me off ever coming home. In any case you've failed, we shall be back semi-permanently before long. In Oz for a few more weeks though. T collecting some award for being greatest cricketer of all time etc. I have one hell of a hat.

Sure enough, by 1980 Victoria and the Cricketer had moved back to England full-time. He had neared the end of his playing career, and would now join his father and Max in their money-making machine. They had a new place in Chelsea, near the Shillingworth house and just around the corner from Max, who was now going steady with a toothy, well-educated girl called Nonie. We took it in turns to visit our parents, and sometimes Victoria would come round to see her niece.

On these occasions Lauren would try to conceal her unsteady moods with a forced cheer which I found almost more draining than its opposite. She laughed too loudly at everything; praised Victoria's appearance with compliments really meant as bitter remarks on her own misfortune. 'Oh, it must be *great* to shop at places like that.' 'Wow, I wish *I* had time to do my hair like that.' Victoria would reply with counter-compliments – about our cosy home, our beautiful daughter – which could not help sounding like consolation prizes.

To make matters worse, Elizabeth seemed to love her aunt. She squawked with delight when Victoria picked her up and swung her around. Victoria brought expensive, exciting toys which made noises and flashed lights. She laughed with glee as Elizabeth clutched at her posh dresses or grabbed her viciously by the nose. When she left, Elizabeth would waddle heartbroken to the door to wave goodbye, and linger there abandoned. For hours afterwards she would keep asking when 'toria was coming back.

One Sunday the parting hug between Lauren and Victoria was so wooden, the cheek-kisses so unfelt, that I had to follow Victoria out to say goodbye properly.

'Look, I'm sorry about Lauren.'

'It's all right, Dom. She doesn't have to like me.'

'She *should* like you. She should love you.'

Victoria laughed. 'You haven't changed. Your lovely blind favouritism.'

I started to take her by the arm, then shrank back, not trusting myself. 'Victoria, between you and me, things are hard. Lauren's not just like this with you. She's really struggling.'

'She could be depressed. Do you know about post-natal depression?'

'But it's been three years.'

'It can last for ages. She should speak to someone.'

'She never will. Her dad was a psycho-something-or-other . . .'

'A psychopath?'

I laughed. 'Not exactly, but it amounts to the same in her eyes.'

We glanced involuntarily back to see Lauren, arms folded, watching us through the window with suspicion in her tired eyes.

'I'd better go inside. Thanks for coming.'

She leaned in for me to kiss her on the cheek, but I didn't dare.

Three weeks later I came back from a wedding notable only for the fact that Daley introduced me as 'Mr Eggs' to the father of the bride, and by the end of the day everyone believed it was my real name. Other than that, the whole business had been soothing in its normality, right down to the tongue-in-cheek way the groom mopped his brow when nobody gave a reason to stop the wedding. The only slight variation was that the awkward silence at the sign- ing of the register was filled with a lisped poetry reading by the bride's nephew, which proved to be considerably more awkward. By the time we approached Archway and home, after a minor jostle with a football car enraged by Daley's new black-and-white scarf, my heart was warming at the thought of Lauren; it was still early, Elizabeth might be asleep and we could spend some quiet hours together. But she was waiting at the door, eyes large and glittering with outrage, a day-long grievance clenched in her jaw.

'Welcome home, *darling*.'

'What's the matter?'

'Oh, nothing, nothing can be the matter. Because it's to do with Victoria, and everyone loves Victoria, so if I take offence, I must be crazy.'

I tried to touch her, but she edged away. 'What? What's the matter, Lauren?'

'You need another clue? Victoria? Going behind my back?'

My knees felt as if they had filled with liquid. I thought for a second I would fall forward onto my face. How could she know? It was impossible for anyone to know. My brain was racing ahead of itself; I felt sick.

'Well, I'll show you,' said Lauren, and produced a post-card as if it were a dagger. *With Love from the Isle of Wight!* My heart thudded. What mad, incriminating thing had Victoria written? And in the middle of this pool of panic, fizzing and flaming like a strip of magnesium in water, there was an awful excitement.

With clammy hands I turned the postcard over and felt my frisking heart thud to a halt.

Was just thinking some more about L. I reckon she could do with someone to talk to – professionally. Tom knows an amazing guy on Harley Street. Expensive but I would think we could 'pull some strings'. Think about it. Just want to help.
V xx

I looked between the card and Lauren's indignant face, quickly assessed a couple of soothing things I could say, and realized they would be no good.

'I'm sorry. She has no right to poke her nose in.'

'Well, obviously she *thinks* she has a right because obviously *someone* has *told her* that I'm whining.'

'It's not a case of whining. Anyone can see you're unhappy.'

'Right. I'm unhappy because I live in a tiny little house with a screaming three-year-old and a husband who's never there, so I *must* be as crazy as Sylvia fucking Plath.'

Elizabeth, woken, began to wail in the nursery. In a well-honed dance of tiny movements we both flinched, acknowledged the noise, and continued.

'No one's saying you're crazy. It might just help you to talk.'

'Of course. If Victoria says so, then why not.'

'This is not about Victoria! I love you and I don't want you to be miserable.'

She dropped her eyes, disarmed for a second. 'Dominic. I am not going to feel better about my life by spending money we don't have so someone can tell me to *work through my issues*.'

'You're judging the whole profession unfairly because of your problems with your dad, and—'

'Jesus! Why don't *you* psychoanalyse me! Shall I lie on the couch right there?'

'Well, it's true.'

'OK, and I guess *you* have the model relationship with *your* daddy. Apart from the fact that nobody in your family has ever expressed any of their feelings because you all live in the fucking eighteen fifties.'

I took a deep breath after this; she had hit a number of nerves with one stroke. 'That's my whole point,' I said, in a voice festering with badly suppressed anger. 'My dad could probably have been treated a lot sooner, but no one admitted there was a problem. So—'

'This is *totally different*,' she spat, but less in anger now than with a helplessness I found even harder to stomach.

Elizabeth cried out again in the nursery, and I heard the man next door scrape his chair along the floor and curse us. We stared at each other for a few moments as if neither of us could quite remember how we got here. Then Lauren, clutching momentarily at her unwashed hair as though on the verge of wrenching out a handful, turned and went head bowed to the door.

We were both at fault for the argument, but it would be Victoria who was remembered as the real villain.

Dad got no worse for a long time, and we all acted as if that meant he was better. One day, however, the phone rang late at night. The sound woke Elizabeth, who started to cry; Lauren, swearing under her breath, rose from the bed and I went to pick up the phone.

'It's Dad,' said Victoria.

She told me that Mum and Dad had been to an event in some fancy West End hotel. Victoria had taken Mum to buy a dress and spent most of the afternoon getting her ready. When they got there, Dad disappeared almost at once.

It took almost an hour to find him. He was in an empty ballroom on the tenth floor, wandering around on his own. When Mum walked in and took his arm, he asked her to dance as if they had just met. She began to cry. He went into the corridor and tapped a bell-boy on the sleeve.

'Can we get a drink for this young lady? She seems a bit upset.'

I drove the Capri home. The family was assembled in a living room which seemed very cold. I hovered around the arm of the Chesterfield.

'Mother,' said Max, 'we are going to have to look at getting full-time care for Dad. There's a place near by, very modern, and—'

'Let's not talk about it tonight, dear,' said Mum faintly.

Max cleared his throat. 'We can arrange the financial side of it.'

She winced. 'There's no need for that.'

'What I think we should do,' said Max, 'is get a doctor, someone to look him over, and if they say it's the right thing—'

'Please,' said our mother. She began a word, broke off and began again. 'Please don't let them take him away.'

'It wouldn't be anyone "taking him away", Mum,' said Victoria. Dad had sat listening to all this with a look of polite interest as if a mutual acquaintance were being discussed. 'We just want what's best for both of you.'

'What's best for *me*,' said Mum, 'is to be with your father. And what's best for him is to be with me. I don't care what sort of condition he's in.'

Max coughed several times. Nobody else spoke. We might have wished in the past that she'd express herself like this more often, but every time she did the rawness of it was terrible, like a cut exposed to the cold. I shivered. Max coughed again. Victoria lit a cigarette.

'Let us at least get someone to look at him, Mum,' I said, to my own surprise. 'It's the right thing to do. It really is. Even if it might not be what you want.'

Max furrowed his brow as if about to put me in my place, but it seemed I'd made an impact by speaking up for once. Our mother nodded, staring at the ground. 'All right.'

It was one in the morning when I left. The wind was whistling dolefully through the terraces outside. Max had gone to bed. Victoria and I looked at each other in the doorway.

'Well done for saying something, OB,' she said. 'I couldn't seem to say anything.'

My breath appeared in white clouds against the night sky, and the smoke from Victoria's cigarette was dragged up by the wind towards it; the trails mingled for a second and were gone.

I shrugged. 'I didn't exactly give a speech.'

'You should believe in yourself a bit more.' She squeezed my arm. As if a button had been pressed, wires seemed to stiffen all the way through me; the blood pulsed through my body.

'I should go.'

'You know, you could just stay here. It's really late. You can crash down in my room.'

'I can't do that, Victoria.'

Victoria looked questioningly at me. She was getting prettier with age, the way I'd noticed a lot of women did. The new shadows around her eyes brought out the sly gleam they had always had. She stood up straighter than she used to, and wore her expensive clothes as if she had been born in them.

I kissed her briskly on the cheek and went into the cold, my heart thudding.

'Goodnight, Dom,' Victoria called after me. I couldn't trust myself to reply, even to look over my shoulder, in case I let everything else go to hell and turned straight back into her arms.

Dad was examined by Dr Etherington once more in early December. As I was about to leave home, already a few minutes late, Elizabeth pulled a bowl off a shelf and smashed it on the floor. I flung myself down to scoop up the pieces.

'Hey, you've missed some of that,' said Lauren.

'I have to go.' I threw the leather jacket over my shoulders. 'I'm sorry.'

'Of course. You *always* have to go. There's always—' But I slammed the door and didn't hear the rest.

Victoria and I saw off a whole packet of cigarettes in the waiting room. On the sofa opposite, Mum fussed over Dad's collar and his hair.

'Max could have bloody turned up,' Victoria grumbled.

'Probably made his first million of the day in the time it took us to drive here.'

She snorted. 'He's not *working*. He's running around with that awful girl of his, the one with the teeth.' Victoria rattled the empty fag packet with regret. 'Wow, we got through those.'

'Remember, last time we were here, you'd given up?'

She smirked. 'You won that one, old boy.'

The door was opened and Dr Etherington poked his bony skull out. 'Kitchen.' He winced slightly as all four of us got up and the three of us trooped in formation behind Victoria. With palpable reluctance he held the door open for the gang of us; Victoria flashed him a cheerful smile. The mere sight of it gave me courage. Inside the room, posters labelled the different parts of the respiratory system, the central nervous system.

'You'd think he would know that stuff already, really,' Victoria whispered. I tried to laugh, but the room was freezing cold. The doctor sat behind a walnut writing desk on which there was nothing but a black book. I looked between Dad and the fussily labelled lungs and nerves on the walls.

Dr Etherington asked Dad a series of questions: how he had been feeling, how he was sleeping, whether he was going to the football. The answers seemed of little real interest to him – indeed, when Dad began to describe a recent Arsenal match, he sighed in quiet impatience. Without being able to stop myself, I laid one of my hands on Victoria's. She took it and squeezed. Mum was holding on to the edge of the desk, as if the doctor might suddenly wheel it away with Dad on top of it.

With each cogent answer Dad gave, I saw Victoria's whole frame relax a little and Mum's grip loosen on the table-edge. Etherington received the responses with a thin, patronizing smile and nod. From time to time he would pause and write slow notes with a fountain pen, leaving the four of us to sit and glance at each other.

'What are you writing?' Victoria asked.

Etherington looked up, his nostrils flaring. 'This is a medical examination, Miss . . .?'

'Mrs Shillingworth.'

He blinked. 'Ah, yes. My wife read about you, I think, in a *magazine*.' He pronounced the word as if it were a poison. 'Don't worry about what I'm writing. I don't think it would be of great interest to you.'

After a sticky, silence-filled half-hour, Etherington sent us all out except Mum, whom he kept back for 'some more detailed questions'.

'The bastard just wanted us out of the way,' murmured Victoria, her eyes fiery.

I put an arm around her shoulders. 'It's all right. Dad was great.'

'Dad can hear you,' said Dad. Victoria gave him a grin; her eyes moistened for a second. Our father wandered off to the corner of the room, where someone had left a copy of the *Racing Post*.

My hand was on Victoria's arm. The main door opened, a man in a shabby suit came in, and my hand flew guiltily away from her.

'You don't have to . . .' Victoria began. 'It's OK to *touch* my *arm*, for God's sake.'

'It's not OK,' I said. My stomach clenched with horror and excitement at what I was about to say. 'Look, Victoria, I—'

'Oh, Jesus,' she said, her mouth dropping open, 'oh, no.'

'Please,' I said, 'hear me out. I—'

'Oh God, stop him!' Victoria cried, and I saw that she hadn't even heard what I was saying; she was looking straight past me, into the corner of the room. Dad had put down the newspaper, unzipped his flies, and, seemingly oblivious to everything around him, was urinating on the floor.

'Dad . . .' said Victoria, and moved towards him, but as if in slow motion; she was frightened by the sight. A dark puddle was collecting on the plush carpet by his feet.

The man in the suit, who had been filling a pipe, said between mirth and disgust, 'Bloody hell!'

Dad looked around and met our horrified stares, narrowing his eyes in puzzlement at the commotion. Etherington's door swung open and for an endless, ice-cold moment everyone was watching our father as he stood there, wetting the carpet in front of him: the stranger amused, Victoria and I inert with horror, Dr Etherington with something close to a sneer on his lips. And next to the doctor, Mum, her mouth slightly open, her eyes pointed anywhere but in front of her.

X

At the other end of a long Christmas, Max called us for a 'council of war' at the Shillingworth mansion. I drove down there on a foggy Monday night after a day taking pictures at a computing award ceremony. I had little idea what a computer was, and wasn't much enlightened by the speeches at the event, which were full of phrases like 'code' and 'artificial intelligence'.

'I'd be more impressed if these people showed some *actual* intelligence,' Daley muttered.

'They haven't got any. That's why they need machines.'

They were uneasy jokes. For the first time I was at the age where the acceleration of technology becomes alarming rather than exciting – though perhaps it was just me who noticed it, as Daley was still cheerfully refusing to use an electric razor and claiming that colour TV was a fad. Everyone but him, though, seemed to be talking about electronics or robots. On the way to school with Elizabeth this morning I'd heard a song whose vocals were chir-ruped by a digitized voice over a backing of synthesizers.

'Is that a *man* singing?'

'Yes . . . sort of.'

'It sounds more like a space alien,' Elizabeth remarked.

'How do you know about aliens? Have you got one in your class?'

'Don't be *stupid*.' There were occasional glimpses, already, of the tart-tongued teenager she would become. 'We've got a hamster.'

I parked the car and we joined the procession: plastic lunchboxes swinging, jumpers sewn inside the collar with name-tags. As I was about to release her into the mayhem of childish motion, like a tadpole into a teeming sea, Elizabeth looked up at me with the poised green eyes unnervingly like her mother's.

'Are you here on Saturday?'

The question felt designed to catch me out. 'Saturday? No, darling. I'm working.'

'It's the Brownies' fair.'

I suppressed a sigh. The Brownies seemed to hold a fair, a concert, a bring-and-buy sale almost every week.

'I have to go to a wedding, I'm afraid, but Mum will take—'

'I don't want *Mum*.' She pouted. 'You always say Mum will go. I want *you*.'

'I know, Bethie. It's just that I have to work at weekends, you know, and—'

'Why?'

I experienced a middle-aged chagrin at being repri-
manded by my daughter. Mothers in their overcoats and
scarves stepped tactfully around us at the gates with final
farewells to their offspring.

'Well, because my job is to take pictures, and . . . and it
normally means I'm busy at weekends. But it also means I
can take you to school and sometimes pick you up.'

'It's meant to be people's *mums* who do that.'

Elizabeth cocked her head, defying me to question the
logic of this argument.

'I'm sorry I'm going to miss the fair,' I said, 'but maybe
we can do something nice soon to make up for it.'

'There's a doll's house I really, really want,' she replied
at once. 'I'll tell you about it later.'

I watched her fall into step with a pigtailed girl, not
knowing whether to be proud or aghast that she was
already able to play me so assuredly.

The morning felt a long time ago when I parked the
Capri, with its chipped paint and dirty hubcaps, in the
Shillingworths' drive alongside the glistering assembly of
sports cars. Conchita showed me through to the library.
Mr and Mrs Shillingworth were away, she told me, in
Provence.

The grandfather clock was lurching its way like a
drunkard through the minutes and hours. The phalanxes
of unread books shadowed the walls. Max and Victoria
were drinking whisky side by side in their armchairs. I felt
a flickering jealousy of their closeness. Victoria reached for
a glass and poured me a huge measure of whisky.

'Is he old enough to drink yet?' asked Max.

'Fuck off, Max,' I said, draining the glass in two gulps, and then fighting to stop myself from coughing as the flames rose up in my throat. It was the taste of the beach in Southwold all those summers ago.

'So,' Max said, 'I've already been through this with Victoria.' Of course you have, I thought, of course you started without me. 'As we all know,' he said, 'Dad needs to be in full-time care. I've got a brochure here.' He slid a booklet across the coffee table towards me: *Dignity for Those in Need*.

'I can pay for it, comfortably,' said Max.

'We're going to make a contribution, too,' said Victoria. 'Me and Tom.'

'I'll put in my share.'

'It's expensive,' Max pointed out, as if to a child.

'I'm aware of that.'

Max smirked. 'As you like. The other thing is, we obviously need to keep an eye on Mum. This is going to be very tough for her.'

'Of course,' I muttered.

'Right,' said Max, 'well, there's not a lot more to say. Let's finish this, shall we?'

He sloshed out the whisky. We drank, listening to the clock and the clanking and whirring of the central heating. The maid was hoovering up non-existent dust in some distant hall. We sat there discussing the Cricketer's new career as a TV pundit.

'He's perfect for it,' said Max. 'Looks great on telly.'

'Don't tell him that. He's good at quite enough things as it is.'

'I bet he is,' said Max slyly, and Victoria giggled and dug him in the ribs. She was wearing a trademark black cloche hat and her fringe hung low above her eyes. She had an old maroon dress on over blue jeans. I poured wine into my empty glass – it mingled poisonously with the dark whisky-dregs – and started to think about leaving.

'I did sort of have another motive for getting you both here.' Max wiped his mouth and broke into a wolfish grin. 'Nonie and I are getting married.'

Victoria clapped her hands. 'Hurray! When?'

'Pretty soon,' said Max. 'Don't want a lot of fucking about. Country house in Hampshire.'

'Can I help her choose the dress?' asked Victoria, grabbing Max by the arm. 'Can I decorate the venue?' For a second I almost hated her.

Max play-punched her. 'You'll be guest of honour, for our sins.' He coughed and glanced up at me. 'And you and your wife are well and truly invited, of course, Dominic.'

'Well, I would think he'd be taking the photos,' said Victoria.

There was a pause. Clunk-CLONK. Clunk-CLONK. Victoria's cigarette burned in her outstretched hand. We both looked at Max.

He cleared this throat. 'Actually, a friend of Nonie's is a bit of a snapper. Got a big . . . a big camera. She's sort of asked him if he's available.'

Clunk-CLONK. I could feel myself getting hot. Vicious remarks streamed across my mind, but I stayed quiet. Victoria stubbed out her cigarette. 'Max, are you bonkers?'

'One of those awkward things,' Max conceded. 'But, Dominic, you're more than welcome to take a few of your own.'

'This is bollocks!' Victoria's mouth was open: I loved her again. 'Are you honestly telling me you're not going to get your *own brother* to take your wedding shots?'

'It's fine,' I said. 'If Max wants to get an amateur to do it . . .'

'Having seen you at work,' said Max with his trademark grin, 'I'm not entirely sure you should be calling someone else an amateur.'

Fury flooded my brain and I shot to my feet. The booze wrapped itself around my head like a damp cloth. I staggered towards him. He got out of his chair and backed away, looking surprised and almost impressed. Victoria grabbed me by the arm.

'Hey. Calm down.'

'Don't tell me to fucking calm down,' I blurted out, although her touch had subdued me.

'Max, you're in the wrong,' said Victoria. 'Apologize.'

'Once a teacher, always a teacher, eh?' Max smirked.

'I don't give a shit about taking your photos,' I said. 'There's not a lens wide enough for your girlfriend's teeth.'

Victoria bit her lip, trying to lock up a laugh, but it curled its way out of her mouth. 'You should probably take that back, Dom.'

'Sorry,' I said. 'I meant, there's not a lens wide enough for your *fiancée's* teeth.'

Victoria snorted and spluttered helplessly, and Max laid his glass down hard on the table.

'I think I'll be off now,' he said. 'You two can let yourselves out, or get up to whatever the hell you want.'

This was said with no intent other than general aggression, but a chill crept up my back and Victoria loosened her grip on my arm. We all looked at each other in silence.

'I'll get on the phone to the care home in the morning,' he said. 'Unless, Dominic, you'd like to do it so that you can be *involved*.'

'Fuck off, Max,' said Victoria.

We watched him leave the room and heard his footsteps in the hall.

'He shouldn't drive,' Victoria said. 'He'll wrap himself round a lamp post one day.'

'We can but hope,' I muttered. Silence fell again in the library. We heard Max's car growl into life outside and roar importantly away into the night.

We sat in the library for a long time, dulled by drink and by the heaviness of everything. Despite the staggering, ever-present clunk of the clock, the room had always had some quality of timelessness about it. After a while, it was hard to believe that anything was happening elsewhere.

'I overreacted,' I said. 'I shouldn't be so sensitive.'

'You've got every right.' Victoria crouched down by the cabinet and fished out the sherry decanter, an enormous onion-shaped thing in solid silver. She came and sat on the arm of the chair: I caught a whiff of peach perfume. 'Anyway, his loss. You're a great photographer.'

'You don't have to say that.'

'You are. God, I should hire you to do pictures of *me*. You should see some of the hideous ones they print.'

'I've got a camera in the car.'

Victoria looked at me. 'I didn't mean . . . I didn't mean now, necessarily.'

'We could, though. I could just do some shots and see how they come out.'

She glanced doubtfully into the mirrored surface of the liquor cabinet. 'I've been drinking for about five hours.'

'Oh yes, you look appalling,' I agreed, 'but as you said, I'm a very good photographer.'

She giggled. 'I've got a couple of outfits in the room upstairs. The room they keep for me. I'll . . .'

'*The room they keep for me*!' I mimicked. 'Do you have your own staff, too?'

Victoria, grinning indignantly, elbowed me hard as she rose to her feet. 'That's enough cheek from you, David Bailey. Fetch your camera.'

The crunching shut of the Capri's boot sounded very loud in the silent drive. I walked back across the gravel and into the house. The drone of the maid's hoover, ever-present like the hum of mosquitoes in some tropical resort, sounded from upstairs. The clock was marching through its unsteady beat in the library. From the Trophy Room came a hiss which reminded me of the old days.

'Psst! Dom!'

My heart accelerated a fraction as the door opened with its creak. The lonely treasures stood to attention; the old Shillingworths in their flat cricket caps stared from the photographs, with the strange melancholy of long-dead portrait subjects. Victoria had changed into a white ball gown, with black and scarlet detail around the bust where it widened like a wedding dress. She was sitting in an armchair, one leg crossed over another. The dress spread luxuriantly over the chair; against its whiteness her hair and eyes looked darker than ever.

'Do I look like Audrey Hepburn?'

'Better; you look like Victoria Kit . . . Shillingworth.'

She grimaced. 'Kitchen's fine.'

'Right, look at my hand.' The flash blinked at her, making her flinch. 'Fine. And now, keep your head still, but move your eyes back towards me.'

'My eyes are part of my head, old boy.'

'I assure you it's possible to move them independently.'

I repositioned her slightly, then snapped her looking away, back towards me. The camera felt heavy and cumbersome in my hands; it reminded me of that first time taking pictures in a church. She took an old trophy down from a shelf, its handles like two giant ears – 'Some old piece of cricketing tat,' she said – and posed with it in her lap. I changed lenses and began to shoot in close-up. Through the little viewfinder I saw, like someone peering through a window, tiny portions of Victoria: the chocolate brown of her eyes, the full lips, the classical frame of her hair around her neck. Each bark of the flash felt somehow too bright, as if rather than being in control of the pictures I was actually the one being snapped. I tried in vain to imagine that it was just any portrait session, that she was just anyone.

'OK, relax for a second. You're doing beautifully.'

She reached across for a cigarette, smiling slightly at my professional tone, and I pounced for another picture as her features softened. 'That's the best one so far.'

Victoria laughed. 'You said relax!'

'I always use that trick.'

Victoria took a gulp of sherry and I, feeling in need of it, did the same. The maid was one floor above us; the vacuum cleaner had stopped, and we could hear the thudding and shuffling of her mysterious empty-house errands.

'So, any special requests?' I asked.

'All I really want,' said Victoria, 'is not to look too fat or ugly.'

'You're beautiful,' I said before I could stop myself. I coughed to cover the moment that followed.

'You've always been so sweet to me, Dom.'

'Don't patronize me, old girl. I'm not being sweet. I think it's fairly widely known how beautiful you are.'

She laughed alarmingly loud. I had a rather nostalgic sense of sounding young and gauche. 'Widely known, is it! It's a shame the news hasn't reached my husband!'

'Is he still not . . .?' I felt helpless. 'Doesn't he . . .?'

'Oh, he's a very appreciative lover.' Victoria looked bitterly at her hands. 'But not an appreciative lover of *me*, unfortunately.'

I could hardly believe the casual way she spoke. 'He cheats on you?'

Victoria was rocking her glass gently back and forth, sloshing the sherry up the sides.

'Cheating is a funny word. It sort of implies that you're both playing the same game, and the game has rules. I'm not sure it was ever like that with us.'

'Of course there are rules. You're married.' I felt that on this subject, at least, I had some authority.

'It turns out there are unwritten rules, Dommo. For example, if you start to feel unattractive and feel self-conscious about sex, your husband is allowed to get it from other people, in other hotel rooms. It's funny, I don't remember that being in the vows.'

I was speechless. My stomach was like a clenched fist. 'How can he . . .?'

'It happens a lot, Dom.' Victoria gave me a sad smile of older-sister knowledge. 'As long as you're married, and respectable, and in the society pages, no one minds how you actually behave.'

'But how can he not want . . . not want you?'

'Why not go and ask him?' She gestured in mock invitation towards the window and the outside world. Her hand caught the sherry glass and jogged it skywards, and the remnants of her drink spattered on the dress. 'Oh, fuck it.'

'Why don't we try some pictures in a different outfit,' I suggested.

My hands shook a little as I packed up the camera. The door creaked behind us. Victoria led us up the stairs to

the room they 'kept for her'; it was high-ceilinged, dominated by a four-poster bed which was immaculately made
up and heaped with plump pillows. I looked out of the
window across the river where the cedars stood watch in
the night. Victoria opened a huge oak wardrobe to reveal
a rail of dangling dresses.

'This one, remember this?' she said, taking the rich material between two fingers. 'This was the dress I wore for—'

'For my wedding, yes. Of course I remember.'

She held it meditatively for a moment. 'Never worn it
since. I was so horribly jealous that whole day.'

Jealous of what? I wondered. Of all the attention lavished
on Lauren and me? Or of something else?

Victoria was holding out a deep blue cocktail dress with
a V-effect at the neck. 'What about this? Bit short?'

'Let's try it.'

She took a step away from me, dropped the dress on
the expansive bed and began to unzip the ball gown at the
back. I turned and looked out of the window, breathing
as steadily as I could. I heard a little sigh from Victoria as
the zip caught her fingers, and then the rustle of satin as
she shrugged off the gown. Every part of me was tense.
Against what I thought was my will I turned around and
looked at her, the new dress draped over her arm. She
stood in her black underwear against the ice-white walls
and bedspread. My eyes went to the fading tattoo, which
was beginning to look like some minor blemish, and
then were arrested by hers. She looked at me, amused.
Impulsively I took hold of the camera and snapped her.

'Ah, you were sizing me up for a photo. For a second I thought you were just staring at my breasts.'

I felt nauseous with the weight of the unsaid and the barely thought. 'I'm sorry. I . . . I don't know. I just wanted to look.'

It felt good to have said it. Victoria sat down on the bed. I stood, quite at a loss, glancing between her and the camera. I waited for her to speak.

'I'm sorry,' I said again. 'I shouldn't be seeing you like this. In this way. I don't know what you think of me.'

She wet her lips with her tongue and motioned to me to pass her a cigarette. Glad of the distraction, I opened the packet on the bedside table.

'The truth is, OB, I rather like being looked at.'

I blocked out all thoughts of Lauren and of anything happening beyond this isolated house. Victoria picked at the cigarette in her hands. 'It's been a long time since anyone looked at me with . . . well, with any sort of desire. You come to miss it, after a while.'

'I'm not the person who should be desiring you.'

'No, well.' Her gaze was still on the unsmoked cigarette as it unravelled in her hands. 'Hard to say what anyone "should" be doing, isn't it?'

I sank down next to her on the bed. My hand brushed against hers on the duvet.

'I've always felt so comfortable with you. You're my *brother*.' Her eyes twinkled darkly for a moment. 'I never thought twice about . . . you know. Even when . . .'

'Even when we kissed?'

'In the library? Well, we were drunk, we were upset. A something-something kiss, as the song goes. I didn't think it mattered.'

'And now . . .?'

'Now,' she said, finally relinquishing the mashed cig-arette and beginning to chew her finger, 'I can see that it's a little more complicated than that.'

For a long while we remained in silence. It was still impossible to know what was really in her head; how much of this dark thing was mine alone.

'It's not as if we're ever going to do anything,' she said in the end. 'We're brother and sister, for God's sake. I saw you naked the day you were born.'

'As you've said before. So you still owe me one.'

'What about on the beach, that time? In Southwold, when we . . .?'

'I didn't really see anything,' I said. 'I was too confused.'

Looking me in the eyes, she unfastened her bra and placed it on the bedspread as if it were an object of no importance. Her breasts, larger and heavier than I im-agined, swung in front of my eyes. I caught my breath.

'I know,' she said, 'I've let myself go.'

'That's not what I was thinking.'

I wanted to touch her so desperately, the urge acted on me like a physical force. I slid my trembling hand across and rested it on her bare knee. This could not be my real life; it was a part I was temporarily playing. In the morning it would be impossible to believe it had ever happened. I watched the rise and fall of her shoulders. My hand went out towards her. Then my heart froze as the maid knocked on the door, pushing it open as she did so.

'Shit,' said Victoria, part-covering herself with one dress, and then squirming to get a hold of the gown. I leapt from the bed and threw myself against the door.

'Wait a minute!' I shouted, shoving the door back the way it had come, so that the maid was thrown back out with it. 'Give us a minute!'

There was a puzzled silence from the other side.

'I'm . . . I'm doing some photographs,' I said. It sounded like the feeblest thing anyone had ever said.

'He's got the camera set up just behind the door,' Victoria called. 'You'll knock it over.'

The maid muttered something in Spanish. Victoria had wriggled into the ball gown.

'Sorry about that,' I called, 'come in.'

I opened the door. The maid walked in, hand on hip, a duster poking out of the other hand. She looked hard at each of us.

'Just saying I finish now,' she said. 'I will finish now.'

'Us, too,' said Victoria, with a pleasant smile. 'You were just leaving, weren't you, Dominic?'

'I was,' I muttered, and started to pack the handheld into the case. The maid gave me one more look and went on her way.

Victoria and I scarcely glanced at each other as I collected my things. We descended the staircase with unconvincing nonchalance, and said goodbye in the grand doorway. She was going to stay the night. As for me, I had to return to my real life as if that was the only world that existed, and what had transpired in the Shillingworth house had once again been a lurid dream.

I drove home past the lighted windows of houses, enviable in their ordinariness; it was hard to believe there could be anyone anywhere feeling quite so alien as I was.

I wondered once more how I had got onto the other side of humanity from them; what was wrong with me. I was drawn to something which nobody I knew would condone or even comprehend. Only Victoria, and perhaps not even she, could ever be on my side. My hands left their sweaty stamp on the wheel and the knot in my stomach felt like something wedged in a machine, something that could never be prised out.

Lauren was wide awake when I slid into bed next to her. 'You stink of booze,' she muttered.

'I'm sorry. Bad night.'

'Sssh. Bethie has only just gone back to sleep.'

'We're putting him into a home.'

There was a pause, and Lauren's arm reached around my shoulders. 'I'm sorry, sweetheart.'

I swivelled and grabbed her. 'I want you.'

'What is this? Are you drunk?'

'No. I told you, I want you.'

Bit by bit she began to yield. Her hands came to rest on my back. I clambered on top of her and started clumsily trying to make it all up to her, to myself, to the love I could never acknowledge. I was ham-fisted and sweaty, bobbing like a cork in a sea of confused desire. For the few minutes it lasted, it was as if life had never moved on from that night in Paris, as if we were indeed living in the sketchy paradise my brain had half envisaged the future to be. In the headrush of climax I fell briefly into a sort of hallucination that everything I felt for Victoria, and the moments of intimacy we had shared, and the trouble with Dad were all part of a dream, and now I had woken to find it all dissolved. This lasted no more than thirty seconds; then Lauren rolled onto her side and fell into instant sleep, and the room grew cold around me.

Dad had settled into his new, reduced life with a mixture of acceptance and defiance. Some days he appeared more animated than he had been for years, flirting with the nurses and bantering with his fellow residents. At other times he was horribly quiet. On the worst afternoons he would not seem to know where he was, and Mum and Victoria and I would glance miserably at each other as he talked about matches he thought he was about to report on, or arrangements for coming home. In the Capri afterwards, the conversation would start brightly – 'He's looking well', 'He seemed perky today' – and fade away as the other cars roared past.

Mum went every weekday afternoon, not knowing what else to do with herself. When no one was able to drive her, Max paid for a taxi. Max himself was rarely there, but now and again he would appear for the Sunday visits. Once he brought his assistant, Smooth Face, overdressed in a grey suit. During the visit, Smooth Face plastered on a huge smile, nodded his head furiously at everything Dad said, and spoke in a voice three times too loud as if he'd been told that senility was the same as deafness. Victoria and I exchanged maddened glances as his head bobbed up and down like some wind-up toy. Just above her right eye was trailing a single, beautiful grey hair. When she saw me glance at it, she swatted it out of view. As soon as we got into the cramped car, Smooth Face let out a sigh of relief, oblivious to Victoria's withering look.

One Sunday Lauren and Elizabeth came along. We inched uncomfortably through the sludgy layers of traffic that seemed to lie in wait for us each time. Elizabeth swung her legs and played I-Spy with her aunt Victoria, who was also training her in the number-plate game. Lauren kept shuffling round in her seat to tell Elizabeth to calm down as she screeched word after word; she fiddled with Elizabeth's outfit, smoothing out her dress. Victoria stared out of the window so as not to smirk at her fussiness, and Lauren read the avoidance of insult as clearly as an insult itself. I glanced in turn at the three women who collectively made up most of what mattered in my life, and wondered why it was so difficult spending time with all of them. This pattern repeated itself until we trundled into the car park, where a handful of vehicles sat in a discouragingly neat grid. Elizabeth's mood seemed to change at once.

'Daddy, I don't want to come any more.'

'We're here now, Bethie. We won't be long.'

'It's frightening in there.'

Victoria gave Elizabeth her sleeve to hold on to. 'Stick close to me, Elizabeth Taylor.' I saw Lauren cringe minutely at Victoria's easy way with her daughter. 'If you want to go out, just give me a tug and we'll make something up.'

'What will we make up?'

Victoria pondered. 'We'll say that, unfortunately, we've left a dog in the car, and he's starting to get too hot.'

The boiled-vegetable smell in the corridors reminded me of school. Dad was sitting in an armchair, studying *The Antiques Roadshow*. He flung his arms around everyone in turn, cackling, and then sat Elizabeth on his knee. She perched there like a cat that would rather be outdoors.

We talked about neighbourhood gossip as if our street were a place Dad had temporarily left. I filled Dad in on Arsenal's recent form; I had been dutifully reading the sports pages where his name used to appear. 'They lost 5–0 to Spurs. Embarrassing!'

'Dreadful bunch.' Dad shook his head. 'They want to get a new goalkeeper, for a start.'

'Yes, that George Wood isn't up to it,' I agreed. I saw Victoria glance admiringly at me.

'You and I will have to go to Highbury, Max,' said Dad, 'once I'm feeling myself again.'

There was a brief collective intake of breath. 'You mean Dominic, Dad,' said Victoria quietly.

'I should think I know what I mean!' Dad protested. 'I was just saying that Max here hasn't had the pleasure of my company down at the football for quite some time now.'

'I'm Dominic,' I said, feeling my stomach begin its now-familiar descent.

Dad staggered to his feet; Elizabeth scampered away and took Victoria's sleeve again. 'Why have you all come here to laugh at me! Are you trying to make me look stupid?'

'No one's laughing at you, dear,' said Mum, trying to take his arm. 'You're just a little bit confused about—'

'I know I'm *fucking confused*.'

Mum swallowed several times as if to clear her throat of some obstruction. We all looked at the big brown television set, where a jolly man was peering through wire-frame glasses at an old milk churn.

Elizabeth had been tugging more and more furiously at her aunt's sleeve. 'I want to go,' she hissed audibly.

'We will in a minute, old girl,' I heard Victoria mutter, and a strange shiver went through me at the term of endearment.

Dad had settled back in his chair. He cleared his throat. 'Sorry about all this.'

'It doesn't matter, Harry.' Mum had taken his hand. The antiques expert said he had some disappointing news: a milk churn like this was more common than you would think.

'Let's have a cup of tea,' Mum suggested.

'Do we have cups?' Victoria was on her feet. I watched Lauren slide off her chair and join her.

'Why don't Victoria and I find some cups.' The sisters-in-law glanced at each other with an unusual shared purpose.

'I want to go,' Elizabeth mumbled again.

'Listen, all of you,' Dad commanded in a voice which froze the attempt at hubbub. All heads turned to look at him.

'I'm not stupid. I know that I'm losing my grip a bit. I know I'm going to go before too long.'

'Harry . . .' Mum began.

'Let me finish. I know I'm going to go before too long and I want to speak to you all before I lose too much more of . . . of what's up here in my head.'

Victoria's eyes were molten. Elizabeth kept looking between her and me, as if appealing to us to reveal that this was all some adult joke. Mum stared at the flowers on the windowsill.

'I don't want you to remember me as this old man who pisses his pants and can't get the names right. I want you to just remember that I loved you. Sometimes things were hard, of course. Dominic, I know you might not have had the same interests. Max and I argued, of course. Victoria, there was a lot to think about.'

I glanced across at Victoria, trying to work out what this meant, but she had turned her face to the wall.

'All I want to say,' Dad continued, 'is try to forget this. This isn't really happening. The old days were when it was really happening.'

A pudding-faced nurse tapped lightly on the door; I had never been so grateful for an interruption. 'Would you like to take Harry out for a turn in the garden before it starts to get dark?' she asked.

Victoria took Elizabeth off to the toilet, leaving my parents and me to walk around the rockeries and inspect the straggly rhododendron bush which Dad tended with two other men. One of them was hunched over the bush as we approached: he straightened up painfully and saluted.

'All ship-shape here,' he said. 'Off to see to the blinds now.' Dad nodded and the man went on his way, his big black coat flattening around him in the wind.

'Stupid old bastard thinks it's still the war,' said Dad, nodding after him.

We stood in silence. Birds were chirping at each other in the last of the light.

'I never heard so many birds!' I said.

Dad's brow lowered and his eyes narrowed as if they were torch-points trying to pick out an object in the dark. I saw him rummage through his jumbled brain for my meaning. It was still there somewhere, but trapped just out of his reach. He had left his life, really, and yet had to keep living it for a while longer.

'Bring some money next time,' he said.

It was Bonfire Night when he died. As I took the phone call from Max, the shrieks and bangs were echoing from Alexandra Palace. I thought of Mum in the old days shuddering at the sound. Elizabeth, face pressed up against the window, was watching the neighbours letting off rockets in their garden. Each one sounded as if it was going to crash straight through our roof.

Very peaceful in the end, said Max; I only caught snippets of his sentences. I was thinking about Dad dictating his reports on long-forgotten games, as I lay in my old bedroom. *Arsenal's performance this afternoon will be talked about as long as men draw breath on the Caledonian Road.* Mum's very calm, said Max. Everything being taken care of. Nothing for you to do. When I told Elizabeth, she gnawed on her thumb and her eyes swirled uncertainly.

'Where will he go now?'

'He . . . he'll be in a nice deep sleep.'

'How will we find out if he's gone to heaven?'

'You might want to ask your mother about that.'

'Don't *you* believe in heaven?'

I patted her on the wrist. 'I like to believe in it.'

'*You'll* definitely go there,' she said, brightening up a bit. 'I bet *you've* never done anything wrong.'

'Well, I'm not . . . I'm not going to die for a while, Bethie.'

'How do you know?'

I coughed, flustered, and Elizabeth moved in with the second punch of the one-two. 'You know that doll's house?'

The magazine ad was still sitting on our kitchen table, and it seemed to pop up again no matter how often it was cleared away. The house itself cost just over £100 – almost worth getting a mortgage for, as Lauren quipped sadly – and was a spindly thing made of pink plastic. There was a 'basic set' of six dolls, the advert explained, which had to be purchased separately. 'New dolls appear every month!' it added breezily, in case you ever imagined the expense might eventually end.

'I've told her she needs to save up some of it herself,' said Lauren.

'You're mean, that's why,' Elizabeth said with a matter-of-fact flutter of her eyelashes. 'What do *you* think, Daddy?'

'We'll . . . we'll have to think about it,' I said distractedly.

'Why can't we think about it now?'

'Are you going to just sit there and listen to our daughter calling me mean?' asked Lauren.

'Cynthia already *has* the house' – Elizabeth flung her arms out, as her mother might, at the injustice of it – 'and three of the dolls.'

'Cynthia's daddy works for Shell and drives a Porsche,' said Lauren, 'and Cynthia's mom lies on the sunbed all day, so, hey, life's tough.'

'My God,' I yelled, 'my father has just died! Listen to the two of you!'

Silence fell, but it wasn't as if I had won a moral point: it felt more as if I was the petulant one. My wife and daughter each got up and left the room. Upstairs, Elizabeth slammed the bathroom door with the ferocity of someone trapping a lion in a cage, something which would become a characteristic gesture in a few years. There was a more moderate bang as our bedroom door closed. I sat in the silence for barely a minute before my feet propelled me towards the phone and the only person whose voice might make me feel better.

Churchill's funeral, that day in the sixties, had seemed interminable; Dad's was over in a matter of moments.

To everyone's surprise Mum gave a speech. She was wearing a hat which he had bought her on their first trip abroad, forty-five years before. She said that Dad had always been the person who made her look forward to the next day, and that she could never hear the name Harry without feeling a little flutter of excitement.

'The day he went into the home, it was the first time in forty years I had woken up without him. He'd made me a cup of tea practically every morning of those forty years. Always too strong. I never liked it.' The ghost of a laugh whispered through the congregation. 'But I came to depend on seeing that cup of tea on the bedside table. That first morning he was away from me, well, there was no cup of tea there. I just couldn't get out of bed. I couldn't believe a day could go on without him.

'Now I shall have to believe that every day.'

When Mum came back to the pew, Victoria took her arm and the two of them stayed like that until the final flowers had been laid on the coffin. Afterwards we drifted through the churchyard, Mum flanked by Victoria and Mrs Linus. Nonie, Max's wife, was pregnant with their first child; she walked with ostentatious care between the headstones, arms folded tightly across her stomach as if someone might try to steal the baby from her. I saw Victoria gazing at Nonie for a long moment, and knew what she was thinking. Victoria was forty-four now; Nonie was a good bit younger. When we got into the church hall, Nonie bared her giant teeth in a consoling smile for my mother and then made an announcement in her boarding-school voice.

'If everyone would like to make their way back to ours now, there'll be some refreshments and a chance to remember Harry together.'

'*Refreshments.*' Victoria wrinkled her nose. 'What does she think this is, a fête?'

'It doesn't make any sense, everyone going out there.' I lit Victoria's cigarette. 'We could have had it at Mum and Dad's.'

Victoria puffed out a slow smoke-trail. 'It's not even as if it'll be *good* food. I bet they haven't got any decent cheese. Last time I was there, there was nothing but Edam. Edam!' She let this damning fact hang in the air.

I thought that if I could just stay with Victoria, things might be all right, but she ended up in a different car. By the time I got to Max's, she'd been swallowed up by a big noisy group and everyone else was talking about cricket. Lauren took Elizabeth into the garden. Mum and I sat in silence, robbed of the one thing we had ever really had in common.

Two weeks later Elizabeth starred as the Angel Gabriel in the school Nativity Play. In the draughty hall Lauren and I perched on child-sized plastic chairs with the other parents, who were talking in low voices about estate agents, the Soviets, *Coronation Street*. There was a tree in the corner of the room and on the walls, felt-tip drawings grouped under the theme CHRISTMAS IN OTHER COUNTRIES. Elizabeth's sandy hair was tied back in a ponytail. Lauren had finished butchering an old nightie into a celestial robe late last night. She watched, swiping at a wet eyelash, as our daughter stood composed, awaiting her moment. Next to her, a minor angel cohort was grappling with a silver tinsel halo which kept slipping down over her eyes.

'You will go to Bethlehem, where a boy has been born.'

Lauren was tensing her jaw to pen in tears, but the overspill nestled in her eyes. I reached for her hand and squeezed against the hard knot of her wedding and engagement rings.

I stole a glance at the faces of the other parents in the sickly school-hall light. Soon they would all be putting up their Christmas decorations, getting the presents assembled under the tree. I couldn't be the only one with my heart weighed down by some impossible secret. Behind all the united fronts of festive jollity, there must be all sorts of resentment and heartache, all manner of buried grudges and regrets. Life was about living alongside these things, rather than trying to run away. What Victoria and I had shared, continued to share, once more felt as if it didn't matter, or could be ignored.

'. . . and he will save mankind.'

Her words crowned with a respectful silence by the audience, Elizabeth turned to leave and the angel beside her, blinded by her halo, walked heavily into her. There was a gasp from the assembled parents.

'And I don't know what you think *you're* doing,' said Elizabeth, the Angel Gabriel, after barely a moment's recovery. A wave of laughter swept around the uncomfortable chairs. Lauren put her hand to her mouth in delight and the two of us sniggered as Elizabeth led her divine team contemptuously from the scene.

Beakers of punch were handed out in the school's gym as we waited for the children to change. The parents of the fallen angel had already sneaked their daughter away. Lauren and I stood in a corner, away from the conversation about catchment areas and rising uniform prices, holding hands tightly.

'I'm going to see someone,' she said.

'Someone . . . ?'

'A counsellor,' said Lauren. 'I think you were right about that.'

'That's great,' I said. 'I think that will really help.'

'You don't sound convinced.'

'No, no, I am. I wanted you to do that years ago.'

'What are you thinking about,' she asked self-mockingly, 'if not me and my important problems?'

'I'm just sort of taking in the festive feeling. You know. It's easy not to appreciate those moments. Bethie in her angel outfit.'

It was half true – the occasion had been a warming one – but really my thoughts were on what lay ahead. Lauren and I had progressed from a truce to a rekindling of genuine affection. In the new year, we would hold hands in the park on Sundays; we would walk side by side at parents' evenings. I'd throw myself into our occasional lovemaking, which would be as amiable as everything else. I would ferry Elizabeth to the inexhaustible events dreamed up by

Brown Owl. On my rare free Saturday afternoons, I would take her to parties where hired entertainers made balloon animals and mothers shovelled lollipops into little bags.

I could vividly remember tearing at Lauren's bra in my airless flat, that summer years before; making love three times in a brief night, in a tent so steamy that the morning air felt like ice-water when we crawled out. But the memories might have been someone else's. To revisit that intensity of feeling I had to think the unthinkable, and the unthinkable had no place in the life I seemed to have chosen.

The next spring Daley and I were hired for a wedding in the chapel of a Scottish castle. A frog-faced millionaire, the father of the bride, was paying for us to get the sleeper train up from King's Cross. This was all the rage, marrying in a Scottish castle; as if it wasn't enough to make your friends purchase a set of kitchen knives, you could now also force them to sit in traffic jams with people they practically lived next door to, and book into expensive hotels. For me it meant another two nights away from home, with all the relief and all the guilt that prospect held these days. We had moved house, and Elizabeth woke every night claiming to be scared of her new bedroom. Just as I was lugging my bag out of the door for the sleeper train and planting a kiss on Lauren's cheek, the weeping began upstairs.

I put the bag down and went up to her. She was sitting desolately in her white nightie, which had a picture of a pony on it. There were ponies on the walls too. The contro-versial doll's house, hardly ever played with, sat like a disused building on the outskirts of the room.

'What's the matter, sweetie?'

She sniffed. 'I can't sleep in this room. I shan't be able to sleep a minute.' Her speech at the moment bore the influ-ence of Enid Blyton and Beatrix Potter.

'You managed to sleep last night. And the night before.'

'No I didn't.' She shook her head gravely. 'I've never slept in this room at all, not a wink.'

I wiped a tear-trail from her cheek. 'Would it help to hear about Cautious Rabbit?'

She nodded. I had begun inventing stories featuring Lauren's semi-retired character and acting them out with an old pink toy. I reached for the rabbit now and Elizabeth slid down under her covers with a sigh of relief. Cautious Rabbit began an adventure plagiarized from Potter, scut-tling through a field to steal a carrot, and I myself would have to run to make the sleeper when I got to King's Cross.

Daley was already in our cramped cabin, sitting on the edge of the lower bunk; by contrast with his sizeable figure the bed looked as if it belonged in the doll's house. He poured me a whisky and the two of us listened to the creaks and chugs as the train crept north in the dark.

'The Authorities and I went in one of these, on our honeymoon,' Daley said. 'France. We had this idea of stay-ing up all night and watching the countryside go by, in the moonlight, you know.'

'Must have been lovely.'

'Ah, it pissed it down for five hours. You couldn't see a thing. We had a great big argument and in the end we woke up the man in the next cabin, and he shouted through the wall, *I will kill you! I will kill you!'*

'And what happened?'

'Well, he didn't.'

I thought of the couple waiting nervously in their castle for tomorrow to arrive, each with their entourage of friends.

'Daley, have you ever had a *really* big row?'

'There was a time I bought a suit of armour without telling her. She came back late at night and I was standing there in the hall with it on. I thought it'd be funnier than it was. She didn't talk to me for a couple of days.'

'I mean, well. Something where you thought the marriage might end.'

Daley was quiet for a while. I heard the bed-springs sigh to themselves as he rearranged himself.

'I did once think that she might be seeing someone else,' he said quietly. 'There was a fella used to go to her painting class. Good painter. Handsome man.' He chuckled softly. 'She used to light up, you might say, when she saw him.'

'Did you ever ask her about it?'

'I did once, and she said there was nothing to worry about, and that was the end of it.'

'Did you ever think, if there *was* anything going on, you'd be better off not knowing?'

'No,' said Daley immediately. 'If there was anything going on, I would need to know, and the marriage would have to end.' He cleared his throat. 'As I've said before, there are certain things you can't do.'

Our train glided on into the night. I could hear coughs and soft footsteps as the guards made their rounds outside. The silence was heavy; I wished Daley would make one of his stupid jokes to break it. Once on a train he'd pretended to have a snake in his bag, so convincingly that a woman opposite us started screaming and had to be restrained from pulling the emergency cord.

When I thought he was asleep, Daley suddenly said, 'You know, if there is anything you want to tell me, I'd not repeat it to anyone.'

There was a pause.

'I wouldn't be scared of you repeating it,' I said. 'I'd be scared of your judgement.'

He laughed. 'My judgement! I'm not God. Fortunately.'

'But you do have high moral standards.'

'It doesn't mean I think everyone should do as I say.'

For a few clanks of the engines, a few crunches of stones under the train's wheels, I thought about telling Daley everything.

'Well, I'll bear that in mind if I ever *do* have a dark secret,' I said at last. 'But rest assured, the only other woman I've ever loved is Victoria.'

Daley's soft laugh rose from the lower bunk. 'I think that's safe enough.'

Before long there was the sound of flat heavy snores from below, and I lay on my back staring up at the ceiling. It was so low I felt as if I might be smothered by it. I fell into a brittle sleep through which I could still hear the noises of the train. When the guard woke us up by banging on the cabin door at seven in the morning, I thought at first it was Daley larking about, and loudly told him to fuck off. On the way off the train I avoided the guard's eye.

The castle was a full-time wedding venue. The signs were all there: the newly fitted power sockets in the medieval hall, the modernized chapel within the grounds; the dutifully kilt-wearing, bagpipe-wielding staff. There were over four hundred guests on the list the bride and groom had given me: so many that a complete stranger could probably turn up and spend a pleasant day there without being challenged.

The castle's many guest rooms had been ruthlessly stripped of their original features and decorated with blocks of primary colour, lots of glass surfaces; what people in the early eighties had thought the twenty-first century might look like. Outside I heard a large merry group arriving, two families up from Kent, exchanging the kind of banter I heard every Saturday: 'Bit of a long haul, isn't it!' 'Yes, found it in the end, though!' 'We actually came up last night, stayed with friends . . .' 'Beautiful spot!' 'They've been lucky with the weather!' 'It's going to be a terrific day!' I stood by the window and looked out; the sun was starting to break through the haze around the peaks. It was, indeed, going to be a beautiful day for a wedding.

The service was early – half past twelve – and several sheepish groups arrived when it was already under way. I stood on the chapel steps photographing guest after guest. Several men had taken the opportunity to wear a kilt. The women tottered in on their heels, children in their itchy jumpers. Wedding fashions had changed less in the course of my career than fashion in general. Someone nudged me in the back.

'Another one of these, eh?'

I looked into the mischievous face. It was the bold lead singer of the ceilidh band who'd led the dance at our wedding. The sight of him gave my stomach a little twist which I preferred not to think about.

'How's married life treating you?' he persisted.

'Oh, pretty well. Pretty well.'

Eventually the groom turned up, burly and grinning, and then after a while the girl: remarkably youthful, as I often thought brides were these days, pretty and pale and swallowed up by her dress. I snapped the service while, outside, Daley set up the Rolleiflex for what would be a challenging group shot. I got a good picture of a hundred heads turning at the 'if anyone knows any reason in law . . .' moment, as some wit pretended to make an objection. During the signing of the register a mawkish pop song was played: *Sometimes when we touch, the honesty's too much* . . . The officiant pretended to pore over a hymn book until the music was over.

Outside, Daley had to use his loudhailer to arrange the group shot. The guests eventually settled into eight long rows. To line up the shot we had to back off so far that the heads of the people on the steps were no more than dots bobbing in the distance. I peered through the viewfinder at them. These two hundred people would never all be together again. A few would be gone by the end of the year. Some would never see the bride and groom again, and the married couple would one day be surprised to spot them in the photo. 'And now smile, those of you who have the necessary muscles,' Daley boomed through the loudhailer. 'Three-two-one . . .' I pressed the button. The moment was frozen for good.

The bride had a long list of photos she wanted: with her brother, arm-in-arm with her bridesmaids, in front of the wedding car with her father and the coat-tailed chauffeur. The car was an old black Bentley.

'One of these wouldn't come cheap,' I said, purely to make conversation as I sized up the shot.

'It didn't,' smirked the father of the bride, and I flushed, realizing it was his own car.

'The number plate didn't make it any cheaper, either.' He pointed out the personalized plate: *BDR 34*, his initials.

'*Brigadoon*,' said Daley.

'What?' barked the older man suspiciously.

'The letters are in the wrong order,' I said to Daley. 'And you can't have a proper noun. It's just a game,' I explained to the car's owner, who was listening to all this with undisguised impatience. 'We try to form words from the—'

'*Bombardier*,' said a voice right behind me. I swung around and almost fell into my sister's arms.

'Victoria!'

I beamed. She was in an enormous black frock-coat and a hat the shape of a fruit bowl. She looked like some eccentric aunt. Her hair had grown a little; it was down around her shoulders.

'What are you doing here?'

'I'm a friend of the Rickettses, thanks to Tom's sterling work for Surrey,' she said.

The father of the bride nodded impatiently; he wanted to get on with the photo. The bride, like many women before, looked cowed by Victoria's presence.

'Is Tom here?'

She chuckled. 'No. I'm on my own.'

The old man cleared his throat impatiently.

'Listen,' I said, 'I'll ... I'll catch up with you at the breakfast.'

But we were seated at tables so far apart they could have been in different countries. Victoria, according to the seating plan, was near the top table. We were at the far end next to some university friends of the groom, who looked disapprovingly at the wine as if it were some fussy delicacy, and then began to drink it in near-pint quantities. Daley and I did our best to keep up with them. Soon the comforting warmth of drunkenness had settled around my brain, and we were engaged in noisy conversation.

'So, you guys go round snapping weddings and that sort of thing?'

'*He* does,' said Daley. 'I'm just his mate. I've got a very different kind of job.'

They leaned credulously towards us. 'Like what?'

Daley lowered his voice. 'All I can say is that, in Ireland, I'm known as Mad Daley.'

The other men eyed him nervously. 'Is it . . . politics?'

'It involves politics,' said Daley, 'but it also involves art, travel and to a lesser extent pop music.'

I silently snorted into my wine glass. Their wide faces were all fixed uneasily on Daley, nobody wanting to call his bluff.

'England – Ireland was quite a match this year,' said one of them. 'Are you into your rugby at all?'

'In truth,' said Daley, 'I despise it and everyone who plays it.'

During the speeches the band had set up, and before long the guests were scampering about like atoms studied under a microscope, scurrying here and there, colliding, grabbing one another, whirling each other around and reeling off at an angle. Sweaty men took the arms of blushing teenage girls; stockbrokers leered at minor aristocrats. The caller shouted out his arcane codes: 'One, two, and a do-se-do!' Daley, who would no more join in with a dance than he would walk across a frozen lake, joined the too old or timid on the fringes of the hall, and took care of the photographs.

I edged my way out of the room and walked down the wide, echoing corridor until I could push open a door and feel cold air on my face. It was almost dark. There was the whining note of a piper in the air; I couldn't quite tell whether it was real or simply stuck in my head. I looked back in through the window at the crowded bodies rocketing around the warm room. I got out a cigarette, searched my pockets in vain for a lighter; I'd left it on our table, I realized, and swore out loud.

When I looked up, Victoria was standing over me, a lit match in her hand.

'Perhaps I can help?'

She perched down beside me. She had taken off her coat and was clad in an astonishing dress, scarlet and royal blue, low-cut and stopping at the knee; like something a movie star would wear, I thought. She caught my eye and grinned.

'Yes, totally inappropriate for a wedding, I agree. And for the season. And for life in general.'

'Have you ever done anything that *was* appropriate?'

She gripped my arm suddenly. I didn't have the strength to pull it away. 'Speaking of which. Let's get out of here.'

'I'm working.'

'You must have enough pictures now. Or Daley can take them.'

'Well, where would we go?'

Victoria cocked her thumb. 'I stayed here last night. There's a pub round the corner. They do food.'

'We've just had a wedding breakfast!'

'It was pathetic,' said Victoria. 'My bit of chicken was so small I nearly had to ask for directions to it. And the starter – sorbet. I mean, I ask you! Sorbet is *not* food.' She shook her head again, in despair at the world.

'Well, what do you want to eat?'

'I want a big fucking chunk of meat covered in a blanket of cheese,' she said.

'Really?'

'Wasn't it you who said I should smoke because life's too short not to do what you want?'

I sighed with unfelt reluctance. 'All right. Give me twenty minutes.'

When I went back into the hall, the ceilidh had already been supplanted by a swing band: it was as though the wedding would collapse if there were even a second of silence or stillness. A muscular Italian-looking man was singing 'That's Amore'. Most people were seated, mechanically topping up their glasses. Daley was unfazed when I said I was leaving.

'We're done here, really. There's no more pictures to be had unless they want some of everyone looking rough as navvies. I'll see you for the train in the morning. And Dom . . .'

'Yes?'

'Don't get too smashed, eh?'

Victoria was waiting in her huge coat at the doors. I took her arm and we walked out of the grounds, onto a winding path where it was too dark to see anything at all. She lit a match to guide us until the lights of the pub appeared around the corner. It was an eighteenth-century cottage called The Auld Turnpike. There was virtually nobody else there; just a couple of ageless men hunched over the bar. Victoria ordered a bottle of whisky and some sort of pasta dish on which she made the barman dump more and more grated cheese.

'More. More. More. Keep going.'

'You're fond of your cheese, eh,' remarked the barman.

'What time do you stop serving drinks?' I asked.

'We stop serving,' he said, with a gap-toothed grin, 'when you stop drinking.'

'What do you think his name is?' Victoria whispered, as he walked away.

'Angus.'

'I bet it's Rab.' She slid a ten-pound note across the table. 'Ten quid it's in the second half of the alphabet.'

We talked about Elizabeth and about Mum. Victoria attacked the plate, as ever, as if it were her first glimpse of food in some time. She poured out measures of whisky and we clinked our glasses together. I noticed I was drunk enough almost to miss her glass.

'I'm glad we got out of that hall,' she said. 'I couldn't take any more. If I ever hear *Love and marriage go together like a horse and carriage* again, I'm going to bloody find someone on a horse and shoot them.'

'And "That's Amore". I must have heard that a thousand times.'

'*When the world seems to shine like* something-something *wine*,' she sang in a mocking drawl.

'*Like you've had too much wine*,' I supplied.

'Funny, isn't it.' She had a forkful of pasta in one hand, a cigarette in the other. 'The idea that love is as good as being pissed. When in actual fact, you get pissed to convince yourself that you're loved.'

I put down my drink and looked into her eyes. 'I'm not

having this conversation again. Why the fuck don't you divorce him?'

She blinked. 'Well, why don't *you* divorce *her*?'

'Because . . . well, for a start, there's Elizabeth.'

'But it's mostly because, deep down, you feel you *ought* to be married, and even deeper down you love her.'

I considered this. 'I suppose.'

'And it's the same for me. I do actually, oddly, love him. I think he loves me. It's just that . . . it just doesn't add up to as much as I would have hoped.'

'What do you want that you haven't got?'

She took off her hat and shook her head. 'When I married him, I wanted to be someone that lived a fabulous life, made a difference, I don't know. Had adventures. Had children. I didn't want to be nearly forty-five, dyeing my hair because it's going grey, doing nothing more creative than buying hats . . .'

'What about your charity?'

'Yes, I dabble in helping kids in India. And I dabble in marriage, and Tom dabbles in it too, and then goes off and dabbles in some girl from the cricket club.'

'Why can't *you* just have sex with other people? Surely he couldn't object?'

'No, he wouldn't object. He'd be quite relieved. But it's different for him. He'll sleep with anyone who looks nice and sounds like she went to Cheltenham Ladies' College. People mostly bore me, Dommo. I want to be made to feel attractive by someone who excites me. That's what I had when I first met Tom. That's not readily available any more.'

My heart was curled in a knot. 'Well,' I said, 'at least you have some impressive hats.'

'Fucking hats!' she said. 'I'll show you what I think of hats.'

She reached for the fruit-bowl hat, grabbed her whisky glass with the other hand, and before I could stop her, had poured out her double measure into the hat. I burst out in horrified laughter.

'Bottoms up, old boy!' said Victoria, and she raised the hat to her lips, took a swig out of it, and passed it to me. Whisky had already started to seep through the bottom of the hat and she shrieked with laughter. The barman came over to investigate and watched as I passed the dripping hat back to Victoria.

'You've no need to share,' he said. 'I'll get y' another hat.'

We screamed with laughter.

'What's your name?' Victoria asked.

'It's Duncan,' said the barman, and I punched the air and collected up the ten-pound note. The man walked away shaking his head good-naturedly. The hat sat sodden on the table, and Victoria and I laughed and laughed and drank and drank.

It was after midnight as we walked, arm-in-arm, back through the grounds of the castle. The celebrations were finally fizzling out in the hall. Staggering across the cobbles and along the winding paths were young couples in various states of inebriation: men with collars long separated from their ties, women in badly creased dresses looking like ice-skaters on their high heels. The chill air was full of cackling and quips. It ran through my head that I should have called home, should have said goodnight to Elizabeth at least, but it was much too late now.

'Two pounds fifty,' said Victoria, 'for your thoughts. That would be on top of the ten pounds you've already earned.'

'I was thinking of that time in Southwold, the first time I drank. On the beach. Hard to believe there was a time when I'd never been drunk. I'll waive payment of the two pounds fifty if you give me your thoughts straight back.'

'I was thinking about Maudie.'

'Is she . . . any better?'

'She's as good as she's going to get. She died a couple of years ago.'

We walked along in silence for a moment. I squeezed her hand.

'Where are you staying, old boy? I would like to use your bathroom.'

I sat on the bed, leaned back queasily against the many pillows, and tried to tell myself everything was quite all right. This was just Victoria and me, brother and sister, we went back for ever: all the usual excuses. The chattering people were returning to their rooms outside. 'Lovely occasion!' 'Long day, wasn't it!' 'Yes, a bit past my bedtime now, I think!' 'Bit of a drive in the morning!' 'Could be more like the afternoon by the time *we* get up!' 'Sleep well!' 'You too!'

'This is a *lot* nicer than mine,' Victoria called from the bathroom. 'Do you mind if I have a bath?'

As I had done once before at the Swan, I thought of all the people who had slept in this room before – servants, grooms, men whose names hardly mattered to anyone at the time, let alone now – and everything that time had wiped from the record.

'Are we going to have to continue chatting through the door,' came Victoria's voice, 'or are you going to be a gentleman and come in here?'

'I don't think that's the wisest idea,' I called back.

She laughed. 'Did you think it was wise to drink out of a hat?'

'All right,' I said, and this perhaps was the moment when I resigned myself finally to having lost control of my life. 'All right, I'm coming.'

Victoria was lounging in the bath, one foot on each tap. The water came up just above the level of her breasts. Her leg rose out of the water; she draped it over the edge of the bath. The green and brown of the tortoise had faded over two decades to a uniform sand-yellow.

'I remember thinking it was the most shocking secret in the world, that tattoo,' I said. 'I guess there are slightly more shocking ones, these days.'

'At the time it *was* shocking.' Victoria ran her wet hands over her face. 'That was as close as I got to being a rebel. The tattoo, a bit of bad sex here and there, and being sick in the hall once with a hangover.'

'And introducing *me* to booze.'

'And introducing you to booze, when you were – what, twelve? Thirteen?'

'Thirteen.'

'I should probably have looked after you a bit better.'

'I've told you,' I said, 'you might as well do it while you can.'

'How far does that philosophy extend, old boy?'

'What do you mean?' I asked.

My heart was lashing against the walls of my chest. We looked at each other in silence. Victoria's brown eyes had an intensity I had never seen before, will perhaps never see again. She leaned forward, her breasts rising out of the water, and yanked the plug out.

'Get into bed,' she said, standing up in front of me.

I went into the bedroom, flung open the door of the little fridge and took out a bottle of white wine. My hands were sweaty and shaking so much that it took a concerted effort to heave out the cork. I drank four straight mouthfuls from the bottle, spluttering and choking on the fourth. I slammed down the bottle on the bedside table, put out all the lights, and lay with my eyes shut, my brain a void.

I felt her get into the bed next to me, her skin still damp. I could hear our breaths tripping over each other, rattling out an uneven rhythm like the ticking of the Shillingworths' grandfather clock.

'We don't have to do anything,' she whispered.

I didn't reply.

'And we will never mention it again,' she said, 'we will never say anything, it will never have happened. In the morning I will have gone. OK?'

I turned and took her in my arms. Her face moved in towards mine and I felt my whole body scream like a firework. I shut my eyes, shut my brain; she could be anybody. We could be anybody in history, this could be any moment in history. It mattered no more and no less than anything else. As she sighed and took my weight on top of her, I clung onto these thoughts and let myself topple over the precipice.

When I woke, it was light outside; birds were singing. The bottle sat by the side of the bed. I squinted at the scene, shut my eyes again, then opened them and sat violently upright. Victoria was gone.

Her side of the bed seemed cool already. I ran into the bathroom, felt the room lurch, sank to my knees and threw up into the toilet. The bathtub was flecked with drops of water. A towel lay crumpled on the floor. I vomited again and then knelt against the porcelain.

It was an hour before I recovered enough even to put my head out of the door. A sprightly wind was blowing in my face. Late risers were leaving with their suitcases and travelling bags. The sky was grey.

I stood in the doorway until a couple approached, their wheeled suitcases clattering behind them. It looked as if they were about to ask if I was all right; I turned and slammed the door almost in their faces. I lay on the bed until Daley hammered on the door, calling me a silly old bollocks, shouting about the train. I felt like a ghost as I walked out of the door.

Part Four

XII

There is a word for what we did, but I never use it in my head. It is a word that pops up in seedy internet jokes, a word that can subdue a room. In a world where most people think what they like, it is the one unthinkable thing.

My desires had long been unthinkable to myself; now my actions were. I had little choice, though, but to go on.

With my throat sore from the vomiting and my empty stomach creaking with cramps, I sat on the train listening blankly to Daley's chatter. That afternoon Lauren, Elizabeth and I strolled to the park to see the ducks as if it were just any Sunday. I tucked Elizabeth into bed, kissed her forehead, and went to bed with Lauren.

At first I was simply preoccupied with getting from one hour to the next, reacquainting myself with normality. I took every opportunity to sit with Elizabeth at bedtime and pop to the shops with Lauren. I sought out the fiddly, attention-hogging darkroom tasks I would normally hand over to Daley. Much as I longed to speak to Victoria, there was no question of calling her: I felt that the moment the Cricketer picked up the phone, he would somehow know. For three weeks there was no contact between us at all.

Then on a Sunday afternoon I drove back to the family home to do some small jobs. Mum was in the garden with Mrs Linus and Hercules the tortoise, who lived at Park Street these days to give her some company. The front door was open; as I walked through the study where Dad used to type his reports, now a resting place of retired artefacts, I glanced out of the back window and felt my heart pause at the sight of Victoria. Just as in times long gone, she was down on her haunches, rustling through a bag of old vegetables. She was wearing a green pinafore dress and a straw hat and her hair, dyed or not, was a deep rich brown in the sunlight.

I remembered Victoria's prediction that the tortoise would outlive us all. Mum looked somehow shorter and less substantial than she used to these days, while Mrs Linus was all too substantial. Her face and legs were flushed with broken veins, and her breath was so short she sometimes broke off in the middle of a sentence. Victoria was nodding with her usual forbearance at some long-winded statement, but as our eyes met her face changed. My heart lurched like a drunk. I began to prepare a normal-sounding gambit. Victoria said something to Mum and kissed her on the cheek. Then she got to her feet and walked rapidly towards the house without a glance, as if I were not there.

'Victoria . . .'

She shook her head slightly and veered around me, not looking back.

'Old . . . can't we just . . .'

She closed the back door calmly and I saw the peak of the straw hat in the window for a moment; then nothing.

'Said she 'ad to take off suddenly,' said Mrs Linus. 'Never know with that one, do you!'

She's just shaken up, I thought; perhaps it's a good thing. If it had meant nothing to her this time, I would feel I was going mad. All the same, I wandered around 40 Park Street that afternoon with a feeling of foreboding. The bedroom she used to sleep in, the bathroom where I first saw the tattoo – still with its wan sticks of soap, its spotless ugly tiles – all these rooms seemed to belong to a museum of a lost past. When I drove home I could think of nothing but phoning Victoria. Lauren was never out of earshot, though, and Victoria would surely be out, and even if she answered I was not sure I could manage another rejection like that today.

After another week or so, however, I felt I had no choice. I waited until Lauren was at her book club and Elizabeth was on a camping weekend with the indefatigable Brown Owl. The house felt guiltily hushed, as if every item in it were eavesdropping on me. On our new push-button phone I punched in the numbers that had come to mean Victoria; it seemed almost too quick. I hung up the phone. I dialled the number and immediately cut off the call two or three more times. Finally the double tone sounded. I was ready to greet the Cricketer in a jovial manner and ask casually as to his wife's availability. Gradually and with relief, as the tones went by, I resigned myself to getting no answer. Then, after a pause, a wary voice.

'Hello?'

'Victoria! It's me.'

'Who is this?'

Her voice was hard and distant.

'Me. It's Dominic. I . . .'

The phone was put down.

Another week went by before there was time to write her a letter. Someone had cancelled a portrait session; I settled down to my task at the desk, shielding the paper like an exam candidate. Daley came and went, observing me with his usual affectionate decorum. I knew there was no chance he would ask an unwelcome question.

It was hard to know where to begin. After a series of false starts I kept the letter brief. I said that, whatever had happened between us, it was not worth ruining our relationship over. I was conscious of the need to avoid details – who knew if she would be the one to open the letter? – and phrased myself carefully so that it sounded as if we'd had a minor falling-out. 'Relationship' seemed a feeble word and I added almost a page describing what she had meant to me; how much I looked up to her. I mentioned the night she took me to the beach at Southwold, then tore up the page in case the reminder of Maudie upset her. What we had was too important, I wrote, for anything to come between us now. I asked her to write back, typing the address on a label – as I did now – to make it look like an official letter. Even a couple of lines would do, I said.

For more than a week I was forced into a guilty, breath-less patrol as the post arrived: every day the same fruitless shuffle through bills for the one thing I wanted. It reminded me of being much younger, waiting for her postcards to arrive; but that had been a purely pleasurable anticipa-tion and this felt like balancing on a wire. Eventually a plain envelope arrived as I was bundling Elizabeth out of the door with her lunchbox. It was impersonally labelled, marked *CONFIDENTIAL*; I knew at once it was what I was waiting for. It sat on my lap as we drove to school, feeling as heavy as a brick. Elizabeth was chattering away about a project on Native Americans.

'Can we go to America?'

'I should think so, one day, darling.'

'When? Next week or the week after?'

I left her at the gates and paced back to the Capri, sat down, scooped up the letter and felt the disappointment like a blow to the chest. It was the same letter I had sent her. She had resealed it, put my address on, and sent it back. The sight of my unread words – *You have been the most important person in my life; I would love to hear from you, even a line* – filled me with misery. I trundled the car blindly up a side alley, away from the eyes of other school arrivals, and sat for a while with tears blinding me.

I had thought at first that the shame of what we did might overwhelm me, but now I started to see that the real price was not shame but loneliness. By following the urge as I had, I had sealed myself off from Victoria. No matter that she had followed it with me. She had made her decision, and I was alone now.

Just for a moment – with the horrible memory of what we had done, and the emptiness I felt at the thought of being without her – life seemed literally unliveable, and the fantasy of ending it swam temptingly into view. But even as I flirted with the thought I knew it had no substance.

I kept taking photos at weddings, going to parents' evenings, ferrying Elizabeth to swimming lessons and birthday parties and hockey practice. I counted the days and weeks and months from those few instants in the Scottish hotel. It was three weeks, then a couple of months, then six months, then a year, and sure enough life went on, just as everyone always says it does.

Around the three-year mark of our separation, I found myself taking pictures at a jazz and dinner fundraiser at the Savoy. By now, without ever really accepting it, I had accustomed myself to the idea that my sister and I were strangers. Lauren must have noticed that I never mentioned her any more, and probably Daley too; but since Victoria had always been in and out of our lives as it was, nobody could have known how dramatically things had collapsed. And, of course, nobody would have dreamed why in a thousand years.

So far this evening everything had gone as usual: parking the Capri, hauling the equipment, studying the seating plan, watching parties of self-confident people descend on the place. With the dithering, dilatory motions seen at black-tie dinners everywhere, the rounds of hand-shaking and indulgent jokes, they settled at last at their dinner places. I was trying to herd some hee-hawing businessmen into a group photo when I saw Victoria and the Cricketer taking their seats at a table. I had dreamed about her so many times in the past months that it took me a few seconds to be sure that it was really happening.

There was the usual queue to slap the Cricketer on the back and to kiss Victoria with varying degrees of familiarity. When they sat down, my eyes met Victoria's through the crowd. I shouted her name. She blinked and turned away.

One of my companions gave a knowing laugh. 'You'll have to do better than that to get a snap of Victoria Shillingworth.'

'No, she's . . . I know her,' I said, fumbling with the camera strap. 'We're related.'

'Course you are,' said the man, 'and Madonna is my next-door neighbour.'

As always, it was hard to miss her: she had on a floor-length dress, fiery red. She wore no hat. When at last she left the hall, I followed her into a cloakroom where an attendant presided over rail upon rail of dark coats. I watched as she lit a cigarette and swung round. Her face twisted as she saw me, but at last she spoke.

'Why are you following me?'

It felt like something Max might have asked me decades ago.

'Look,' I said, 'I know that you—'

'Not here,' she hissed, and pulled me out of earshot of the concierge, who pretended not to have seen us at all.

'I know you don't want to discuss it . . .' I began again.

'I think it's best if I pretend I don't even know what you're talking about,' she said, her eyes glinting ferociously at me. 'Don't you?'

'Please.' I reached out to touch her sleeve, but she shrank away as if from a snake.

'All I want is . . . well, just to know if you're going to keep this up for ever.'

'What else do you suggest I do, Dominic?'

'Old girl, I—'

'Don't call me that,' she snapped, and began to walk away.

'Just please stop ignoring me,' I called after her, my voice rising in desperation. I saw the attendant tap the receiver of his telephone in readiness, in case someone was needed to take me away.

'Victoria!' I yelled.

'All right! Jesus. Don't make a scene.' With a sigh she came back towards me, arms folded across her chest. I remembered for a second what she had looked like that night in the Trophy Room, in the photos that were never developed; and afterwards, up in the bedroom. I felt disgusted with myself for thinking about it. She flashed a brilliant smile at the attendant. There had been a time when only I could get a smile like that out of her. Or had there? Had I imagined it all? Was it always a one-sided thing, which she humoured somehow until it went too far? The thoughts jostled like assailants.

'Look, I'm . . . I'm sorry for the way things are now,' she said. 'You understand why and you understand I've got little choice but to keep going.'

'It's not as if it was *just* my fault,' I said. 'You did actually say that it wouldn't matter, and that it—'

'I have to get back to Tom.'

From that night on she never cut me dead again, but if anything, what replaced her hostility was worse: grudging eye-contact at family occasions, polite enquiries about Elizabeth, a formally phrased invitation to drinks at the Shillingworths'.

Did she ever think about what we had shared in that exciting, destructive night, or everything we had felt for each other in the thirty-six years before it? Again I wondered: *had* she felt for me what I felt for her? And if so, how could she bear to be like this?

I still saw her in magazines from time to time; I heard her name come up in gossip. It came to seem less and less likely that we could ever have been devoted brother and sister. She had promised to shield me from a nuclear blast on the beach in Southwold. I had stood by her at the football and sat with her in the doctor's surgery and lit her a thousand cigarettes. But it was all like a story now, one I only part believed. Perhaps that was how she remembered it, too, and perhaps that was how she was protecting herself. Or perhaps, I continued to think on long nights, the parts of the story I most treasured had always been in my head.

I could not escape the name. *VICTORIA* was printed boldly across buses' destination blinds; it sat proudly on the Tube map. 'Victoria' by the Kinks came on the car radio; we drove past the Victoria and Albert, up Victoria Road or Victoria Avenue. On the edges of grey towns I spotted the Victoria Exhibition Centre, Victoria Playhouse, Victoria Cinema. Sometimes in the foyers of the municipal venues that bore her name I would see a bust or portrait of Queen Victoria herself, looking grimly over the world which still bore her fingerprints. I would think of my sister's old bedroom laden with junk, and then think of anything else I could.

On and on through those years I carried the knowledge that I had lost my favourite person, and could never dream of telling anyone.

Seven years to the day after the morning I woke to find Victoria gone, I sat in a packed church in West London watching the christening of Hugh and Charlotte, Max and Nonie's twins: their third and fourth children. After going a long way through life without asserting his masculinity in this manner, my brother had belatedly turned into a prolific father. To one side of me, Lauren watched dutifully, saying the 'Amen's and standing up at the right moments. On the other side was Elizabeth, now known as Beth. She had grown taller than her mother already. She wore a baggy black T-shirt and tight black jeans. Although she'd inherited Lauren's silky blonde hair, at the moment it was jet-black too;

every week she beat the life out of it with a new colour from a packet.

Max, with a Savile Row suit and greying hair, stood at the front next to Nonie. Next to them stood the godparents. Smooth Face – my brother's assistant, Roly – was now an agent in his own right. His face and chin still gleamed pinkly, but his forehead had acquired a couple of new lines, his eyes had a certain cynicism learned from my brother. He was now good-looking in a hearty, sporting sort of way, and well-dressed in a shirt and tie from Max's tailor. To his left was the Cricketer, stockier now, and flushed about the face; and finally, short-haired as ever and armed with the old expression of genial mockery, Victoria. At the vicar's prompting they chorused the words printed on their service sheets.

'Do you believe and trust in the Lord your God, who made all things?'

'We believe and trust in him.'

'Do you renounce evil?'

'We renounce evil.'

In the crush to get out of the church door before being spoken to by the vicar, I brushed against Victoria so closely that for a second I could smell peaches, but we didn't make eye-contact. I glanced back a moment later in the churchyard to see her embracing someone else, some former cricketer. Beth, her eyebrows arched, followed my gaze.

'Have you and Toria fallen out?'

'What?'

'When I was a kid, she used to be round all the time.'

I grinned, in spite of myself. 'Are you not a kid any more?

'I'm fifteen, and please answer my question.'

'She's just . . . she's very busy.'

'She used to be so, like, always into talking to me and now she's just kind of polite. And the way she looks at you. She's constantly giving you evils.'

'Giving me what?'

'Giving you evils, Dad.' Beth sighed. 'Giving you the evil eye. Um, I'm trying to think of a more old-fashioned way of phrasing it.'

Beth's voice had a slight mid-Atlantic note, either a genetic borrowing from her mother or a teenage affectation, or a bit of both. Her speciality was disdain. Among the current targets were school, any music recorded longer than a year ago, virtually all clothes including her own, and nearly everyone she met. If we were able to discover any bands, TV shows, schoolfriends or foods she approved of, they were automatically added to the disdain list, like Party members found to have been collaborating with the enemy. She carried herself through life like someone forced to participate in a time-consuming ritual. To Lauren this felt like a continued insult. I tended to be spared the worst of Beth's ire: I was useful for getting her home.

She went out every Friday and Saturday with gangs of teenagers, all of them staring at their shoes and sneering uncertainly at everything that came by. They swigged economy-brand supermarket cider on Hampstead Heath;

they faked IDs to get into sticky-floored pubs in Camden
Town (Daley had made Beth's for her); they had parties.
Sometimes she would crash through the front door at two
in the morning, waking us with her customary fierce shutting of the bathroom door. On other occasions the phone
would sound like a siren in the night. I'd jump from sleep,
worried that the noise might wake up Elizabeth, and then
realize it was Elizabeth calling. Lauren would slur, 'Go get
it. What if she's . . . what if she . . . ?'

The call would be from a payphone, which bleeped to
be fed more money every ten seconds; or from someone's
parents' house in Kilburn, with shrieking people and bassy
music forcing her to raise her voice.

'I said if you *could* come and get me' – she hated the
phrase 'pick up' – 'then, yeah, that would be cool.'

I could never resist teasing her. 'When you say that
would be cool, do you mean please come and get me?'

'Yeah. Whatever. If that's . . . yeah. OK, see you.'

'You might have to give me the address.'

A sigh. 'Oh. Yeah. OK. I'll find it out or something.'

When I got to the venue – a miserable bit of wasteland
by a railway bridge, or a house unwisely left in the hands
of a fifteen-year-old for the weekend – I had to ensure I
didn't park where anyone could see me. Under no circumstances could I go and ring the doorbell. My job was to sit
in the car until a dark shape appeared and made its way
towards me.

Only recently, a couple of weeks before this christening, I'd fished her out of a dark neighbourhood on the

other side of the river. Lauren had been particularly rest-less that night. The papers were full of stories encourag-ing people to worry about 'drug culture' and 'raves' and other things which took me back to the days I used to lie in bed wondering what Victoria was up to. When the phone rang, I sprang mechanically out of bed. I was dressed and in the car in less than five minutes.

It was a friend's house, she'd said on the phone, but it looked more like a warehouse than anything. There were few houses or shops around, just a couple of silent cul-de-sacs paved with puddles and dog shit. How the hell did she end up here, I wondered, feeling a rare tug of alarm.

In the years since Victoria disappeared from my life, I'd tended to panic less, think less about what might go wrong. You could say that I'd learned to conquer my emotions – that was what Lauren said – but really it was just the absence of emotion. With Victoria, I had experi-enced the purest excitement and joy, but the cost had been disaster. I could never go there again, or acknowledge I'd been there in the first place. I could only live in perpetual denial, and denial meant shutting off most of my mind, existing in the sort of edgeless half-happiness that most people around me seemed to maintain: watching soaps, sitting down for dinner, paying the mortgage.

What this meant was that it took me by surprise when I felt anything really acute. Worry for Beth had just started to inject chills into my spine when she emerged, walking too quickly and in zigzags, and stumbled into the back of the car.

'Nice night?' I asked.

'I'm fine,' she said. 'Can we just drive?'

'I was planning to stay here all night, actually. It's such a pleasant spot.'

'Very amusing.'

I glanced back at her pale face and dark-rimmed eyes. 'Sure you're all right? Not going to be sick?'

'I'm fine, Dad.'

We drove home to the creamy chords of seventies ballads designed for people to go to sleep to: songs Daley and I had laughingly listened to before Lauren was born, now introduced as 'an oldie, but a goldie' or a 'blast from the past'.

'You know, you don't *have* to come and get in the car and drive me,' she slurred, halfway home. 'I could have perfectly happily just done whatever.'

'Your mother worries about you.'

'Whatever. Can you go slower?

'OK. Are you . . . ?'

I was cut off by spluttering and choking as she threw up suddenly in the back of the car. Swearing under my breath, I pulled over.

'Sorry. I was trying to angle it out of the window.' She coughed. 'Think someone put something in my drink.'

'Someone put something in which of your sixteen drinks?'

She coughed. 'Don't tell Mum.'

'It will be our secret,' I said.

'I owe you one, Dad.'

'What will you do in return?'

She wiped her mouth with the back of her hand. 'To be honest, I'll probably just make you pick me up all over again in about a week's time.'

'Oh, you're *making* me, are you? And there was me thinking I had free will.'

We shared a grin. 'You just keep on thinking that, Dad.'

Now, two weeks later outside the church, it was her turn to keep a secret. 'All right,' I said suddenly, lowering my voice. 'Between you and me, yes, Victoria and I fell out quite badly. We don't really speak now.'

'Fascinating.' The irony in her voice was too thickly laid on to be convincing.

'Well, there you have it.'

She sighed at the indignity of having to betray further curiosity. 'OK. So what did you do to her?'

'Nothing, I . . .'

'Did she do something to *you*?'

'No. It's just, you know. Sometimes things go wrong, in a family.'

Beth grimaced. 'Does anything ever go *right* in a family?'

We were interrupted by Smooth Face, who had sidled up behind us; he had Max's knack for making it seem as if he were in charge of proceedings which had nothing to do with him.

'Bubbly?'

'I'm all right, thanks.'

'*I* will.' Beth seized a flute from his hand. Smooth Face raised an eyebrow and said something I didn't quite hear.

Beth gave a short laugh and the two of them moved away slightly to continue the conversation. I was left looking over the ranks of gravestones at Victoria, arm-in-arm with the Cricketer. She crouched down to grab one of Max's older children and whisked him high in the air and the two of them laughed with glee.

It was 1993. The sun had gone behind a cloud above the churchyard, and Dad's grave was in shadow. I saw Mum stop and gaze at it, leaning in close to inspect the stone she'd seen thousands of times, as if some new blemish were presenting itself. Beth was still talking to Smooth Face. Victoria and the Cricketer laughed as Max slung a twin under each arm, and Nonie with her huge teeth chirruped for everyone's attention and announced refreshments.

There was meant to be a recession, and marriage was meant to be an outdated idea, and nobody was meant to believe in God any more. But as at every other time people had said these sort of things, weddings went on. It was not unknown now for us to take pictures at the second weddings of people whose first weddings we'd also photographed. Daley called these people 'repeat customers'. At one wedding in Croydon, we were listening to the self-penned vows of the pink young couple when Daley gave me a nudge and whispered.

'Recognize her parents?'

'No. Who . . . ?'

'I'm pretty sure we did *their* wedding. Early on, like. Seventies.'

It was the beautiful, dark-haired couple who had been among our first customers as a team: the ones who had thanked each other over the register. They glowed with a time-refined, somehow classier version of the lustre I remembered from twenty years ago as their daughter – barely older than Beth – joined hands with her good-looking Pakistani groom.

'Christ. I need a drink.'

Daley clucked his tongue. 'When have you not needed a drink?'

It was a fair, if needling, point. Part of the reason I had bonded with Beth over her many drunken nights was that I was drinking more myself now than at any time in life, and I suspected she knew it. I'd once made it a rule not to touch alcohol before six; then it was three; after what happened with Victoria, there was no rule. At weddings I usually had a good few swigs from the flask to steel myself for the ceremony, then a good few more as the guests milled around afterwards, then a couple of champagnes at the reception venue.

Daley had begun to drive again. He was as bad at it as ever: heavy-handed on the wheel, wrenching the gearstick like Arthur pulling the sword out of the stone. He would weave in and out of lanes as whimsically as a fish swimming upstream, and grin ruefully as we were shelled with the blasts of angry horns. Still, he now was a better bet than me.

I slouched into the shop one lunchtime to take pictures of a young family, and reached for the whisky bottle stashed in a cabinet of spare camera parts. I twisted off the cap, raised the bottle to my lips, and felt my body heave. A stinging taste filled my nose and mouth as if I were being forced face-down into a vat of acid. The mouthful shot out of my throat, splattering the wall.

'What the fuck was that?'

Daley appeared serenely from around the corner. 'Ah. I took the liberty of replacing the liquor with something more industrial.'

I sniffed the bottle. 'What the hell is this? Turpentine?'

'Give me some credit, man. Turpentine could kill you. This is just a low-grade paint-stripper.'

I walked coughing and cursing to the sink for a glass of water. 'What are you trying to do?'

Daley cocked his head to one side and looked at me, his wide forehead furrowed. He was wearing the latest model of the grey pullover, and his hair, now grey-white and as close-cut as ever, looked like a coating of frost on his head.

'I'm trying to make the gentle point that you might be better off not drinking quite so much.'

'And you decided to make that point by poisoning me.'

'You're poisoning *yourself*, Dom. *That's* the point.'

'Oh, fuck off, Daley.'

I felt my ears burning, the blood-rush of someone defending his right to be in the wrong. Everyone knew drinking and smoking were a bad idea, but all the same, everyone was following Victoria's old advice and doing it while they could. Everyone knew adultery was wrong, but people did it. I was more and more convinced that the world relied on a kind of doublethink, whereby everyone agreed to turn a perpetual blind eye. There were only a handful of acts so appalling that morality couldn't stretch to allow them in. Mine was one of them, but the tide of events, oiled by drink after drink, was gradually eroding it from the record.

It seemed like barely a fortnight after my nephew and niece's christening that we were on our way to celebrate their second birthday at the Shillingworths'. A pale, hungover Beth sat in the back seat, resentfully glaring out of the window. Lauren was checking her make-up in a pocket mirror. Her hair had lost a little of its sparkle and the skin was sagging around her eyes, but she was no less beautiful. We lived harmoniously independent lives now, coming together to sleep and eat, but for little else; her counsellor, Angela, probably influenced her decisions more consistently than I did. She did breathing exercises and had 'de-clogged' our lives by taking around half of my possessions to a charity shop while I was at a wedding.

Old Man Shillingworth was standing in the entrance hall, shaking hands and playfully insulting new arrivals. He had hired a squad of caterers who bustled smoothly around under the supervision of the Spanish maid. She must be in her late thirties these days, and had been with the Shillingworths half her life. I wondered if she had a boyfriend, what her plans were. Nonie, heavier and caked in make-up, hawked the waddling twins from one guest to another. 'Charlotte, say hello. Hugh, show everyone how you do a fire engine. That's it! Nee-naw, nee-naw! And now say hello to your Uncle Dominic and Auntie Lauren!'

Max stood in the kitchen bantering with a little cartel of slim, long-nailed women. As I entered the room he glanced up, twitched his eyebrows in recognition, and turned his attention back to the girls. 'How *dare* you!' one of them was screeching. She threw a playful punch and left her hand where it lay, on his chest.

I found an unguarded bottle of wine and spent a pleasant hour with it. As I poured the dregs into my glass I caught sight of Beth at the edge of the room. She was toying with her hair and shifting her weight from foot to foot. I saw her glance around, pour herself a generous measure from a bottle of schnapps and down it in three gulps. That's my girl, I thought, and shuffled over to her.

'Sorry about this. We'll go soon.'

'Sorry about what?'

Her eyes were green ovals. She's very pretty, I thought, with a swell of pride.

'This whole thing. Bit of a drag.'

'A *drag*.' She shook her head. 'Has anyone said that since 1969?'

And then her eyes swam across the room to the doorway, where Smooth Face was standing with his arms folded and a strange, thoughtful expression on his face. I saw him pretend to be looking at a vase on a shelf and then allow his eyes to creep over to Beth. The two of them, my eighteen-year-old daughter and my brother's thirty-five-year-old assistant, stared at each other across the room.

Then he left, and she – after a few moments' calculated pause – went after him.

I watched them go, recovering my breath only after they had disappeared. Even then it was uneasy, seeming to stick in the lungs.

I made for the Trophy Room. The door opened with its familiar drawn-out creak. Inside it was strikingly cold, and although the maid had dusted recently, it felt as if nobody had been in there for some time. I looked at the armchair Victoria had sat in that time, long ago. There was a new certificate framed on one wall: for 'Lifetime Services to Cricket'. Otherwise, the room was as it always was.

There was quiet. I sank down into the armchair and thought about Beth in the arms of the shiny-faced man twice her age. Who was I to take exception? I could feel blood throbbing in my head and my lungs crumpled suddenly into a rollicking cough.

The door gave its showman's creak again. I froze. What was I going to say if Old Man Shillingworth came in now, or the Cricketer? What *was* I doing in here on my own? A hesitation, and then the door was pushed open.

It was Victoria. She had a grey dress on, and her hair was streaked with grey, too. For the first time ever I saw her as a middle-aged woman, a woman past her best. The moment soon passed and I looked at her once more with the usual emotions, the fondness and remorse and the ache of separation, stacked up like the layers of the earth.

'Should have known I'd find you here.'

'Why would you want to find me?'

She coughed. 'Look. Mum is seventy-five next month. You know that.' Her mouth relaxed into a half-smile. 'Did you know there's a new gentleman on the scene?'

'What?'

'She's been seeing a man called Ernie from the pub.'

I laughed, and she laughed too; then we both went quiet.

'That's great,' I said. 'At least . . . is it great? I guess it is.'

'I guess it is, too,' said Victoria. 'Look, here's the thing. I'd like to take her and . . . and the man to Southwold for her seventy-fifth. But of course, I . . .'

'You can't drive, and you'd like me to do it.'

She nodded. 'Max is going to be away.'

'That's fine,' I said.

There was a long silence.

'Great,' said Victoria, 'so, I'll give you a call about the details.'

We looked at each other with the awkwardness of people who had only been introduced that afternoon.

'Great,' she said again, and closed the door.

It had been a good while since we'd spoken even at this length, and a very long time indeed since we had made any sort of plans together. There was a tingling relief in the air: I could feel it coming off me like sparks, though I was indignant as well. Why was it her alone, not me, who could choose when we came back into one another's lives?

But of course I had never been able to question Victoria like this. I told myself to be grateful. It looked as if I had another chance, after all, to put things right.

*   *   *

Ernie was a white-haired gentleman who had very nearly been killed while parachuting into Germany as an eighteen-year-old: a bullet entered his chest and flew out of his back, missing all 'the big guns in the middle', as he put it. As a result, he said, he had lived the rest of his life as if it were a bonus. Mum rolled her eyes at everything he said and gave him a series of her small smiles. Victoria sat in the passenger seat, not smoking, looking straight ahead. Ernie, in a blue blazer and very narrow trousers, kept up a cheery monologue for most of the drive. 'Southwold! Haven't been there for almost twenty years! Mind you, haven't been to *North*wold at all! Wonder what Northwold's like? Same thing, but a bit colder, I suppose!'

'Oh, Ernie,' said Mum, smiling and looking out of the window.

The monkey-puzzle tree, the sign for freshly picked vegetables, were all still in place as we approached. When I was younger I used to think how quickly things changed; now I found it more surprising that things could avoid changing. Ten miles out of Southwold, as the road narrowed, a sports car thundered past us. I glanced at Victoria, hesitated, and then read its number plate out loud: 'A-D-S.'

'What? What?' said Ernie.

'Oh dear,' muttered Mum.

'It's a game, Ernie,' I explained. 'You have to take the letters of the number plate, and then ...'

'And then make the longest word you can which includes all of them ...' Victoria took it up.

'But they have to appear in that order,' I said.

'Mission understood and accepted,' said Ernie.

'So, for example, you could have *adenoids*,' I said.

'I don't,' said Ernie.

'Or *addresses*, which is longer,' said Victoria. I glanced at her and the two of us almost smiled at each other.

'Or . . . or *addendums*.'

'Yes, yes,' said Ernie. 'All right. *Antidisestablishmentarianism*.'

There was quiet in the car for a few moments, and then everyone burst out laughing.

'Beginner's luck,' said Victoria, grinning.

Southwold was becoming fashionable. A whole strip of beachwear shops now catered for families zipping up from London for the weekend. There were upmarket fish restaurants and a sign advertised 'seafront villas' to go on sale in 1996.

The afternoon light glared off the sand as we walked along the front. Weekenders were swarming over the beach, eating ice creams with their trousers rolled up. Kids with cricket bats whacked tennis balls into the water, and eager dogs raced into the waves after them. We went up to the old hut and looked down at the sand-castle-makers dotted over the site of our midnight swimming adventure. The hut had long since been sold by our parents' friends, and it was red and white now. Ernie unfastened one of his blazer buttons. A seagull shrieked above and I pointed my camera up and caught it whirling down towards us.

'Dad used to love it here,' said Mum, looking at the

flattened sand by the entrance to the hut. 'I can just see him now sitting here with his . . . those silly shorts of his.'

We all pictured him for a moment.

'I've still got them,' she said. 'The shorts. Quite a few of his clothes. I washed them all after he died, and then . . . well. I couldn't quite bring myself to take them to a charity shop or anything.'

'Dive, boys!' said Ernie, throwing the remainder of his ice-cream cone for the bird to pounce on. He made a low noise like a plane coming in to land as the bird alighted next to his shiny shoes.

'Perhaps we should have a cup of tea?' Mum said, looking down towards the pier. It was being refurbished; a couple of cranes stood lazily around as if they could not quite be bothered in this heat.

'Why don't you two go down,' Victoria suggested, 'and Dom and I can join you in a little bit?'

'Oh, we don't want to break up the gang,' said Ernie, oblivious to any nuance in the conversation. 'Let's all . . .'

'Lovely,' said Mum, taking his hand with an ease which surprised me. 'Come on, Ernie. We'll leave the kids alone for a bit.'

She shuffled him down the gentle incline. Victoria and I watched them go. What now? I took out a cigarette and waved it at her, but she seemed not to notice.

'She seems to really like him,' I said.

Victoria nodded, then put a hand to her stomach. 'I'm bloody starving. I would ask if you had any cheese, but I've always been disappointed in the past.'

'I stopped carrying it around with me,' I said, 'about the same time you stopped answering my calls.'

This was meant to provoke, but she hardly seemed to have heard it. 'I bet they won't even want a proper dinner. Mum eats less than the tortoise these days. She's practically disappeared.'

'We could go to the chip shop.'

She grimaced. 'I'm not sure how much nostalgia I can take.'

'So why are we here?'

Victoria leaned back against the side of the beach hut and looked right at me.

'Old boy, I have something to tell you. I have cancer, unfortunately.'

'What?'

'Lung cancer.'

'What do you mean?'

She smiled fondly at me. 'Well, very much what I say, really. Lung cancer.'

'What?' I said again. She reached an arm out to steady me and I let my weight slump against the side of the hut. Her arm stayed on mine.

'Are you all right?'

'You can't,' I said pathetically.

She chuckled. 'On the contrary, given the thirty-plus years of smoking, the specialist said it was something of a wonder it had taken this long.'

I couldn't reply.

'It's so fucking *tiny*,' she said. 'That's the annoying thing. You should see the X-ray. I mean, it really just looks like a little smudge on the photo, like a tiny little knot in the bone or something. It's preposterous that you can be killed by a thing that looks—'

'You're not going to be killed by it,' I said, gripping her hand. 'You're not.'

'Well, the good news is that, thanks to cricket money, the best specialists in the UK, the world and Mars are on the case,' said Victoria, patting my hand. 'But the thing is, being the best ones, they tend not to fudge things. So they're quite upfront about my chances. Which are fifty-fifty . . .'

'Well, that's something,' I said. It felt as if the words were shards of glass trying to force their way out.

'. . . fifty-fifty of getting through to this time next year,' Victoria concluded.

All I could think of were the cigarettes. That first one I smoked with her on the beach below and the many, many more we had shared. But above all the one I made her smoke when she had almost given up.

'And after that?'

'Well, after that the odds will change again, I suppose. Max is your man for betting. But the long and short of it, old boy, is that I am probably going to die.'

Seagulls called above; two were still snapping at each other over the fragment of wafer.

I sank down onto the sand, feeling Victoria's arm around my shoulders. I looked up, her face was very close; a shudder went through me of a different kind from any before.

'Apart from Tom, you're the first person to know,' she said. 'Well, and the doctors. I sort of had to let them in on it.'

'What about Max?'

She grinned. 'For someone who hates sport, you were always so competitive. No, Max doesn't know yet. I felt you should be the priority.'

'Why?'

'You know why, Dom.'

Some minutes passed before she got any further with the sentence.

'You were always my favourite, and I'm well aware that things . . . things happened between us which . . . you know. I reacted badly. I didn't know what to do. I did what our family does and wouldn't talk about it. But now, none of it seems important. All that's important is that I'm alive for the moment, and . . .'

Our fingers were locked together; hers were icy to the touch. Although the sun was still presiding over the beach, and the sky was a superb blue, it felt very cold.

She kissed me lightly on the cheek. 'Come on,' she said, 'let's get chips.'

As we were helping each other to our feet, a tall man in a Hawaiian shirt approached. I had a quick unpleasant memory of a wedding where everyone had been dressed like that. He looked us briskly up and down. Under one arm he had an inflatable crocodile; he carried a picnic basket on the other.

'Can I help you?' he said, not pleasantly. 'This is our hut.'

'We're just leaving,' I said. 'It used to be ours, you see. Well, our friends'.'

He peered sceptically at us. 'Right. Well if you wouldn't mind moving along, I—'

'I've got cancer, I'm afraid!' Victoria cut in.

The man wrinkled his nose. 'What?'

'I said I've got lung cancer,' said Victoria, 'so you ought to show a little bit of respect.'

The new owner of the hut gaped at us as we walked away from him, up onto the path. 'Is this your idea of a . . . of a sick joke or something?'

'Stay away,' Victoria yelled, 'you'll catch it.'

I glanced back at him, open-mouthed, and started to laugh. 'Look at his face!'

'Oh dear,' she said, 'I'm not doing a great job of keeping it a secret, am I?'

We laughed more and more, relishing the sound, wanting him and everyone else to hear it. Then she fell behind and gave a kind of heaving gasp as if choking on a drink, and I turned to see her weeping.

'Victoria . . .'

She had one hand across her eyes and she tried to wave me away with the other. 'I'm fine.'

'You aren't fine.'

The low, snuffling sounds she made were eerie. She doubled over, head in her hands. I felt as if someone was going to stop and accuse me of mistreating her in some way. I straightened her up, pulled her face into my chest and stood, feeling the beat of her heart and the sudden iron tension of her body.

'It's just such a bloody fucking shame, really.' She jerked her head back, looked at me through the film of tears, half laughed and half sobbed. 'I really don't feel all that brave about it, actually.' She wiped her nose roughly with the back of her hand. 'I'm terrified, old boy.'

We stood there in silence. The afternoon was beginning to cool at last. Someone went cycling past on the other side of the road, ringing his bell energetically. A man in a string vest was sitting in the doorway of a souvenir shop amongst the rusty racks of postcards, listening to a sports commentary on a transistor radio. I thought of all the people in the world getting on with perfectly ordinary things while this was happening. Then of Victoria at her wedding, and feeding the tortoise, and in a thousand other places, when it was still possible for things to play out differently.

She pulled herself away from me, wiped her eyes and smiled sheepishly.

'Well,' she said, 'in the circumstances, I'd better not have a cigarette.'

The chippy owner had no monocle these days, in fact was almost blind now, his wife told us. He sat in a deck-chair behind the counter taking the orders and relaying them to his wife, although she could hear them perfectly well. She moved more slowly these days, though, bending with an effort over the fryer and narrowing her eyes to peer inside.

'Two cod and two large chips, please.'

'Two cod, two large chips, Hettie.'

'Thank you, dear, I heard the gentleman.' She had already started shovelling the chips, folding the newspaper into a parcel, packing the parcel into a plastic bag.

'How's business been?' asked Victoria.

The old man's sightless eyes seemed to twitch in amusement. 'People will always want fish and chips.'

In the window of the shop was an enlarged photo, artlessly arranged in an ugly frame. Lauren could have done a better job of that, I thought. The old couple stood hand-in-hand, surrounded by a smiling group in a village hall. *JAMES AND HETTIE, 60 YEARS!* Next to them still hung the obsolete advertising plates for pies and Craven 'A', which would not affect your throat.

Victoria handed me one of the greasy packages. As I opened it, a few chips squirmed straight out onto the pavement and lay there to await the birds. The strong salt-and-vinegar smell was suddenly sickening. I almost dropped the whole bundle on the floor.

'Are you all right, old boy? Look, let's sit on that bench over there.'

I sank heavily onto the bench and Victoria perched next to me. She licked a tissue and dabbed at her pink eyes. 'Need to smarten up before Mum sees me.'

'I'm sorry,' I said, 'so much is my fault.'

'Don't be stupid, old boy. How can cancer be someone else's fault?'

I gazed at the cheery display in the window. 'You'd given up, you were going to give up, and then I wheedled you into starting again, just because of this nonsense about only living once, which ended up being the most stupid thing I ever said.'

'It wasn't stupid. I always talked about making the most of life and I never really followed my own advice. You made me realize that.'

'I made you realize that, and so you smoked till you got cancer, and you let me do . . . whatever happened in the hotel, and . . .'

She put a finger to her lips. 'Shush. I smoked those cigarettes myself and I came to your room voluntarily that night. I'm a big girl. No one lived my life for me.'

'I wish you'd stop talking as if your life were already over. You can . . . they can cure anything these days. You could still make it to a hundred.'

'Even if I did, I'd still be blaming our parents or the previous generation or Adam and Eve. It's not good enough in the end. You've got to take responsibility.'

She started to sing. '*Non, Je ne regrette rien* . . . something-something, something-something, something-something . . .' She gestured dramatically. We were both laughing. 'Something-something-something. Beautiful song.'

Our laughter died away and a salty sea breeze crept down the street. The man in the string vest snapped off the radio and got to his feet. Victoria stood up too. 'Come on,' she said, 'they'll be wondering where we've got to.'

XIII

It was eleven at night by the time I had dropped Ernie off at his bungalow, Mum and Victoria at Park Street. When Victoria and I hugged goodbye in the doorway, she held on for a long time; I noticed again how cold her hands were. The streaks of grey in her hair seemed more pronounced: perhaps the day of sunshine had brought them out. Within six weeks she would start chemotherapy and her hair would be shaved off.

Lauren had gone to bed, but there was a note on the kitchen table: *Welcome home. Beth out with boyfriend. Food in oven.*

I sat at the kitchen table watching the clock and reading the paper without taking anything in. The middle sentence of the note had made me feel much sourer than it should have. I imagined the conversations Beth and Smooth Face might have: Smooth Face talking about wonderful Max and the Cricketer and the steamrollering might of their business empire, and gently undermining Beth's old scruffy wedding photographer of a dad. I imagined Beth, only just old enough to drink legally, laughing her sudden girlish laugh at his wisecracks, getting into his car. Her teenage cynicism had often been awkward and frustrating, but now that she was suspending that cynicism for a man twice her age I wished it back.

A bottle of whisky was waiting faithfully for me in the drinks cabinet. Twisting open the top felt as joyless as taking off the clothes of someone you're bored of sleeping with. As my throat braced itself for the flat hit, I hesitated, mouth to glass: what if Beth called needing a lift? What if there was an argument and he left her in some miserable spot? But no, there'd be no argument. The traditional irritation of the 2 a.m. summons had been more important to me than I realized. Knowing that she was now in the hands of someone who could drive her anywhere made me miserable. I slugged the whisky and brought out a bottle of wine as well, just in case.

It was well after two when she came in. I was still sitting at the kitchen table, an empty bottle in front of me. After her keys had rattled in the door there was a lengthy exchange of whispered goodbyes. I could hear Smooth Face's clipped vowels, his closing witticisms. I tried to force back my irritation as finally she left him and came clumping into the kitchen, blinking in surprise to find me there.

'What sort of time is this?'

'Can you not tell the time, Dad?'

'Do you think half past two is an acceptable time to be coming home from a date with someone twice your age?'

She walked straight past me, took a can of Coke out of the fridge, opened it with a finger hooked into the ring-pull, and took a long mouthful, all without looking at me.

'What the fuck,' she finally asked, 'has his age got to do with the time that I'm allowed to come back?'

'Do you have to use that kind of language?'

'Do you have to be that much of a cliché of a dad?' She took a big noisy gulp of Coke. I blocked her way as she tried to leave.

'That man is not the right person for you to be with,' I hissed into her face. 'He's thirty-five.'

'Thirty-six, actually.'

'He wants to . . . to sleep with you and take advantage of you and then he'll leave you to deal with it.'

Beth rolled her eyes theatrically. 'How the hell do you know what he wants?'

'I am your father,' I said, in a rising voice, 'like it or not. I do not want to see you going out with someone practically as old as me . . .'

'You don't want to see me happy, is what you mean.'

'Oh, don't be such a teenager.'

Of everything I might have said to her, this was the most insulting. She looked at me, her oval eyes filled with fury.

'Get out of my way, please.'

But I hardly had to; she brushed past me easily. I noticed with pained affection how she slipped her hand inside her sleeve to turn the door handle.

'You better get used to it,' she said, turning back on the threshold – her voice twanged American for a second – 'because me and Roly are going to see each other whatever anyone thinks about it.'

Roly. I hated him even more by his real name. It was an absurd reason to hate someone, but really no more absurd than my other ones. I heard Beth clatter up the stairs, the slam of the bathroom door and the raking sound of the lock angrily pulled across. I rested my head in my hands.

Tomorrow's hangover was already hardening just behind my temples; I wished I could have the first part of it now, to get it over with. But hangovers, like all aspects of drinking, were less sensational these days: there was no bloody retribution for my excesses, just small dull reminders of my mistakes. A creak of dehydrated muscles, a brief complaint of a headache.

From upstairs came the sound of Lauren roused from sleep by her returning daughter. I heard her trip confusedly out onto the landing.

'Glad you're safe.'

'Course I'm safe.'

'Dad come get you?'

'No. Roly drove.'

'OK. Night.'

For a second I smiled at the sound of their voices, oddly similar, one like a remix of the other. Why was I so bad at dealing with both of them? There was only one woman that I had ever got the hang of, and soon – it seemed incredible I had only found out today – soon we might be parted: not in the way we had been, on and off through life, but for good. There was no way for my brain to get a grip on a separation with no end. I shut my eyes and let it all swim out of focus.

We were driving to a wedding with the radio on. The IRA was thinking of calling off its current ceasefire. 'Stupid bastards,' muttered Daley, leaving the steering wheel more or less to its own devices as he gestured out of the window. 'Some people will never let it go, eh.'

'You need to get in the other lane.'

'You know, the world is safer than it's probably ever been. No Berlin Wall. No problem with Russia. No need for bloody wars. But some people, they don't know what to do unless they're fighting. They –'

'You could say all this while still keeping your hands on the wheel, you know.' We got a blast from the horn of someone who, by the look of him, was heading for another wedding.

'Or *you* could drive,' said Daley, 'but you can't because of the drink.'

I had begun the journey with a couple of beers. By now, at midday, I was on whisky. I slipped off the top of my hip-flask and waited for the familiar sting in the throat. The traffic moved slowly on all sides of us.

There had been a whole summer of fiftieth-anniversary documentaries about the war. When I went to Park Street on a Sunday afternoon, Mum would be watching expressionlessly as her youth was put to bed as history. Images of the war seemed so antiquated now that it was hard to believe anyone could have lived through it and still be here.

Whisky is like a friend, I thought, who always embraces you a bit too hard, breathes too close to your face, but whom you can rely on. The road opened up in front of us at last, and the ageing Capri ground its way noisily through the gears. It had narrowly passed its MOT with some warnings to get this and that done, all of which I ignored. Its engine rattled and whined and the suspension was worn out; on a slippery road it felt like riding a horse across a frozen pond. The worse a car it became, the more attraction it held for Beth.

'Remember, any time you want to get rid of it, I'll have it.'

'Very kind of you, Beth, but the thing is, I do sort of need a car.'

'But you don't need one like *this*. Just get a normal car.'

'And what's a normal car?'

'You know, the sort of car grown-ups have. A Volvo or something.'

I'd been hatching a plan to give her the Capri for her nineteenth birthday. Two days ago, though, Roly had turned up with the keys to a vintage Mini. I could hear Beth's cry of excitement from indoors. The two of them had taken off in it and hadn't come back that day.

Lauren had started to worry about the relationship, just as I was trying to resign myself to it. 'Do you think they're serious?'

'Well, she's only eighteen. She's got a lot ahead of her. And she's beautiful.' The two of us glanced at each other for a moment, briefly warmed by the thought of her.

'But do you think she *knows* she's got a lot ahead of her? What if she . . . settles for this guy?'

'She'll be OK,' I said.

In bed last night we'd made one of our occasional forays into sex. It had begun as a discussion about Victoria. The circumstances had naturally softened Lauren towards her.

'Are you thinking about her?'

'I'm just scared about what's going to happen.'

Lauren swivelled onto her back and pulled me onto her. The pure feline green of her eyes still stirred the old awe in me.

'It's going to be OK,' she said quietly. 'They have the best treatments ever, now. So many people survive . . . recover. You know.'

I let myself sink into her and kissed her neck. I reached for her and felt my way between her legs and we wrestled our way through it. She fell asleep straight away and I lay on my back thinking of Victoria, a few miles down the road in her million-pound home, staring at the ceiling and wondering what was to come.

Daley and I trundled westwards towards another pair of hopeful young lovers, their expensively printed invitation in my lap: *Richard and Victoria*. I refilled my hip-flask from the bottle, glancing at Daley in case he tried to tell me off. But he had spotted something else.

'Fans alert!'

This was a particular group of Arsenal supporters whom we'd exchanged insults with so often on our respective Saturday travels that we were almost friendly with them. As we pulled up alongside them, they honked their horn and Daley fished in the glove compartment for his blue-and-white scarf, almost sending us once more into the path of a car trying to overtake. The two men in the back seats offered us genial V signs and I returned the compliment. We laughed as they sped off, the back-seat fans clambering up to continue giving us the finger through the window. Daley chuckled.

'I think football fans are going soft like everyone else.'

The wedding was signposted by two hundred yards of balloon bunches. When we got out of the car, I left Daley to heft the bags out of the boot and went straight into the church to find a toilet. The organist, a young, owlish fellow, was warming up his Mendelssohn; I aimed a cheery salute towards his loft and went out to capture the crowd.

The ushers were all in grey morning suits; the bridesmaids' dresses were cornflower blue. One of the bridesmaids, a curvy girl of about twenty-five, was gesturing wildly as she made some joke or other; her bouquet went flying out of her hand. As she stooped awkwardly to pick it up, her breasts filled my eyeline for a second and our eyes met.

'Oh dear. I hope you didn't pick that up on camera.'

'Luckily, the lens cap was on.'

'Oh good.' She had a low, posh, effortlessly suggestive voice. 'I don't think I'm the best bridesmaid in the world. We've already had one in the pub! Victoria will kill us!'

'I've seen worse,' I said.

'You must have seen a lot of weddings.'

'Too many to count,' I said. 'You'll be fine. Just walk when you're told to walk. And stay quiet when they say if anyone knows any reason in law . . .'

'Have you ever seen someone *do* that? Just stop it?'

'Never. I've seen a few where they probably should have, though.'

She giggled. A blue hydrangea had come adrift from her bouquet. She bent again to fish it up from the ground, and put it between her teeth for a second as she turned the bouquet in her hands.

'Enjoy the wedding,' I said. 'Perhaps I'll see you afterwards.'

We weren't allowed to go into the church; the vicar was the old sort, thinning hair, bad breath, 'respect'. We watched this Victoria, arm-in-arm with her proud father, getting out of the Aston Martin. Her dress had to be manhandled through the door in several stages like water being bailed out of a boat. She and her father walked slowly towards the church. His smile was so wide it looked as if his face could hardly contain it. They were the sort of father-and-daughter team you sometimes saw at weddings who were unnervingly close, more like friends, as the father would unfailingly remark in his speech. I posed them in front of the church, took three shots and then said, 'All right, thank you,' and waited for their features to relax. It was then that I got the best picture, the bride's face lighting up as they shared some joke or other.

The father and the bride stepped inside – the bridesmaids picking up the bride's dress – and the door swung shut behind them.

'It's like some magic trick, isn't it,' said Daley, nodding at the door, 'like when they go into a trunk and disappear.'

'And now for a magic trick of my own,' I said, bringing the hip-flask out of my pocket. Daley glanced at me and closed his eyes for a moment.

We stood in the churchyard. The dregs of uncertainly sung hymns wafted through the rafters towards us. *'Love divine, all loves ex-CELL-ing.'* The organ tootled away. There was a blast of Whitney Houston for the signing of the register.

I swigged from the flask.

I was floating in a whisky haze by the time we lined them up along the church steps, Daley marshalling the crowd with his ancient shtick: 'Tall people at the back . . .' Click. 'And smile.' Click. 'And a little to the left.' 'Check the light, Daley.' And click. Then a short drive down the road to a dowdy hotel. Speeches. The new wife, Victoria, was the happiest girl in the world. Her father could recall several humorous scrapes she'd got into as a girl. The best man had some jokes he'd got from a book. There were toasts. The meal unravelled into dancing, shuffling, wandering, smoking. I drank a bottle of wine as if it were a cupful. Daley glanced at me from behind the camera; the longer a wedding day went on, the more he tended to cover the photography duties. I found the bridesmaid from earlier, a little dishevelled herself, the dress slipping down one shoulder. She drifted away from her friends and offered me a light.

'Are you staying at the hotel?'

'I'm not,' I said, 'Daley ... my partner is driving us home.'

'Partner?'

'Not in a romantic sense,' I amended. 'People didn't say that in my day. It was husband or wife.'

'What if you were gay?'

'That wasn't invented in those days.' We both laughed. She touched my arm. 'It's a shame you're not staying.'

'Why?'

'Well, it would be nice to spend some time together.'

'We could spend some time together now.'

That was it all took; neither of us would see it as our finest moment. I followed her back through the hotel, past the horrible floral carpet in the reception, the photo of Queen Elizabeth above the desk. The girl's room was on the ground floor. Her name was Amy, and I could still just about remember my own; it seemed polite to get that out of the way. I helped her out of the cornflower-blue dress. For a few minutes I was away from Beth and Roly and the horror of what was happening to Victoria. Amy cried out gratifyingly loudly and grabbed my hair. Afterwards we pulled the covers up over ourselves and lay there in our very separate thoughts.

'Should get back out there,' she said eventually.

Putting a suit back on less than an hour after it was glee-fully discarded is one of life's most slyly discouraging feelings. The cold of the shirt, the irritant nibble of the zip at the fingers. I straightened my clothes half-heartedly in the mirror. There was an old cup of tea on the dressing table. Amy stepped into the bathroom and began to run the shower. I opened the door and walked straight into a familiar face.

'It's the photographer! My word, I could have sworn that bedroom was being used by one of the bridesmaids earlier . . .'

It was the bald ceilidh caller. It sometimes felt as if they were deliberately following us around the country. At this moment I was even less pleased to see him than usual.

'Excuse me,' I muttered.

'Unless,' he went on, 'you and the bridesmaid were in there together? A few "mood shots", perhaps?'

'Get out of my way.'

'I do apologize for disturbing you. It's just, I have such respect for the art of the photographer.' His little bald forehead was screwed up in amusement. 'You go into areas which most of us wouldn't even think of.'

'Get out of my way.' I could feel my heart's wayward thumping, my breath speeding up. I caught sight of Daley and a couple of others appearing as the conversation warmed up.

'I mean, you were just as thorough at the wedding in Scotland, weren't you? Disappearing with Victoria Shillingworth, of all people!'

'Victoria Shillingworth,' I said, taking a step towards him, 'is my *sister*.'

He raised an eyebrow. 'Your sister! That's not quite the impression I got!'

'What the fuck do you mean?' My heart was pumping at treble speed. I felt overwhelmingly sick.

'No, nothing,' said the little man. 'If she's your sister, then my information must be incorrect.'

I grabbed him by the lapel and shoved him backwards against the wall.

'Hey, hey, hey!' said someone, taking my arms from behind immediately and with a certain glee, as if he had been waiting all this time for a fight to start. 'That's enough of that, I think!'

'I'd be very careful if I were you, mate!' said the little musician, flailing with his free arm. 'I know things about you!'

'All right, Brian,' said the man who'd gripped my arms, 'leave it now.' There were other people talking, all at once. Amy peeped out of the room, her hair in a towel; she shut the door again at once. I shook off my detainer and forced my way past the bald man, not looking at him. Daley beckoned me with a disdainful sweep of his hand.

'We're going home.'

It was the first time I had ever really known him angry. The silence in the car was like cold treacle. When the football results came on the radio, Daley let the sombre-voiced man plod all the way through without a single comment, a snort, anything. We sat there while the seemingly endless list of names and figures trickled by. *Darlington 2. Leyton Orient 1. Scunthorpe, Rotherham, Scarborough . . .*

I wriggled in my seat. The motorway, fringed by dried-out grass, nodded off slowly. There had been a crash up ahead; a van was jack-knifed. Daley scratched the side of his face and sighed. On the radio, an American was talking to a plummy-voiced presenter about O.J. Simpson. The traffic eventually moved at a crawl past the roadblock. My bladder ached.

'Daley, can we stop somewhere?'

'We were stopped for half an hour back there.'

'Yeah, in the middle of the road.'

'There's no services now for twenty miles. You'll have to wait.'

'I'll piss in your car.'

'It's *your* car,' he said, looking straight ahead.

'Oh yeah.'

But there was no glint of fun in his voice. I left it for half an hour before trying again to puncture the silence.

'Look, I'm sorry, all right? I got drunk . . .'

'You don't say.'

'I know it was unprofessional.'

The car crunched as his large hands wrestled with the gearstick. 'You're bloody right it was unprofessional,' he said at last. 'That's putting it mildly. Turning up at weddings like we're a pair of pikeys. Getting pissed, having fights, climbing into bed.'

'*You* don't look unprofessional. Just me.'

'I don't know if you've noticed these past twenty-five years, but we actually work as a team.' His face was spotted with colour. 'I would also remind you that you are *married*.'

'I've had a hard time.' I felt like crying. 'Victoria . . .'

'I know, Dom, I know. But before that, you got drunk because of not being able to communicate with Beth. And before that it was your marriage. And before that, I don't know, you were drinking because it was a Wednesday or something.'

This had the sting of a well-aimed blow, but it seemed a low one. It was all right for him to be high and mighty, with his ordinary, changeless marriage, his contented life, his seemingly unquestioned universe of right and wrong. What did he know about me, really, for all the time we'd spent together? It was the unfairness, the nail concealed in the boxing glove, that bit me.

'Well,' I said, looking petulantly out the window as Daley stepped on the pedal, 'it could be that I've been having a hard time for longer than you realize.'

'What I realize, Dominic, is that you've been losing control of yourself for quite a time now. I always gave you the benefit of the doubt, but now there isn't really any doubt.'

'Any doubt about what?'

'Any doubt you have a problem, and you need to—'

'You've not got a clue what my fucking problems are!' I shouted, thumping the dashboard.

Daley glanced warily at me.

'Why don't you try me,' he said.

'Because you wouldn't understand.'

He gestured in exasperation with both hands. We veered as if by magnetic force towards a parallel car, and the two vehicles nearly scraped together for a second, like two bodies on a dance floor.

'Careful.'

'Don't tell *me* to be careful,' said Daley, looking me in the face. His eyes were tired. 'You always seem to have this idea that you're the first guy in the world ever to have a problem, and it's somehow too much for an ordinary person to grasp.'

'Because it *is*.' My eyes were full of tears.

HOW'S MY DRIVING? asked the back of a delivery lorry as Daley tried to jink past it. His large head had turned to look at me. 'How the hell am I supposed to help you, Dom, if you won't—'

'Put your hands on the fucking wheel!'

'I'll put my hands where I like! Just like you did today!'

I lunged across at him, he backed away. There was a screech and a blare of horns and then an explosion. That's the last thing I remember thinking: nobody tells you this about a high-speed car crash, how terrifyingly loud it is – like a bomb going off.

XIV

The next thing I remember thinking was that I had been lucky not to die, and luckier still not to have been seriously hurt. In fact, as Lauren reached over the side of the bed to take my hand and kissed it with a trace of her old ferocity, I realized I was hardly injured at all. A nurse confirmed that I would only have to stay one night, and even this was a mere precaution. Daley was in a somewhat worse state, a couple of breaks, a handful of what the nurse breezily referred to as 'internal knocks': he'd be in for a few days.

'But nothing permanent?'

'Nothing permanent.'

I was amazed – almost embarrassed – by my good fortune and spent a couple of days in a state of something like wonderment. The more my memory filled in the initially hazy sketch of what had happened to cause the accident, the more of a fluke it seemed that I, and to a great extent Daley, had dodged the possible consequences. I lay quietly in my bed reflecting on what seemed a fresh start: a chance to give up drinking, to concentrate on Beth and Lauren and all that was ahead, to be a better colleague, husband, father, all of it. It was only when I went to see Daley on the third day that the price of my reprieve was revealed.

When I arrived, there were two visitors by his bed already. I stood clumsily in the corner.

'This is Dominic,' he said, 'who was in the car with me.' Not *friend*, not *colleague*.

We bantered about the crash as if it had happened to some other people. 'They said it was lucky my head was so hard,' said Daley. 'And the brains are buried a nice long way inside.'

'I thought at first you were dead,' I said.

'Nothing so dramatic, eh.' Daley gestured at his legs, dangling impotently in their casts. 'These fellows'll take a bit of time to get back to normal. I might have to give up my hopes of a soccer career.'

We laughed at that. 'I'll be able to take care of everything till you're better,' I said, tripping over the words a little. 'I can carry all the stuff, I can . . . you don't need to worry about anything.'

Daley looked away.

'What is it?'

He rubbed his face. 'Look, Dom, this isn't such a pleasant subject, so I'll be short about it. I don't think you and I will be working together again.'

I looked into his wily old eyes, a new nest of criss-crossed lines beneath them. He looked back with a regret and affection which made me so uncomfortable that I had to stand up.

'Daley – Roger. I know I've been a mess. I want you to know I'm going to give up drinking and get myself together. I've had some time to think. You were right about . . .'

He held up a hand to stop me talking.

'Dominic,' he said, 'you know I'm a plain-speaking man. I don't want to work with you any more. I've had time to think too, more time than you, I'd wager. And I think this is the right thing for both of us.'

'Don't . . . I know you're angry, I know it's my fault, but please don't start talking like this. It's been thirty years. We're an incredible team.'

'We were, yes.'

I sat back down, feeling numb. There was silence for a few minutes; then someone shouted from another bed and Daley muttered something derisory. As if with a physical effort, we shoved the conversation elsewhere. A member of staff came in to tell me visiting time was nearly over.

'Have a think about it, Roger,' I said, rising very slowly to my feet, 'and maybe we can talk when you . . .'

'I've had a think about it, Dom,' said Daley. He cleared his throat and looked away as I left the ward. I felt wobbly-legged as I showed myself out, past the kids' drawings on the wall and the notice reminding patients not to miss appointments.

Daley and I had been colleagues since I began to take photos; we'd never been less than good friends. But time could take anything away from you, I should have learned that by now. Not that time had anything to do with it. It was true what Victoria had said. In the end, no matter who you blame, your life is your own business. It adds up to what you make it.

Beth was going away to university in Newcastle. Her subject was film and television studies. 'Sure you're up to it?' I asked cheerfully. 'It can be tough work, having to go to the pictures.' Beth's face was like granite.

'That's exactly what I expected you to say.'

'It was only a joke,' I said. 'I'm really proud that you—'

'Whatever.'

It felt like a long time since I could get a laugh by making Cautious Rabbit hide under the bed. I asked meekly whether she would be wanting a lift to Newcastle.

'Roly's driving me.'

Of course he was. He saw her more often, the closer she came to going away. Sometimes he took her to members' clubs with the Cricketer and good old Max. Nobody seemed to think this was odd, her and her twice-as-old boyfriend and his even older cronies hitting the town. Not the Cricketer who had a seriously ill wife he left at home; not even her uncle Max. Perhaps it wasn't odd for anyone but me.

The day came: another warm Saturday, like the one that saw Max off to Oxford over thirty years before. Roly was due at ten in the morning; he arrived almost to the second, as the chimes of Big Ben sounded on Radio Four. Beth was thundering around upstairs, swearing. She'd been out for a valedictory piss-up with her old schoolfriends, returning at four with the familiar stumble and crash on the stairs. I'd miss those noises in the night, I realized.

Now she stood on the stairs, pasty-faced, still in pyjama bottoms. Her myriad belongings, boxes half-packed, bags hanging open, stood in the hall.

'I'm going to need a while yet,' she said.

Roly looked up at her, his hairless face poised in a poor impersonation of an understanding smile.

'We do kind of need to get going as soon as poss,' he said.

'Well, I'm not dressed and I haven't finished packing.'

Roly's face suggested a claw was digging him in the ribs. 'Sure. My point is just, there will be quite a lot of traffic today.'

Beth sighed and disappeared. I offered Roly a consoling slap on the back.

'You know,' I said, 'I can always drive her, if you're in too much of a hurry.'

'I wouldn't have thought you'd want to get back on the road any time soon,' he observed. 'How's he doing, your mate? Bearing up all right?'

'He's doing well. He'll be out of hospital soon.' I ushered him away from the stairs. 'Come and have a sit down. I'll make you a coffee.'

Eventually the moment came when everything was ready, the boxes and bags stashed in Roly's revoltingly clean company car; Beth's red-purple-brown hair washed and bullied into submission with hot air. Lauren and I took turns to hug her and I shook Smooth Face's hand again. Then they climbed into the car which purred competently out of our drive bound for the North Circular, and that was that.

Lauren and I stood outside for a while after the car had disappeared, in an unacknowledged wait for them to come back – some crucial forgotten object, maybe a change of heart. I glanced across at Lauren's eyes, a thin mist over the green beam. I suspected she was feeling something like me. This was meant to be one of those pivotal times, the moment we lost a girl in order to gain a woman a little further down the line; yet in fact Beth was already a woman. It had happened without our permission.

Lauren made lunch in the kitchen. Radio Four was chatting on politely to itself. I had no wedding today; I'd kept the date free in case I did get the chance to drive Beth to Newcastle. Besides, work was likely to be rather slower for a while.

My wife stood at the sink, tossing salad in a bowl. Her hair, rather colourless these days, was in a long ponytail. She was wearing a grey cardigan and a black woollen dress: she wore a lot of black now, it was slimming, according to magazines.

'I just can't get to like him,' I said.

'Who?'

'Roly.'

She glanced over her shoulder at me with a small smile. 'No. Me neither. But, you know. Young love.'

It was twenty years ago we'd met. It was strange that she could be so identifiably the same person that it might as well be twenty-four hours; and yet in other ways so changed that it was hard to believe the original person ever existed.

'Do you want to go and see Victoria today?' she asked. 'I'll be fine here. I have things to do.'

'No, she's asked me to . . . not to come too often.'

Victoria was holed up in the bedroom we once visited in very different circumstances. The chemotherapy had been going well, by her account at least; I wasn't sure if I trusted her. The first time I went to see her in the Shillingworth mansion, the Spanish maid ushered me up the long staircase. The room felt too warm. Victoria was propped against a mound of pillows, wearing a green silk nightgown. There were shadows around her eyes which reminded me of Beth's make-up, but she winked at me as if it were all part of the plan for her to be here.

'You mustn't come too often. You can't start coming every Wednesday or some nonsense like that. Because then I'm a patient and then I might as well roll over. I don't want to be someone that people *visit*.'

'So how do I know when I can see you?'

'Oh, I'll let you know.'

And she did. I took her to exhibitions, to Hyde Park, shopping at Harrods where I had to talk her out of buying a parrot; but it was always at her request. I could not drop in unannounced. I must not ask how she was.

'I still think it doesn't seem right,' I persisted now, as Lauren stood at the sink, and Beth whizzed further north with her grimly smiling driver.

'It doesn't seem right?' Lauren sat down opposite me.

'Come on. Admit it. The age gap, the . . .'

'The what?'

'His *motives*. I don't trust him.'

Lauren drizzled oil over a piece of lettuce. 'Well,' she said, 'I guess she'll meet boys her age at university and decide for herself if she wants to be with a guy in his late thirties.'

'I suppose.'

'But, you know. Who are we to ask what's natural in a relationship?'

She put her fork down and looked at me, cat-like, and I felt cold.

'What do you mean?'

Lauren looked coolly at me. 'I've been talking to Angela a lot about acceptance, you know, moving on from what-ever's happened in the past. I just want you to know that I know there have been other people.'

I looked at the glass of water in my hand.

'I know things have been hard at times between us,' she continued, 'and you've found your solutions. And, you know, that's OK. We're OK. I don't care what you've done.'

I coughed. 'Thank you.'

'OK, good,' said Lauren. She got up and went to the fridge, took out a cucumber, chopped it, tossed it into the salad bowl.

'I always loved you,' I said.

'I know,' she said, 'I know I was always number one. If I didn't think that, I would have been out of here years ago.'

My stomach twisted uneasily. Of course, she *had* been 'number one', if you discounted the love which could never be acknowledged. And perhaps that was enough. But it was a painful sensation to be forgiven for a sin she considered serious enough to talk about like this, when the true crime was so much worse.

The Shillingworth place was as dauntless as ever from the outside, but inside, it now bore the marks of Victoria's residency. The Spanish maid tiptoed around outside her room with a decorum Victoria would never have wanted. I was on first-name terms with her now, Conchita; she pronounced Dominic 'Dominique'.

The kitchen cupboards were stacked with fruit, sachets of herbal tea, anything else the Cricketer had heard might be beneficial. In the huge silver fridge were cheeses and cakes, things Victoria had requested but was only allowed to eat in moderation, and at times of others' choosing. She was engaged in a never-ending battle of wits with Conchita to get access to the treats, while Conchita and the Cricketer worked with equal cunning to make her take the vitamins.

'One time she come down, three in the morning,' said Conchita, 'but I have heard her on the stair, I am waiting for her. She opens fridge, bang! I come out like police. She screams, we have a laugh.'

'I was saying to Ian – Ian Botham,' the Cricketer said, 'you would make a good prison guard.'

The Cricketer welcomed me these days with a certain respect. How is she? I would ask. Not bad, not bad. A little better. Bit of a long night. Yesterday was quite tough, I think. And so on. He had filled out into a big, heavyish man, still good-looking but roughed up by the years, his golden hair patchier, his polo shirts and loafers old-fashioned in that insidious way all our clothes suddenly were. Occasionally when we were discussing Victoria, a pained look would come into his eyes, the panic of not knowing what to do, and at those times I would feel as if we'd really been on the same side all along.

Beth came home for Christmas with a new haircut – short, boyish, Victoria-like – as well as a dozen new outfits and the old penchant for not telling us anything. On Christmas Day we went round to see Mum, who asked about university and nodded thoughtfully at Beth's responses. 'I've never been to Newcastle,' she said, as if surprised. 'I don't suppose I shall, now.' We went to Dad's grave on New Year's Eve. The next day I took Victoria to Finsbury Park in my new car, a blue Escort. We walked around and around for a long time. Eventually we sat down on a bench and she fell asleep on my shoulder, jerking upright after a few minutes. 'We shouldn't stay here, old boy,' she said, 'it's bloody freezing.'

In March of the next year, a couple of weeks before Beth was due home for Easter, the doorbell rang one Friday night. I had been sifting through negatives from a portrait session I did with a hockey team the previous day. Jobs were a little thinner on the ground since Daley and I had parted. The hockey girls were all long-legged and wry, looked at me as if at forty-six I were the oldest person they had ever met.

I opened the door to see Beth hand-in-hand with Roly. Her hair was a screaming purple. She was wearing a dress and boots, as if they had just come from some function or other, though it was only eight o'clock. I ushered them in. Roly cleared his throat a number of times.

'To cut to the chase. I'm here because I want to ask for your daughter's, as it were, hand in marriage.'

Lauren and I looked at each other. Beth looked at the ground.

'I see,' I said.

'Bit of a formality, I suppose,' said Roly, 'but we wanted to do things by the book.'

'Beth?' asked Lauren. 'Is this what you . . . ?'

'Yes.'

'You're not nineteen yet, I mean, it seems a bit . . .'

'It's what I want,' Beth confirmed, almost as if speaking under hypnosis. I could just hear the radio from the kitchen. Lauren and I looked at each other again. What was there to say?

'Well, I can't . . . I won't stand in your way,' I said.

Roly grinned and grabbed my hand with an enthusiasm he had never shown before.

'Good man,' he said.

'Wow,' said Lauren, 'so . . . wow. You'll be engaged!'

'Quite a few people at uni are engaged,' said Beth. 'There's this stereotype that everyone my age wants to sleep around and whatever, but you know – a stereotype is what it is.'

It sounded like a prepared speech.

Roly nodded approvingly. 'You've either met the right person or you haven't. If you have, why wait?'

'Why indeed,' I said faintly.

The radio prattled on in the kitchen, as it had the night we brought Beth home from the hospital, a scrunched scrap of a person in a basket.

'So,' I said, 'have you thought about a wedding photographer?'

Naturally, the engagement party was held at the Shillingworth place.

Max wore a white suit. His hair was all grey now, but in his fifties he looked healthier than ever: the children had kept him young, Nonie enthused. I couldn't remember his ever being young in the first place. He sported a new pair of designer glasses and had lost some weight. He was about to go out to the Caribbean for five weeks on one of his extended cricket-watching, flesh-pressing errands. The Old Man Shillingworth was going with him. He too looked in his usual demoralizingly robust health.

Victoria had a woollen hat over the remains of her hair, her eyes were watery, and she was thin. The once-full contours of her hips and thighs were swallowed up now by her clothes. She sat chatting to Beth, the two of them occasionally breaking out into girlish laughter. From time to time Beth would grasp her aunt's hand or put her arm carefully around her shoulders, the two of them looking more like conspiratorial sisters than aunt and niece. I wished I could hear what they were saying.

As afternoon gave way to evening, the guests began to filter outside, where the Cricketer was presiding over a barbecue. Lauren and I chatted to Roly's parents. He was the youngest of their kids, which meant they were close to seventy, which made the age gulf between our betrothed children loom even larger. I bashed my way through a conversation with the father, a recently retired doctor, who – like a lot of people – had opinions on photography. 'They're saying it's all going to be digital, soon.'

'Yes. Well, we'll see.'

'Take some of the skill out of it, I suppose,' he mused. 'People will just take as many snaps as they want. Be able to take hundreds in one go.'

I wanted to retort that perhaps there would be robot doctors in the future, too, but he meant no harm. I glanced across; Lauren was doing a better job at nodding amiably at Mother Smooth Face.

When it was still fairly early, Victoria took me aside. 'I think I'm going to retire upstairs, Dommo. I'm not quite as energetic as I was.'

'Don't go yet. Just stay for half an hour. Beth loves seeing you.'

She let me take her arm and lead her out to the quiet cedar-tree corner of the vast garden. The Cricketer, doling out meat with his tongs, looked up as Victoria neared.

'Are you sure you should be . . . ?'

'I'm fine,' she said. 'Dominic's looking after me.'

The Cricketer nodded and saluted, and again I couldn't quite remember what I had ever had against him.

Her arm felt flimsy now, and I held it with an unaccustomed gentleness. We sat at the foot of one of the trees and she sprang immediately to her feet again.

'I think I'd rather stand, actually, old boy.'

'Right you are.'

Together we watched the party guests buzz around the focal point of the barbecue, where the Cricketer stood flourishing sausages and chops at one person after another. Victoria sighed. 'Look at him. What a poser.'

'Well, he's earned it.'

She looked at me in genuine surprise. 'That's the first time I've ever heard you be nice about him. My God. I'm not *that* ill.'

I blushed. 'I just mean . . . at least he's a poser with something to pose *about*.'

'Unlike Roly, you mean.'

We fell quiet for a moment.

'Am I going mad, old girl? I'm not, am I? It's lunacy for her to be marrying him, isn't it?'

Victoria took a long breath out. 'He is a bit of a twit, as they used to say,' she conceded. 'But a harmless one.'

'But we're not talking about going on a date or something. This is *marriage*. This is for life.'

She laughed. Her teeth were a little yellow, her lips cracked. 'It doesn't always mean exactly that, does it?'

There must have been forty, fifty people in the garden. One of the leaflets in Victoria's bedroom said one in four people would get cancer at some point.

'I admit, though,' said Victoria slowly, 'I would really like it if she doesn't end up stuck in a marriage where her husband regards her as a sort of . . . amusing possession that doesn't get used all that much.'

I looked across at the Cricketer, booming laughter at some bon mot of his father's, and hated him all over again. Victoria was about to add something, but she broke out coughing. I watched her with concern.

'Are you OK?'

'Yes, Dom, I'm fine. Main problem is people asking if I'm OK the whole time. Look. If you don't think she ought to be marrying Roly, you could tell her. Have you thought about that?'

'That's a good one. She won't let me advise her to put a coat on when it's pissing down with rain.'

Victoria grabbed my wrist with the strange sudden urgency she'd always been able to communicate. 'Listen, OB. If I can give you one piece of sisterly advice, which I'd like you to remember in the future.'

'Don't talk shit. You're not going anywhere.'

She put her finger on my lips and my words turned to ice flakes in my throat.

'Indulge me, then,' said Victoria. 'If you *do* find you're not able to call upon me or anyone. You are capable of doing important things, Dom. You've never allowed yourself to believe that. There was always the joke about being the same size as life and everything, but you can be larger. You . . .'

She broke off, coughed, put her hand on my arm and took it away again; then doubled over and vomited at the foot of one of the cedar trees.

She retched three more times, dropping to her knees. I sank down next to her and put an arm around her shoulders. A stench rose from the yellow-orange stew across the base of the tree.

'Does that help with the plants growing,' she asked faintly, 'or is that just shit?'

I squeezed her hand; it felt like metal. She began to say something else, then put her head in her hands. I sat there with her. Before long the Cricketer came striding over, tongs still in hand.

'I said you should've taken it easier, Vic,' he said, jocular, shooting a momentary glance at me as if it was my fault for overstimulating her. Then he shouldered his way past, and helped his wife up by the arm and led her away, leaving me by the trees.

They were going to tie the knot at a registry office in Central London where I'd been photographing people for years, with the reception at the Shillingworths'. Lauren and I had had some idea that she might go cold, meet some other boy in Newcastle and throw in the engagement. Or that they might remain engaged indefinitely, the way people sometimes did these days. But no, there it was: 29 March 1997. As the summer of '96 went by and I stood on church steps and outside dark civic rooms, finger on the shutter, it felt more and more as if I were rehearsing for Beth's wedding. Even though they weren't going to be doing it in a church, the familiar words of the religious service sounded particularly portentous suddenly, re-acquiring an old High Church sternness which decades of repetition had rubbed away.

It is not to be undertaken carelessly, lightly or selfishly, but reverently, responsibly and after serious thought.

Till death do us part.

For all the custom-written vows and the pop ballads, these ancient promises would not go away. It was at these moments that I wished I had Daley to bring everything down to size; these moments, and the moments I found myself alone as the service played out, smoking my silly little cigarettes as if somehow this constituted an act of defiance. I missed him in particular when it was time to go home: when I packed the camera into the bag and slouched off towards my characterless new car to sit in silence on the road.

It was a strange summer of nationalism, brought on by a football tournament which briefly obsessed the nation in a feverish, meatheaded way. There were St George's flags in windows; the motorways were strangely quiet on Saturday afternoons. The radio was full of members of guitar bands singing with exaggerated Cockney accents songs like the ones I used to hear in the back room of Victoria's corner shop. At one wedding, the reception was entirely over-shadowed by a match being played out on a big screen. The unfortunate bride smiled bravely as seventy or so of the hundred guests clustered around to yell at the pictures from Wembley. *Get it in the box! What the fuck are they doing!*

The tournament ended, the weddings came and went, the year got old. One afternoon early in October I was summoned to the Shillingworth place. I'd seen Victoria now and then in the few months since the engagement party, and we spoke on the phone a lot, though our outings had become less frequent. There had been no shocks, no obvi-ous worsening of the state of affairs. But today Conchita laid a warning hand on my arm as I arrived.

'Not so good.'

I plodded up the stairs with lead in my legs. Victoria was sitting on the bed in a pair of blue satin pyjamas that looked three sizes too big. After a moment I realized they weren't too big, but she was too small. She had withered in the weeks since I last saw her. A hat was pulled tight over her head, as usual. There was a bucket next to the bed, and a glass of water on the bedside table, and packets of pills. The room stank of synthetic pine. Victoria smiled wanly.

'Sorry about the state of me.'

I fumbled in the carrier bag.

'This is for you.'

It was a huge gold-wrapped Brie. Even in its paper, it smelled so pungent that for a moment I feared it was the last thing she would want in the room. But her face relaxed and she laughed in delight.

'At last! After all these years of you not having cheese on you. At last.'

'Sorry it took so long.'

The laugh gave way to the grinning silence that settles over old friends, and then there was a perceptible shifting of the air in the room as she looked into my face. Her dark eyes were the only thing about her not physically diminished. They looked into mine with that old urgency and I felt myself shifting slowly backwards.

'What? What is it?'

Victoria folded her arms across her flattened chest. 'Old boy. I have two important things to say to you this evening. Both of them are going to be rather difficult.'

'I can't see what can be more difficult than ... than what's already happened.'

'That's the spirit. Right.' With a little sigh of effort she straightened herself up.

'What's first? The rather complicated one, or the very simple one?'

'Complicated.'

'Naturally. All right. Well, I was over seeing Mum the other day. Ernie came and picked me up. The two of them really seem to be tight as you like.'

She licked her lips. 'You and I have talked quite a bit in the past about the fact that communication in our family has been rather, er, Victorian.' I watched, with no idea where this was heading, as she took a slow sip from the glass of water. The slowness of her every action these days was something I never quite got used to. 'Sorry. Mouth is always so dry. Anyway. Because Mum is now of a certain age, and I am, how can I put it nicely, dying – don't argue, please – she and I have had some pretty frank conversations recently. Franker than ever before. I perhaps wouldn't even call them conversations. She talks, mostly, and I listen. I think Ernie has released her ability to . . . well, to talk. I don't know, perhaps you've been finding this as well.'

But no, between Mum and me things were much as they always had been. We talked mostly about the wedding.

'So,' said Victoria, examining the chewed stumps which were once her fingernails. 'The other week I stayed over there, despite Tom's gravest threats, and we talked all night. Amazing! Mum didn't even get tired. I don't think old people sleep much, and nor do I these days – not when I'm meant to. Anyway, so we were talking about Beth getting married. And about regrets and . . . and unfinished business. Not specifically, I mean, there was no blackboard with these topics on. But we somehow got onto her and Dad.'

She took another drink of water. Conchita was hoovering downstairs.

'She let slip,' said Victoria, 'well, no, it wasn't a matter of "letting slip". She seemed quite anxious to tell me. She told me that in the early days of the war, Dad was sent out to India. I never knew that. It turns out he wasn't always short-sighted. He was out there for six months and got discharged with, well, something like shell-shock. He went a bit batty out there, was the way she put it. I don't know if it was related to . . . what eventually happened to him.'

'With him going out of his mind?'

'Yes. You're right. It *is* better to just say it. But obviously, that's the whole point, they never talked about it again. Not to me, not to Max, even to each other. There was a stigma. He had come home like he was injured, but he wasn't injured, there was no foot blown off. You know. No wound to show the neighbours. So his mental health remained something they could never discuss. It was a source of shame. That's why him cracking up was ignored for so long.'

I took a long breath. 'That's interesting. I'm glad you told me that.'

'I haven't got to it yet, old boy.'

'Oh.'

'I had to read between the lines a bit, but in short, I think their relationship became a bit of a no-sex zone for a while. He was still ashamed, whatever. You know. So they stopped. It happened in my marriage, it happened in yours – they just kept living without. They got on with it.'

And now suddenly I knew why I was being told this, and it took an effort to stop myself from falling off the bed. Victoria glanced at me wryly.

'You've guessed where this is going. One weekend he went up to Manchester to cover some match. She slept with someone else. The arrangement ... well, maybe arrangement is too strong a word, but it happened several times. She got pregnant.'

It was one of those huge truths which are no sooner out in the open than they feel permanent and familiar. But it was no less astounding for that. The moment was a long one, maybe the longest that even we had ever shared. I had to say it out loud to make it more real.

'Dad wasn't your father?'

'No.'

'So you and I . . . ?'

'Yes. Half-brother, half-sister.'

There was nothing, and everything, to say.

'Me and Max, likewise. The only one hundred per cent siblings are you and Max.' She smiled. 'The ones who don't get on. I suppose that should have been a clue.'

My brain was frothing as if hundreds of fish, each one a question, had been tipped into water. It was the obvious one which came to the surface first.

'Why the hell didn't she ever say?'

Victoria raised her eyebrows. 'I'd like to give you the usual explanation, no one in our family ever talks, blah blah. But specifically, she wanted Dad to be gone before anyone ever knew. Maybe she and Dad agreed they'd never bring it up until . . . you know, until it didn't matter.'

'Dad knew, though?'

'Oh, he knew all along. But what were they meant to do? It would have been a scandal.'

'But surely *you* would have liked to know this before?'

She gave a helpless, amused shrug. 'I would have been pretty fucking interested, yes, old boy. But what can anyone do about it now?'

'So you didn't shout at her when she told you, or . . . ?'

'I just gaped at her the way you're gaping at me now.'

I tried to imagine a version of Mum I had never known, and struggled to summon up. Young, pretty, frustrated, tied into a marriage, trying to loosen the knot just enough to admit a newcomer. Suddenly pregnant: all the options horrifying, except to act as if everything was absolutely normal.

'How did she meet him? Who was it?'

She stared down the bed at her legs and her slippered feet, and smiled to herself.

'It was Mr Linus.'

'No.'

'It was Mr Linus. Ed Linus.'

Of course this made far more sense than if it had been some dashing French stranger. Given her lifestyle who was Mum more likely to have slept with? Nonetheless, it made everything feel a great deal odder even than it already was. I felt as if I'd fallen through the floor and had barely settled before the new floor in turn gave way.

'This is . . .' I said, and found there wasn't a word.

'It is indeed,' Victoria agreed, and silence fell, the eternal moan of Conchita's hoover downstairs only seeming to make the room even quieter.

'Hey, shall we go out?' She tugged my elbow, though so feebly it reminded me of the eight-year-old Beth. 'Do you want to go for a walk?'

'Really?'

'We could just go a little way, have a picnic. We've got Brie. Just go down to the river. It's only five minutes.'

For a second it felt like the spontaneous Southwold trip, but that feeling abated as I saw how hard it was for her even to get out of the door these days. I helped her up from the bed, trying not to notice once more the dismaying cold of her skin, or how close her bones felt to breaking through it altogether. I had to fasten up the toggles of her large duffle coat. She picked up one of the pill packets, and a mobile phone. 'I know, I know. Absurd little things. But I'm meant to take it everywhere. You know.'

Then we had to clear it with Conchita, who watched tight-lipped as we shuffled through the hall, past the Trophy Room, past the huge dining room. 'Not back in one hour,' she said, 'I call police. And then you, Dominique . . .' She made a comical, but alarmingly accurate, mime of my head going into a noose.

'All right. Half an hour. We'll just be round the corner.'

Although it was a pleasant, mild afternoon and she was wrapped up in the Paddington Bear coat, Victoria shivered as we walked across the giant drive, between the gleaming and now barely used vehicles.

'Is it cold, Dommo, or. . . ?'

I began to lie and was hauled back by a sharp glance. 'No. *You're* cold.' I put an arm firmly around her waist and she winced.

'A little bit gentler. Sorry. I feel more ninety than fifty-five.'

'I refuse to even believe you're fifty-five.'

'What, because I look so good for my age?' She laughed sadly.

It took us fifteen minutes to get to the river at Victoria's new speed. By the time we made it, the sun had gone behind a cloud. '*Now* it's cold,' I said. 'You were just ahead of your time.'

'As usual.' She pulled the Brie out of the bag but then seemed to recoil from the sight of it. The scant remaining colour drained from her cheeks. 'You know, just at the moment, I don't think I can actually . . .'

'It's all right,' I said, hastily shoving it back into the bag. Of all the upsetting sights the past few months had produced, the spectacle of her unable to eat a piece of cheese was in its tiny way the worst of all. We stood looking at the river, where a couple of mallards were floating about. *What lovely luck, to see a duck.*

'So Mr Linus. He just continued living there, even though . . . ?'

I thought of big, pink Mrs Linus waddling out to the line with the washing.

Victoria nodded slowly and gazed out at the water. 'According to Mum, once they'd decided what to do, they all just kind of got on with it. They probably weren't as good friends as we thought, but Mum and Mrs L always did that talking-over-the-fence thing pretty well. And Dad and Mr L got on great, thanks to football. Classic stuff, stiff upper lip, don't mention the war. *Terribly sorry about knocking your wife up that time. Don't mention it. See the Arsenal score?*'

'But then he left?'

'Once me and Max were older, it got difficult. It got tenser. And apparently the Linuses were getting on worse by that point anyway. You know. Poor old Mrs L, she was already the size of Gibraltar by that stage. Anyway, what's for sure is one day he just left, started a new life in South America, and Mum and Dad said righto, we won't mention him again. And they didn't. Until the other night.'

I thought again of all the decades of banal exchanges we'd had with Mrs Linus, without the slightest inkling.

'Jesus,' I said, helplessly, 'it's . . . I just can't . . .'

'No, nor could I,' said Victoria.

'Have you tried to contact him, or . . . ?'

'Mr Linus?' She put her hand over her mouth for a moment and swallowed. 'He's dead. He died in Brazil four years ago. He . . .'

A single tear crept onto her cheek and I grabbed her hand.

'Sorry. Stupid thing to cry over.'

I began to contradict her, but suddenly a huge shudder ripped through her body. 'OB, I know we've only just come out here, but I'm going to have to go back in. I'm so sorry.'

'It's fine. Don't be silly.'

'It's the fucking medication. I can't do anything without feeling ill.'

'You don't need to explain.'

We walked back in silence. I kept glancing at her, the woman I had in some way shared almost every moment of my life with. 'A tenner for your thoughts,' she said as we got onto the Shillingworths' drive. 'Twenty even. I can afford to splash it around at this point.'

'I was just thinking . . . well. You know. What does this mean? In terms of what happened?'

'As in?'

'With us. I'm sorry to bring it up, it's just . . .'

'It's just that I cut you off for years over it.' She smiled ruefully. 'Yes, I've been thinking about it myself. Obviously.' She gripped my hand. 'Well, we're half-brother and half-sister. We're half as related as we thought.'

'Still in the wrong.'

'Still definitely in the wrong, but . . . shall we say we were half as bad as we believed we were, and leave it at that?'

We stood motionless together on the drive. In the couple of hours since I'd arrived, what I thought of as my history had been rewritten. The shiny assembly of cars, the looming ivy-covered house before us seemed for a minute as if it might all disappear like a film set whisked away.

'I guess that's about right,' I said. 'I mean, half as bad is a definite improvement.'

'It's around a fifty per cent reduction, I believe I'm right in saying. Shall we shake on it?'

I seized her gloved hand and then relinquished it quickly, bothered even now by the idea that someone might be watching, someone might know.

Part of me would never adjust to the idea of having to help with tasks which she was no longer equal to, and she was equally reluctant to ask. It took several moments of her grappling vainly with the lock, swearing at increasing volume, until I took the key without speaking and swung open the big door.

Conchita watched inscrutably as we plodded up the stairs. As we got back into the clammy room, Victoria was already grappling to remove her coat and gloves; she dropped the lot onto a chair and pushed open the door of the en-suite bathroom. Inside was more of the paraphernalia of illness: pills, a discouraging clinical sheen.

'Are you all right?'

'Yes, yes. Sorry. Give me a minute.' A hacking, rasping cough. 'Ignore any noises. I would turn a tap on, but I can't grip them properly.'

I went and looked out of the window at the oblivious world: the trees forming their checkpoint against a paling sky, and beyond them the busy city going about its usual business. It was the sort of time Victoria used to come home from teaching, bound up the stairs to get changed, slam her door with relish. There would be kids spilling out of her old school right now, and out of my old school, by the gates where she once hit Rowlands with the boot.

The toilet flushed and she came out of the bathroom, shaking the water from her hands, and now wrapped up in a green nightie. I got a glimpse of the faint outline of the tortoise tattoo. She looked like a skeleton in a museum display and her cheeks were white, with angry spots of red.

'It's funny, you still try to do everything by the book. You still wash your hands to keep the germs off. Even though half your body is infested with disease.'

'I've heard funnier things, old girl.'

I took her arm and helped her back onto the bed. She reached out and took my face and held it inches from hers. Her hands, damp and cold as clay, pressed into my cheeks. They were shaking wildly, and I began to shake as well.

'Right.' She looked down for a moment, then fixed me with her dark eyes. 'I said there were two things to talk about. Here's the second. I have to ask you to do something for me that you're not going to like.'

'Anything.'

'It's going to be unpleasant.'

'There's nothing I wouldn't do for you. You know that.'

'Let me be honest with you, Dom. I am getting worse. I'm afraid that from now on, it is going to be mostly this.' She cast her hands around the room. 'Throwing up in the garden, running to the toilet. Coughing up blood. Et cetera. I'm trying my best, but much as they talk about fighting cancer, I'm afraid you sort of can't. It gets you or it doesn't. It's getting me. I don't want you to watch.'

My throat felt as if something had been wedged sidelong in the middle of it. 'So . . . ?'

'So, I don't want you to see me decline any more. I don't want you to come again.'

Maybe I had half known what was coming, but it felt like being hit in the stomach by a wrecking ball.

'Please don't say that.'

'We'll talk on the phone. We can talk every day. Just, I don't want you to come. You're the one person I can't . . . can't wither in front of. Do you get that?'

'I can't do this.'

'Please, old boy.'

I was clenching my teeth with the effort of not crying. I forced myself to nod.

'Larger than life,' she said after a while. 'Never settle for less than that. Remember? You promised.'

'OK.'

My eyes were brimming; I swatted angrily at them.

'Is there even a chance you'll change your mind?'

'You know me, Dom. There's always a chance I'll change my mind. But this is the rule for now.'

'All right.'

We held each other for a long time, until Conchita knocked on the door.

'You need anything?'

'I'm fine, thanks,' Victoria called.

'Mr Tom called, he will be back in an hour.'

I wrenched myself cell by cell out of her grasp and got to my feet, sliding off the bed. She stayed where she was, her head back against the heap of pillows. We joined hands one more time.

'I love you.'

'You too.'

'Goodbye, old boy.'

'Goodbye.'

I closed the door behind me and walked quickly down the long staircase, breathing in-out, in-out, trying to concentrate only on that. Conchita was at the bottom. She grimaced in sympathy and took my hand, the hand that had just been in Victoria's, and held it for a second.

'It's very difficult, Dominique.'

What a shame Victoria had never called me Dominique, I thought as I stumbled out of the front door. For a second I wanted to turn back and hare up the stairs to tell her. The joke became the first note in a long line of conversations we wouldn't be able to have, a line stretching off endlessly to the distance.

I stood in the drive for a moment looking up at the Shillingworth house. She was still so close, but if I got in the car, she never would be again. Sitting in the driver's seat, starting the ignition, putting my foot on the pedal, each act felt another step into a pitch-black tunnel. I slammed my foot down and hurtled down the narrow mews, out into a horribly bright world where the sun had just emerged again from the clouds. I can't remember now where I drove to, or how I eventually got home that night.

We spoke again a week later. I told her that I'd been to see Mum.

'And did you discuss the life-changing revelation?'

'No. We talked about this recipe for soup she's got.'

We laughed and I pretended not to notice the coughing that followed. It was true: my two hours with our mother hadn't seen us stray beyond our usual conversational boundaries. I'd brought her a handful of magazines and a new kettle. Next week, I was taking her and Ernie to see *The Bridges of Madison County*, back by popular demand at the cinema in Belsize Park. Amongst all this, when was the right moment to begin discussing what she had done fifty-odd years ago? What purpose would it serve?

'That's the thing,' I said, 'it's not exactly life-changing. Well, it is, but . . .'

'It changes the past, not the future.'

'Exactly.'

I told her that I'd been to the bottom of the garden and turned down the temperature in the vivarium. I would keep doing this until Hercules' body temperature was so low that he stopped feeding. Then I would line a box with old newspaper and fill it up with loose soil and Hercules would bury himself in it and go to sleep for the winter.

'It sounds a very nice idea, that,' said Victoria.

'Hopefully, he should wake up just in time to start making his preparations for Beth's wedding.'

'Gosh,' she said, 'it seems a long time till the end of the winter. I mean, the thought of being asleep all that time. Missing everything. Christmas, and . . .'

A car had pulled up on the street outside and the driver was impatiently honking the horn for a passenger. 'Can you hear that?' I asked. 'The number plate's D-R-G.'

'*Derangement*,' she said at once.

'I can't think of one. All I can think of is *drugs*. Remember when Maudie couldn't think of the word "horse"?'

'Horse! Horse!' She laughed and coughed. 'I'd better go in a moment, old boy. Keep calling, won't you?'

'You know I will.'

I was alone in the house that night. Lauren was out at her book club. She read a lot these days; she went to the gym, did yoga, and recently I had caught her working on sketches for a new children's character. I was cooking spaghetti Bolognese for when she came back. The meat sizzled in the pan as I rained red wine on it, put the bottle back down on the worktop, then took it to the other corner of the room, out of temptation's way. As I gazed at the browning meat in the pan a slow panic rose in me, something I always experienced now while trying to avoid drinking. It was the instinct of a boy wading into water, further and further from safety. I suddenly had to speak to Victoria again.

The Cricketer answered the phone. 'I'm afraid she's asleep.'

'I just really want to talk to her. I don't think she'll mind.'

'I thought you spoke to her earlier,' he said.

'It's not rationed, is it? Please.'

'She's asleep. She gets tired out, as you know. You can call her in the morning. I'm not going to wake her up now.'

'Please, Tom.'

'Goodnight, Dominic.' The hard clunk of the receiver being put back in its place. My heart pounded with fury for a moment and I redialled the number, but it rang and rang to no one. The next time I tried, there was a single flat tone: it had been taken off the hook. I sat on the stairs until the smell of smoke summoned me back to the kitchen.

Lauren came back tipsy from the book club, where not much literature had been discussed, by the look of it. She undressed in front of me in the bedroom, shaking loose her long hair. Blonde was giving way gently to ash grey; at the moment it was a silvery mixture of the two. We lay together talking about the wedding.

'You'll be such a handsome father of the bride,' she said. 'I'm so proud of you not drinking.'

'Proud of your husband for not being an alcoholic?'

'Shush.' She kissed me on the cheek.

As usual, Lauren fell asleep very quickly. I lay with my eyes open. The red digits of the clock laboriously took each other's places: the lines making up the electronic 3 shuffled into a 4. The streetlights dropped their glare in the end and light was shaded into the sky. Engines started to cough outside, milk vans, postmen; the new morning building layer by layer. I escaped at last into a vague, threatening dream, only to be hauled back out by the wail of the phone. Lauren groaned and sighed and turned over. The clock was at exactly half past five.

'Maybe it's Beth,' Lauren slurred through sleep.

'I'm sure it's OK,' I said, but my stomach was curling into a ball, and as I walked downstairs to the phone in the hall my legs threatened to fold up beneath me. When I heard the voice at the other end, all the jitters flattened out into a single deadening fact.

'Dominic, this is Tom.'

As his voice began to frame the words I could not quite bring myself to hear, I wandered into the living room.

Daley would be opening his shop down the road; I still walked past now and then, knowing I could not go in again. Mum would already be attending to her knitting, the new kettle racing to the boil in calm silence. In the garden shed Hercules would be shuffling and burying his head, and three hundred miles away Beth would be doing much the same in her student room. Victoria had died in the night, yet everything else was going on as it always did.

XV

She had left detailed instructions for her send-off, in a handwritten note.

> *None of this business of a cheerful funeral! I want them miserable as hell! Dressed in black! But no flowers. Give to a kids' charity instead. Toast me and put me next to Dad. Over and out. V.*

All this was carried out. More than six hundred people turned up: they crammed into every corner, peeped through the door, lingered in big groups outside the crematorium. Max called her the best sister anyone could have had; the Cricketer described a marriage of unbroken happiness.

As the service progressed, I wished I'd had the gumption to volunteer to speak myself; as it was, I had the strange sensation, just as I had at her wedding, that the person being spoken about could not be my sister. How could it be that I had known her better than anyone, yet now was just one reverent face among many? Had I imagined everything that ever happened between us? If not, how could it be that someone could ask me afterwards, 'And how did you know her?'

Max ruffled my hair, the Cricketer was courteous, Daley slung his huge hands around my back in a bear-hug. At the Shillingworths' afterwards, I was close to breaking my new vow of sobriety as guests picked awkwardly at a huge tray of assorted cheeses: I even felt that to drink would be, as people say, what she would have wanted. But if I opened the floodgates on this of all days, there would be no way to stop. Around several of the rooms the Cricketer had arranged photographs of Victoria. I stood for a long time looking at a shot of her in that lampshade of a wedding dress, snapped with my little camera just before I went to rejoin the congregation. About to drop the cigarette to the floor, she was glancing to her left with a mischievous smile on her lips. Beth came up and touched my arm.

'Are all these pictures yours?'

'No. This one is. Most of the younger ones are. I didn't get as many chances later.'

'You never told me what you fell out over.'

'I'll tell you one day.'

'Yours are the best.' She squeezed my shoulder. 'You're an amazing photographer.'

It came as a surprise, and was closer to bringing tears out of me than anything else that day, a day I had got through with a shutting off of my heart.

'Thank you, Beth.'

'I mean it.'

She hugged me at the foot of the stairs, thirty paces from where Victoria and I had parted for the final time.

By the time I saw her next, the wedding campaign was quite far advanced; invitations had been sent out. Max was, of course, to be Roly's Best Man.

'How many nineteen-year-old brides have their *fifty-four-year-old uncle* as best man, Lauren? It's creepy.'

'That's a swell thing to say about your brother.'

'Still, I suppose what's really creepy is that she's marrying a man who's nearly forty himself.'

'Are you determined to ruin this?'

'You don't like it any more than I do. You're just in denial.'

'Supportive, Dom. It's called being supportive.'

Relatives and well-wishers chimed in with suggestions for the big day, as it was incessantly referred to. Had Beth and Roly thought about 'favours' for the tables? Where did they want the receiving line to form? Had they considered hiring a toastmaster? Might they like a chocolate fountain, an ice sculpture, a karaoke machine?

'God,' I said, 'weddings are more complicated than they used to be.'

'I just wish she'd talk to us about some of it,' Lauren fretted.

Beth had a mobile phone and encouraged us to call her on it, at a remarkable rate per minute, rather than what she called 'doing it the old-school way'. But calls to this hyper-evolved phone seemed to last a maximum of twenty seconds before her voice began to break off into short snatches of sound and we were cut off.

Weeks could go by, in other words, without our knowing much about what was on Beth's mind. This was normal among the parents of undergraduates, but what was not so normal was for those parents to be preparing for a wedding.

The dawn of the first New Year without Victoria was a painful one. The pre-midnight hours ticked by with a special slowness, the usual assortment of BBC clowns jabbering away, clip after clip of Princess Diana. My thoughts turned insistently to Southwold, where the beach would be empty and silent, our old beach hut peering up at the big cold starry sky. It was hard to believe that with every day that passed in 1997, dozens of new things would happen that she could never know about; and so it would go on.

When finally the new year got under way, Lauren began to call Beth more and more often, but the snippets of new wedding information she received only made her fret more. Beth was going to keep her hair short, and it would be bleached and then dyed black (Roly liked it, apparently). They would be writing their own vows. They were proposing to walk in to a hideous piece of dance music called 'Firestarter' (to show, according to Beth, that they 'weren't taking it too seriously'). I hated to see how worried Lauren was after these conversations, and once or twice tried to call Beth and reason with her, but the outcome was always the same: a sigh, a measured response. 'It's what we want, Dad.'

Lauren was getting more fearful almost by the day. The weekend before the wedding she went to the hen night in a restaurant. She came back later than I'd expected and much more sober than I'd hoped. She opened the door, hand tucked in her sleeve, and came solemnly in.

'How was it?'

'Awful.'

'What?'

'Dom, she doesn't love him.'

She sat down and pulled her hair loose. Her tongue flecked her lips; her eyes were like moons seen through mist.

'Based on . . . ?'

'She just seemed so distracted all night, so unhappy. And eventually she went to the bathroom for ages. When she came back, I could see she'd been crying. She didn't want to talk about the wedding. She didn't join in with any of the jokes. I tried to talk to her about it and she shook me off and we had an argument at the cab rank. Then she went.'

'She's probably just nervous.'

'She's nervous because she's making a mistake and she knows it.'

And in customary style she got to her feet and left me with a dramatic utterance to digest. But maybe this one was right, I thought. Whether I could do anything about it was another matter. Time was short now.

I called her mobile almost every day. 'Are you all right? How are you feeling about things?'

'What do you mean, how am I feeling about things? Are you Oprah now?'

'I'm just trying to—'

'I'm busy and stressed, how do you think I'm feeling?'

'Sorry? Not the best line.'

'I said I'm *busy and stressed, what do you think, I'm about to get married.*'

That was all there was to it, I tried to reassure Lauren; jitters. Collywobbles, as Victoria had once said. But there'd been a good reason for her reservations, and I feared there were good reasons for Beth's. Neither Lauren nor I slept much as the week went by.

The night before, we were entertained by Max and Conchita; the Old Man and his wife had gone to a hotel for the night, and Smooth Face was dining there with them and his own family. On best father-of-the-bride behaviour I declined wine again and again and did my best to laugh at the procession of jokes about last nights of freedom and balls-and-chains. The conversation was led by a couple of Shillingworth employees, friends of the Cricketer's. They laughed raucously, topped up their glasses. Beth smiled politely at everything and toyed with her raven-black hair. She went to bed early.

Lauren drove Mum home soon afterwards, shooting

me one of her sad, imploring looks as she left. The house soon took on its thick, unsettling night-time silence, the grandfather clock clunking away in the library. The Shillingworth men went off into some corner of the house to drink. I headed instinctively for the library and sat there for some time in a newly reupholstered armchair, looking at the drinks cabinet, the books, all as they had been on that night. Where before I would have had a drink in my hand, now I just stared off into the past.

Staying here on the eve of the wedding had seemed a good idea somehow. I'd be close to Beth, I thought, and in some odd way close to Victoria too: much as I resented it, I now associated her with this house as much as our childhood home. Shortly before the clock's long-winded declaration of midnight, I began to realize that it had been a mistake. There was no possibility of sleep at all; my stomach was performing its familiar contortions. I was beginning to wonder how I would pass the night when the two men from Shillingworth Enterprises, still up and now loudly drunk, came clumping towards the library. I slipped into the ante-room, not wanting to see them.

'I know where there *is* some,' said one of them, and I heard him wrestle with the door of the liquor cabinet and haul out a bottle. The other deposited himself noisily in a seat. The sound of glasses filling made my mouth water with yearning, as it always would from now on.

'I tell you,' said one after an interlude of swigging and sighing, 'Roly's bloody shitting himself!'

'Nerves, mate,' replied the other in a Lancashire accent, pausing to hiccup before re-making his point. 'There's bound to be nerves.'

'Well,' said the first, 'if you can't stand the heat, get out of the Kitchen!'

They spluttered with laughter. My face warmed as if it had suddenly been shoved in front of a fire. 'Don't let Max hear you say that!' warned the northerner.

'I bet there was a few jokes like that when Tom married – you know, what's her name. She was a Kitchen, wasn't she?'

'She was,' said the northerner, 'and by all accounts he *did* stay out of the Kitchen, most of the time.'

'What?' A low cackle. 'You're having me on!' Clunk-CLONK. Midnight. The other raised his voice over the chimes.

'No, no. Common knowledge. In fact he not only stayed out of the Kitchen, he visited quite a few other rooms, if you know what I mean.'

Their laughter went on some time. I sat there trembling. I felt a powerful desire to cause them physical harm. I'd believed this kind of impulse was one of the symptoms of my drinking; it turned out I was quite capable of mustering it sober. And clear-headed as I was, I knew exactly how I would do it: God knows I was familiar enough with that library. I'd march straight in, pick the sherry decanter out of its cabinet and smash it over the man's big head, beat the hell out of him.

I sat there in silence, my heart like the pedal of a bass drum, as they talked more about the way the Cricketer had 'made a lot of runs' away from Victoria, 'played some lovely shots' with a woman he met in India, and so on.

'Still, speak ill of the dead, and all that,' said the northerner in the end, and the conversation turned, apparently without irony, to how marvellous a player the Cricketer had been.

It was coming up to one o'clock on the morning of my only daughter's wedding. I listened as they picked themselves out of the chairs and plodded up the long staircase.

I went into the Trophy Room. The door seemed to creak more quietly than usual. The room was as cold as ever, and gave its usual, now unbearable impression that nobody had been here since I photographed Victoria with the trophy in her lap. There was a picture on the wall of the Cricketer accepting one of the many prizes that lined this room; she stood next to him, beaming.

I stayed there for as long as I could bear, until I had broken the back of the night. At six o'clock I washed my face and changed into my suit and helped myself to breakfast. Then I sat and waited.

The women started to arrive by nine. A woman to do the hair, a woman for the make-up, and a woman who seemed to be doing nothing except reporting the weather forecast ('Brightening up later, they say. Overcast now, they say'). The bridesmaids, Max's little daughter Charlotte among them, began to assemble in a sitting room and were pounced upon instantly. Their hair was curled and prodded, their skin examined like plasterwork. Various rooms were being decked out with flowers and streamers; Conchita moved about the house so quickly she might be on skates. Lauren was on her way with Mum. Everyone was here except Beth. The knot in my guts was so tight I could hardly move.

Invisible amid all the activity, I made scrambled eggs on toast and took it up the staircase, pausing on the landing to glance up to where I last saw Victoria; but only for a second. I knocked on Beth's door and was groggily admitted.

She sat up in bed. 'Is that for me?'

'Of course. It's your wedding day.'

'Breakfast in bed, wow.' She rubbed chunks of goo from her eyes. Her hair was matted from the pillow. She was wearing a band's T-shirt: *blur*, all in lower-case. She's so young, I thought.

'What's going on downstairs?' she asked.

'All in order,' I said, sitting on the edge of the bed; to my surprise she seemed not to mind. 'Make-up people and so on are all here. Bridesmaids are being done.'

She sank back against the bedstead with a low groan.

'Are you all right, darl . . . Beth?'

'I just don't quite fancy all this hassle,' she said. She reached for the tray, somehow missed and upset it, dumping the plate of eggs onto the duvet.

'Oh, fuck!'

'It's all right,' I said, 'we can soon . . .'

'Fucking hell!' She looked close to crying. I wished I hadn't brought the eggs. 'Now I've spilled fucking eggs on the bed and everyone's waiting downstairs, and . . .'

'It's all right.' I was desperate to avoid winding her up further. 'Do you want to have a bath or something, and I'll clear this up? Or I can just leave you alone completely. Whatever you want.'

'I don't *know* what I want,' she said, staring down at the yellow-brown mess in front of her.

'I'm sorry. I shouldn't have woken you up. It's your day.'

'You didn't wake me up. I barely slept.'

So gently that she could hardly have felt it, I touched her on the shoulder. She looked up. Her eyes were watery, her breath morning-stale as I leaned closer to her.

'Beth, can I ask you a stupid question?'

She almost smiled. 'You don't normally ask permission.'

'Do you really want this?'

'What?'

'Do you really want to marry him?'

Moments passed. Cars were pulling up outside, the doorbell rang, a bath was running. Beth began to speak. 'I did want to. When he asked me. I was happy to be asked. I thought I wanted to.'

Suddenly she was crying. I put my arm out, but she shoved it away.

'Why are you asking me? When you know . . .' She half choked; her eyes stung me. She snatched a tissue from a box on the bedside table, cast aside the stained duvet, and brought her legs defensively up underneath herself. 'When you know there's not a fucking thing . . .'

'It's not too late, Beth.'

'Of course it's too late!' She looked just like Lauren all of a sudden.

'Well, do you want to or not?'

'What the hell has that got to do with anything?' Beth yelled. 'What am I going to do: just walk away now?'

'If you want to get out of it,' I said, 'I can get you out of it.'

Beth sniffed and shook her head contemptuously. 'Well, I'd like to see you do that, Dad, I really would.'

I took a deep breath.

'If you don't want to do this,' I said, 'I swear on my sister's grave, you are not going to do it.'

This might have been hammy, but it shut her up. We sat there listening to the commotion downstairs.

'You just have to give me a sign,' I said.

She looked at me for a long moment.

'I'm going to have a bath.'

Beth padded halfway across the room in her oversized T-shirt, and stopped. 'Dad. Do you mean it?'

'I've never meant anything more.'

I felt light-headed and wobbly as I came down the stairs. Lauren, with my mother in her new green hat, was waiting in the hall.

'How is she this morning?'

'She's all right,' I said, 'a bit anxious.'

'Not a bad day for it!' Mum announced. 'Clearing up later, they think!'

'They're saying sunny intervals, now,' replied the weather expert from down the hall, and the two of them fell into half-deaf conversation. I took Lauren by the sleeve of her expensive faux-fur coat.

'You were right.'

'About what?'

'About her and him. I'm on the case.'

Lauren laughed mirthlessly. 'Yeah, Dom. You're always on the case.'

Nobody believed I could do anything, as usual. I was smaller than life. I was a footnote on the wedding day, even my own daughter's. I heard the laughter of those men last night, and thought of the new knot tightening now around Beth, and around me. My heart was chafing at it, writhing, trying to loosen me from its grip.

The big clock's sad strokes brought us second by second towards the arrival of the wedding car. I took strings of photographs. Beth responded in bright monosyllables to the endless chatter. 'Yes, getting close now!' 'Just want to get there!' Lauren hovered around the circle of primpers-in-chief, struggling to get a word in.

Sympathy for my wife, and a pulsing love not felt for years, muscled in alongside all other sensations. She deserved more than to be this: someone's fussing mother, about to hand over her most prized thing to an undeserving man. My heart pounded on, but I felt calm.

The car would arrive at one. At half past twelve, the bridesmaids – lined up miserably against a wall like suspects in an identity parade – were approved. They were shown to vehicles poised in the drive, and the rest of the party began to transfer itself gradually outside. Lauren had taken Mum out into the garden to look at the crocuses. The Shillingworth grounds were a riot of pink and blue. In the humbler garden on Park Street, Hercules the tortoise had roused himself a fortnight ago, oblivious to the loss of his second owner.

At ten to one, as cars began to crunch and growl their ways out of the drive, I was alone with Beth again. Her smile was bright and synthetic. Her eyelashes had been stuck on. Her black hair had been blow-dried and stacked in a rough pyramid, and her voluminous dress enveloped her like a tea-cosy. She sat in the chair she had been placed in almost two hours ago, listening for people outside.

I stood beside her and tried to find her hand in the cascading folds of the dress. It was sticky to the touch, and shaking.

'Did you mean what you said before?'

'Yes.'

Up, up, up went the speed of my heart.

'Dad, I don't want to do it. Get me out of here.'

'Are you absolutely sure?'

She nodded, and put her hand over her eyes.

'All right. We're going outside. I will seem to be photo-graphing you. Go and stand by the Escort, all right?'

The day was still grey, with a light wind tossing the tree branches. The last few guests were being loaded into cars. Everyone waved at Beth, or sent some chipper remark her way. She replied in kind. She was walking like a drunk, like someone who would keel over any moment. The wedding car was due.

I looked at Beth and saw Victoria, thirty years ago, at the crossroads of her life.

'Stay there,' I said to Beth, 'stay there two minutes.'

'Dad, don't leave me.' The last car had slipped into the narrow road and gone.

'Dad . . .'

'Three minutes.'

I walked back into the Shillingworth place, knowing it was the last time I would ever set foot in there. I went into the Trophy Room: the door, like a drugged guard dog, barely creaked. I pulled down a cricket bat from a shelf, one of the Cricketer's bats. I swung it at random and knocked a cup down from its shelf. Swung it again and hit a photo; there was a tinkle and a nasty crack as it landed face-down in front of me. I swung it again and again, sent showers of glass through the air, sent ornaments flying. I sought out the picture of Victoria with the Cricketer and buried the bat in it. It slid slowly to the ground.

My hands were shuddering on the handle of the bat. The whole thing had taken no more than a minute. The silence was full enough to swallow someone. I looked around at the damage, the wrecked treasures lying thick on the ground. I dropped the bat and ran outside. Beth was pacing furiously by the Escort.

'What the hell were you doing?'

'It doesn't matter. Come on. Get in.'

I opened the passenger door, but there was the wedding car now, its tyres massaging the gravel, its driver in his hat and double-breasted jacket. Beth looked at the shiny car in despair and I felt my insides slide.

'I have to go with him.'

'No you don't. Get in.'

I was grabbing her arm now, bundling the dress inside, there was so much of it. She sprawled across the back seat of the car, the dress all around her, her mouth slack with fear.

'They're going to kill me.'

'No one's going to kill you,' I said. 'If you go to that wedding, it might kill you.'

'And what's going to happen to *you*?'

Her voice was as small as when she was four years old. I glanced in the mirror and saw her eyes, enormous and terrified and exhilarated. The smallest smile came onto her face, a grin of possibilities unbound.

'I think I'll be all right, old girl,' I said, and slammed down on the accelerator to take her past the startled driver of the classic car, out of the drive, out onto the open road.

EPILOGUE

It is ten years now since I drove you out of the Shillingworth place. It's fair to say that it has taken most of those ten years for the storm to blow over. We can agree now it was the right thing to do. We can also agree it was wrong to smash up the Trophy Room. That's life: you don't get everything right.

It could be another ten years, or longer still, before you read this. It might be that you never read it. I'll make sure that I'm long gone before you even have the option. But at least you *will* have the option. So many people leave life without having explained everything, without having said even half of what they'd like to say.

As I said at the start, you have been to a lot of weddings since the one you absconded from, and you'll go to plenty more. Eventually you'll get married, I'm sure – maybe to the admirable man you're dating as I write, maybe to someone you don't yet know. Now it's legal for you to marry a woman, if you want. Whatever you choose, I suspect it will turn out better than your first engagement. I hope to be there, snapping away on my fancy new Nikon. If for any reason you hire a different photographer, pay attention to him. When you see him clock off and head for his car, think about all the stories he might be carrying around.

What happened between Victoria and me would never be forgiven by most people. She was right that a couple of decades are enough to change the world's mind on most things, but not on this. It would be nice if, if you read this, *you* forgive me. But I didn't write it all down for that. I just wanted a record to exist somewhere.

There's a record in my mind, of course, but that mind is not a photo album any more. I've started to forget things, I notice: little things, phone numbers, people's names, what I'm meant to be doing. Lauren has to remind me of appointments I don't recall making; reminisces over memories I have to pretend to share. These could just be the minor embarrassments of age, or there might be more to it. What happened to Dad could happen to me.

If it does, I'll forget all this: it will be removed from my brain one memory at a time. I'll forget everything from Victoria throwing the football boot at Rowlands' ear to you and me barrelling up the motorway, not daring to stop for a hundred miles, breaking into wild giggles, the two of us whooping with fear and joy on the hard shoulder. I'll forget everything that came after, too. I'll forget Max writing to me last year to suggest a reconciliation, and the handshake on the beach at Southwold which sealed it; the awkward way we stood around afterwards, making small talk, his laugh when I suggested a game of cricket. I'll forget why on the same beach, if you go onto the pier where hundreds of little public-sponsored gold plaques stretch out over the sea, you can find one that simply says *Old girl*!

That's why I wanted you to have this, even if having read it you end up thinking less of me. If you want, you can destroy it, you can allow yourself never to think about it. But it will live on somewhere in your mind, long after I have slipped quietly away, like a photographer leaving a wedding.